Beneath a Camperdown Elm

Janet C. Bly

OTHER BOOKS BY JANET CHESTER BLY:

TRAILS OF REBA CAHILL SERIES:
   WIND IN THE WIRES
   DOWN SQUASH BLOSSOM ROAD
   BENEATH A CAMPERDOWN ELM

THE HIDDEN WEST SERIES:
  (CO-AUTHORED WITH STEPHEN BLY)
   FOX ISLAND
   COPPER HILL
   COLUMBIA FALLS

CARSON CITY CHRONICLES SERIES:
  (CO-AUTHORED WITH STEPHEN BLY)
   JUDITH & THE JUDGE
   MARTHELLEN & THE MAJOR
   ROBERTA & THE RENEGADE

THE CRYSTAL BLAKE SERIES:
  (CO-AUTHORED WITH STEPHEN BLY)
    (8-14 YRS OLD)
   CRYSTAL'S PERILOUS RIDE
   CRYSTAL'S SOLID GOLD DISCOVERY
   CRYSTAL'S RODEO DEBUT
   CRYSTAL'S MILL TOWN MYSTERY
   CRYSTAL'S BLIZZARD TREK
   CRYSTAL'S GRAND ENTRY

THE HAWAIIAN COMPUTER MYSTERY /
THE ISLAND MANSION MYSTERIES
  (8-12 YRS OLD, MAKING CHOICES BOOK)

STUART BRANNON'S FINAL SHOT
  STEPHEN BLY'S LAST NOVEL, COMPLETED BY JANET
  CHESTER BLY, RUSSELL BLY, MICHAEL BLY & AARON BLY

"LIKE WHERE YOU ARE GOING WITH REBA. LOTS OF HIDDEN SECRETS ... YOU HAVE ME HOOKED."
   GABE A.

"YOU CAN ALMOST SMELL THE DUST AS YOU ENTER THEIR WORLD. I CAN SEE THIS SERIES FEATURED ON HALLMARK MOVIES ONE DAY."
   JUDY B.

"REBA IS A VERY LIKEABLE CHARACTER ... I WOULD LIKE FOR THINGS TO GO PERFECTLY WELL FOR (HER), BUT THEN THERE WOULDN'T BE A STORY!"
   SANDY K.

"YOU HAVE A GREAT TECHNIQUE FOR BRINGING IN WHAT MIGHT OTHERWISE BE BORING FACTS ABOUT RANCHING, GEOGRAPHY, AND GREAT IDEAS FOR A ROMANTIC CONVERSATION. MAYBE I CAN GET (MY HUSBAND) TO READ THIS!"
   BARBARA H.

"YOUR WRITING IS MESMERIZING. I HAVE TROUBLE STOPPING ONCE I START AND I FEEL THAT I AM IN THE MIDST OF THE CHARACTERS, AS IF THEY ARE REAL."
   CONNIE SUE L.

"LOVE THAT (THIS STORY) TAKES PLACE AMONG PLACES I'VE TRAVELLED THROUGH AND EVEN GREW UP IN ..."
   DEANNE G.

Beneath a Camperdown Elm

Janet Chester Bly

A Trails of Reba Cahill Novel
Book 3

Beneath a Camperdown Elm

Janet Chester Bly

A Trails of Reba Cahill Novel
Book 3

Printed in the United States of America

Bly Books, P.O. Box 157, Winchester, ID 83555

Visit our website: www.BlyBooks.com

Includes Reader's Guide for Discussion and Characters & Places List

"For he will bring our darkest secrets to light
and will reveal our private motives."
1 Corinthians 4:5 NLT

I will give her back her vineyards,
and will make the Valley of Achor (Trouble) a door
of hope.
Hosea 2:15 NIV

Dedicated to:

Henrietta Mears of Hollywood
who inspired
Pearl Cahill of Road's End
to bloom where she's planted

ACKNOWLEDGEMENTS:

Heartfelt thanks to many folks who've helped me to make this book possible...

Cover & Interior Design: Ken Raney

Miralee Ferrell, Edit & Developmental Critique

C. J. Darlington, Beta Reader

Michelle Bly, Critique & Copy Edit

Michael Bly, Critique & Copy Edit

Jan Grueter, Proof Reader

Resources for farm and ranch scenes ...

Richard 'Dick' Pentzer: Camas Prairie, Idaho ranch advisor

Cole Riggers, Camas Prairie, Idaho farm advisor

Roger Riggers, Camas Prairie, farm advisor

Sheila Hasselstrom, Targhee sheep rancher

A special 'thank you' to ...

Dr. Harold D. Crook, Ph.D., Professor of Nez Perce Language, Lewis-Clark State College, who provided the correct, updated Nez Perce language transcription and pronunciation for the audio and hard copy editions of the "God Be With You" song used throughout the series. Find the full rendition by search on the BlyBooks.com website blog.

And much appreciation for readers who previewed the original draft of the first three chapters and provided valuable comments, critiques, or suggestions:

Edward L. Arrington, Jr.; Gabriel Asenas; Sharon Ann Bahr; Judy Brady; Molly Noble Bull; Dorothy Bullard; Robin Bunting; Marilyn Carvin; Marilyn Eudaly; Dolph & Carol Frisius; Anna Gregory; Deanne Grubb; Barbara Hallmeyer; Sandy Kozol; Connie Sue Larson; Gill Lillford; Ethel Lytton; Brenda Morgan; Karen C. Riley; Jorie Story; Bonnie Wheeler

Most of all, thank You, Heavenly Father, for the precious privilege of being enabled to publish books in the Name of Your Son, Jesus.

May each Bly Book in some way prepare a reader's heart to receive Your truth.

Chapter One

*O*n the goat trail known as Highway 95, halfway between Winnemucca, Nevada and Road's End, Idaho, otherwise known as home, Reba Mae Cahill relished a rare bit of joy.

"A God hugged day", she whispered, even in the swelter of noon heat. She'd like to bottle it up for an on demand repeat.

She hadn't felt like this since as a kid she escaped from Grandma Pearl's spider and rat-infested root cellar. Or as a teen when she finally broke the wild black stallion, the love-of-her-life horse, Johnny Poe. Almost giddy, her dark fog vision from the past broke up, turned to mist, and vapored away.

"What did you say?" A male voice intruded. Sitting next to her in the driver's seat, on red Naugahyde seats, in the cobalt blue convertible '55 Chevrolet, white top rolled down, Jace McKane kneaded the muscles in Reba's warm neck as they drove down the highway.

Her fading, Regal Red hair tied back in a ponytail, whipped around in the blast of wind. Any remnants of her Road's End hairdresser's Curly Cue treatment, now nonexistent and straight as a stick. "I meant to say, I was thinking about the future and it looks fine."

Mighty fine.

She scanned Jace's profile, more deeply embedded in her getting-to-know-him file. The boyish mug belied his thirty-two years. She'd learned an important tidbit on this four-some car trip from the southern California coast. "I love being on the road with you."

He grabbed her hand. "From now on, you're stuck with me."

Finally, a dream come true—her very own rancher husband.

Soon.

Very soon.

"You're still gonna help me and Grandma Pearl fight to save our ranch from Champ Runcie and the crazy lawsuit, right?"

"Oh, yeah. That's top on the agenda."

"Good. But first, I'll teach you how to ranch, the Cahill way. That is, in between Grange Hall dances, movies, dinner out, and long horse rides on the Camas Prairie."

She knew all too well Jace could be top executive in a high paying company anywhere. Or own the company. In fact, he did for a while. But he wanted a different lifestyle. He decided to try the wild outdoors and landed in Road's End, a small place with ordinary folks. He traded his Gucci's and Nikes for cowboy boots.

Scooched down in the backseat corner, in the rear-view mirror Reba's mom, strawberry-blonde Hanna Jo, looked confined. But she had dozed off and on for hours, which helped pass the time. Light and shadows through the window played on her face to trick an image of youth for her forty-four years.

"How you doing, Mom?" Reba asked.

"Couldn't be better." Hanna Jo appeared to be in good spirits, but Reba suspected the taunt of self-doubt within, if not pure panic.

Reba hoped this return to Road's End, after twenty-two years away, would untether her mother's heart from a slew of bad memories. Perhaps somehow stop the trauma without erasing the history of who she is. And loose the grip of poor choices—hers and others.

Finding out about her real parents.

The years on the run.

Could she endure the challenge of responsibility and stick it out on the ranch?

The previous night they endured an upsetting episode, the first since they left Santa Dominga three days before. In a sweaty, humid Winnemucca motel room, Hanna Jo woke with chills as she yelled, "Get the monsters! They're chasing me."

Reba held her tight to try to stop the shivers and she finally quieted down. When they turned on the lights, Reba gave her the nightly dose of pills prescribed by the Reno Desert City Mental Health Institution.

But that was last night. Today brimmed with optimism.

Behind Jace sat his ten-year-old half-brother, Abel. She turned to peer at his round as marbles dark gray eyes as he held down a pack of Topps Desert Storm trading cards that scattered on his lap. She glimpsed pictures of 'Stormin' Norman Schwarzkopf, and Saddam Hussein, along with a Huey Cobra helicopter, framed in brown camouflage borders.

"Are we almost there?" Abel asked for the umpteenth time, his eyes glazed.

Reba sucked in her breath. Smoke swirled from several controlled stubble fires. "Couple more hours. Box those cards before they ..." One flew out and littered the road before she finished her warning. He tossed them to the floor and tried to stomp on them, straining against the seat belt.

"Better put the top up." Reba peered in the mirror. "Besides, I'm getting freckles."

Jace stroked his thumb across the back of her hand. "You've got them all over."

She blushed. He didn't know that yet. "Yeah, but I don't like them on my face."

"Wouldn't hurt to make a pit stop anyway."

They took a side trip to a gas station off the highway. A dry summer breeze whipped through rolling hills and wheat fields, as stalks ground against a combine's whirring blades. Semi-truck wheels crunched while carting grain to town.

"Watch out, everybody," Jace called out as the white vinyl top with the zippered plastic rear window slowly rolled over them.

Jace filled the tank with gas, while the rest used the facilities. When Reba returned, he wiped the windshields and a couple muddy spots on the Belair's hood and tailgate. "She needs a good bath and polish after this long drive."

Reba knew how proud he was of this car. He found the Chevy for what he considered a bargain price at Oliver's Fire Sales & Salvage, along a Nevada country road. They hopped back in the vehicle and Jace drove them back on the highway.

After tracing long miles along the Salmon River, the Chevy chugged up White Bird Hill. At the top, they could see the Camas Prairie stretched long and wide over the mountain. Reba scanned grazing cows, horse tails whipping flies, and wheat fields spilled with shiny shades of gold with heavy heads shouting, *harvest payday!*

Her mother mumbled something.

"What?" Reba said.

Hanna Jo leaned forward with a lazy smile. "I've got it figured out for the ranch. I'll train and care for most of the horses. Reba, you take charge of the cows. Jace can oversee planting and the machinery."

"But I've got dibs on Banner to re-train." Reba thought of the buckskin mare promised her by New Meadows horse trainer, Soren Patrick, to replace her beloved black stallion, Johnny Poe. She had her sights set on the cowboy earlier that summer, before Jace, and before Valery.

Soren said he'd bring the horse to Road's End after they arrived home from California. She looked forward to bonding with the buckskin and Soren again. As well as his fiancée, Valery, of course.

"And how does Grandma Pearl fit in, Mom?"

"Same as always. Whatever she wants, when she wants."

More than she could imagine or hope for—a team of cowgirl Cahill women *plus* the man of her dreams. Reba quickly added, "These days, she prefers caring for the yard around the house, her mares, and the dogs and cats. That's her domain with her bad knees and hips. I know the Younger boys have been helping off and on with other chores since I've been gone. And Michael left for Alaska.

Plus, Vincent had business in Boise."

Reba realized they'd need to tweak duties and roles on the ranch with adding her mom and Jace to the team. Might as well spell it out from the get-go. "We'll take turns with mending fence, birthing calves, and all those numerous other duties. We can hire students to move the half-ton of field rocks."

"We'll see." Her mother yawned, stretched her arms, and leaned back in the seat.

So nice to return to Idaho, away from the crazy congestion of California. Their only other traffic: a truck driver with a "Please Drive Carefully" sign on back whizzed past them. Reba noted several crosses and wreaths on top of roadside mailboxes, reminders that fatal vehicle accidents happened anywhere, even in rural, country places.

Less than an hour later, the '55 Chevy pulled off the highway to Road's End as summer shadows crossed before them. Checkered patches of dry, tan wheat and verdant grass surrounded them, touched with golden highlights.

Reba stole a lingering glance at her mother. She kept rubbing her cheek and then her shoulder blades, back and forth. A nervous gesture. Sorry she agreed to come? Scared? Anxious how she'd be received? Maybe more than a little trepidation.

Reba tried not to worry potential problems into circles—that she might neglect her meds, not be able to deal with the pressure. With her present exuberance, Reba determined to do all she could to help her mom with the transition, despite her stubborn, independent streak.

For the sake of family.

For the sake of the ranch.

They passed Road's End Lake, with only two fishermen settled in a canoe, fishing poles held near the bow. A bald eagle soared down, snatched and swept away a flopping catch, clutched in talons.

The one-time logging mill pond, now converted to a State park, signaled full campsites with smoke from campfires and dozens of row boats tied to the dock.

"Hey, Abel, don't be a GUBERIF," Jace said.

"What?" The boy sat straight up.

"The message painted on the road. No GUBERIF allowed here!"

"What's that?"

"Firebug spelled backward, which is someone careless with fire, who has never learned from Smokey the Bear how to prevent forest fires."

"Mom doesn't let me play with matches."

"That's good. Neither do we."

They eased into Road's End's rambling, rustic village. The 400 residents mainly divided between loners with privacy issues, retirees from Seattle or California, and generational farmers and ranchers. Many owned a past that never got settled, still in the middle of their stories. Rumors of hidden gold or promise of cheap rent enticed others. Some not hardy enough to stay soon moved on. They left single-wides and cabins behind, when they discovered the long winters too primitive a lifestyle.

Road's End—the only way to get out: retrace the way in.

They cruised down Main Street past Paddy's Trailer Park, the two-story hotel, and in front of McKane Outfitters where small flags flew from log posts showcasing huge elk horns. A slanted, tin roof covered the log building. The year before, Jace bought the shop, experimented with the slower paced rural life, then handed the business to his struggling half-brother, Norden, for a start at a new life. Norden rose to the challenge, seemed to fit in, tribal tattoos and all.

They stared at a shiny, red Harley Davidson parked in front of the store.

"Norden got a new motorcycle?" Reba asked.

"I'll check in there later," Jace commented.

Reba peered up the hilltop at the alley between the Outfitters Shop and Whitlow's Grocery where Seth Stroud used to live with his late niece, Maidie.

Hanna Jo followed her gaze. "I spent a lot of time at their place growing up."

"Grandma said you did a lot of caregiving for Maidie, during her sick spells."

"I'm sure glad I did. That's one thing I don't regret. Do you think

Seth and Hester are still here?"

"Don't know. Didn't see the purple Model T parked out front." Reba mused about the elderly newlyweds and their wedding in Goldfield, Nevada weeks before. "They said they wanted to honeymoon here. But did you know the house burned down? All that's left is the garage, small apartment above it, trees, and remnants of Maidie's garden."

"Did they figure out what happened?"

"Gas leak."

Town seemed deserted. No cars lined the only paved street, not even in front of the saloons, Delbert's Diner, or The Steak House. Reba noticed 'Closed' signs on business doors and windows.

A stricken Hanna Jo, crumpled face paler than usual, whispered, "Please! Mom didn't plan a homecoming party, did she?"

Anxious her mother might bolt, Reba felt she needed assurance. "Nah. Besides, the whole town wouldn't attend."

Or would they? Most everyone she knew told a Hanna Jo Cahill story. She seemed well-remembered, whether they actually knew her or not.

They rolled to the end of Main and turned left at Cahill Crossing to reach Stroud Ranch Road. Her attention turned to a woman who strolled, then tottered down the road toward them, like she walked in heels over gravel. But this woman wore tennies on asphalt.

Blair Runcie?

What was she doing out here, alone, without Champ, her invalid husband?

They got closer and stopped. Hollow cheeks. Gaunt face. A dazed Blair stared at them.

Reba climbed out. "Blair, are you all right?"

"I don't know you," she said.

"Sure you do. I'm Reba Cahill. I just returned from California." Had she been gone so long a lifetime neighbor wouldn't recognize her? Was Blair suffering a bit of dementia?

Blair straightened, eyes alert. "Yes, of course." She looked at the Chevy. "Is your mom with you?"

Hanna Jo rolled down her window and waved. "Hi, Blair."

The unsmiling woman stomped away without another glance. So unlike the steady, faithful, quiet but friendly mayor's wife the whole town sometimes admired, other times pitied.

Jace slid out and called, "Blair, can we give you a ride?"

The woman shook her head, slung a hand in a "keep away" move, and kept walking.

Reba peered down the road from where she'd come from, looking for evidence of an event, possibly at the Grange Hall. But why didn't she drive a rig?

As they turned down the long, dirt trail into Cahill Ranch, Reba studied the terrain. No sight of red bovines or Grandma's mares. Moss-covered wood post and barbed wire fencing included a stack of tires filled with large rocks to hold the barrier in place. A long extension of parched lawn beyond that.

Jace slowed the Chevy to a crawl as they approached the Cahill's Camperdown Elm tree, the site of Grandpa Cole's death by heart attack, beside an axe embedded in the trunk. Layers of velvet looking, but sticky feeling verdant leaves, much like sandpaper, provided summer's lush covering over knobby, twisted branches.

"I didn't realize how flat the top was," Hanna Jo commented.

Reba glanced in the rearview mirror at her mother's face, taut and tense. She wished she could reach out and assure her everything would be all right. She focused on the old elm tree instead, that familiar, mutant pillar from her childhood that now seemed to leer at her. Not as tall as a regular elm, the crooked branches contained many gnarled knots for a foothold. Often her safe haven, a great place for a kid to play. She loved to rest in the twisty branches and hide from the world among the rough leaves.

"An upside-down tree," Grandpa Cole called it. "Things are not what they seem," he chided with a curse, the only time she heard him say those words.

At other times, he admonished her when things went wrong, "Get used to it, girl. Life gets pulled inside out, just when you least expect it." And he'd point his cigar toward her favorite toy, a topsy-turvy, two-headed flip doll made of rags.

But now, blood flowed like sap through her body as she inhaled the sweet perfume of lilacs blooming nearby, despite signs of drought elsewhere.

Pearl's Blue Heelers, Paunch and Aussie, yapped from their confinement tied to the wrap-around porch, pushing each other into the shrubbery. The black and white barn cats moved their heads in tandem as they passed. Scat, the long-haired calico cat, observed them all from a tree.

Reba ignored them to scan the familiar two-story, dull, ivory white house. Windows closed up. Paint peeling more than she remembered.

As Jace dragged suitcases and bags from the Chevy, she reached for the extra house key under the cats' water dish. Abel stayed on the porch to play with the dogs. Hanna Jo hastened to her old bedroom beside Reba's.

"Grandma Pearl!" Reba shouted, as she burst into the living room. "Grandma!" she called again.

All seemed in place as she whirled through—ottoman, roll top desk, shades down like usual; worn, overstuffed couch and matching armchairs; wall of dusty books and fireplace. The things of home.

"Grandma!" A hint of echo reverberated.

She rushed to the kitchen, Grandma's bedroom, and her own room. Then, to Hanna Jo's, decorated in purple and cream, with black framed senior class picture, and a running wild horses watercolor on the walls. Her mother's attention seemed fixed on the many items in the closet and drawers she had opened, while holding her old Kodak Brownie camera.

But where was Grandma Pearl?

Signs of her scattered everywhere among the pine and oak furniture, the casual clutter, the stacks of newspapers and magazines.

Reba knew her shoe size, the brand of bleach she preferred, the smell of her hair like apples or cherries after a shampoo. She knew the scent of her favorite Jean Naté powder, and the intriguing contents of her bathroom drawers—dozens of pairs of screw-on earrings, old cologne bottles, and grandpa's collection of pipes. But she had no clue why she didn't greet them right now with ample hugs.

Especially to welcome home her prodigal daughter.

In fact, the bunkhouse looked deserted too.

A clamor from the kitchen distracted her.

"Reba, come here," Hanna Jo yelled.

She scooted through the dining room to the kitchen where her mother pointed to the fridge. She pulled off a scrap of paper attached by a magnet with her grandmother's penciled, pinched, and pithy handwriting.

Apply mulch.

Fertilize.

Assess lawn.

Summer Camp Road 7:00

"What's happening on Summer Camp Road?" Hanna Jo asked.

Reba peered at the rooster clock on the wall. "It's after 7:00 now."

"Let's check it out," Jace said.

Hanna Jo held up her left hand. "Wait, look at the calendar."

Under a picture of clustered white daisies with gold centers, Tuesday, July 30, marked with a big red X and circled.

"That was two days ago," Reba said. "She didn't mention anything special happening when we talked before we left Santa Dominga."

"What *did* she say?"

"See you when I see you."

Chapter Two

$\mathcal{R}$eba lingered a moment before she locked the door behind them.

She realized how much she missed the place. She'd been gone more than she'd been home this past spring and summer. She felt like hugging the timbered walls. This house etched with many memories seemed to welcome her. At one time, she'd felt pressed down here, nearly choked by a sense of desertion.

Today wasn't one of those times.

She muscled open the stubborn, stuck garage doors and found Pearl's two-tone green 1958 GMC Carryall in the stall. Reba's pickup parked in the place of her grandmother's missing deep red 1953 Willys Jeep.

She patted the hood and peered all around her rig, which, in addition to a horse trailer, constituted her main earthly possessions. The keys still tucked above the visor. Inside and out had been washed and cleaned recently.

They pulled Abel away from the rambunctious Paunch and

Aussie, then Jace drove them down Stroud Ranch Road, past the Grange Hall and Mosquito Ridge Cemetery. He turned east on Summer Camp Road. Around them, a few farmers still worked harvesters, until it got too dark.

A half mile down they spotted a field crammed with vehicles. Most of the town's citizens and a passel of strangers crowded lawn chairs, as though to watch an impromptu baseball game, but with no bats or bases or players on display.

Jace parked beside a broken place in a fence and they scrambled toward the mystery event. Reba searched for Grandma Pearl among the crowd as they rushed forward amid shouts, cheers, applause and a blast of musical sounds. Then she gawked at the activity among the native boulders, rocks, and fallen logs.

Piles of lumber of varying heights scattered the uneven ground, along with a row of saw horses, one of pallets, and another of ladders. Bricks stacked near a cement truck and bulldozer. A backhoe. A dump truck. Slabs of cement. Several tractors. Large concrete pipe and hay bales. Yellow and red 'Caution Keep Out' signs surrounded this semblance of a construction site.

In the middle sat an out-of-place, old phone booth, like the non-working one at Delbert's Diner. And a teardrop camper trailer, an unattached flight of steps, and a big brass bell which she guessed to be the Maidie Fortress Memorial Bell that Champ Runcie sponsored.

The most amazing part of the display ... two persons wearing hard hats rode squatty, thick-tired bikes rolling over everything—jumping, sticking, and balancing, including on the machines. They smooth-wheeled on each of the objects, then added flips and sideways twirls, before they leaped over spaces. Mesmerized, Reba stared when the pair rose up on their back wheels, synchronized, on opposite sides of the huge display.

A ballet of trick riding, up and over the obstacle course, to music from a boom box, a medley of jaunty, pulsing instrumental tunes that included a bagpipe.

When the music stopped, the bikers bowed to claps and cheers. They pressed forward to shake hands and take pictures with all who wanted. The matronly Mathwig triplets, identical in looks, different in height and stature, owners of the Road's End Hotel, stood in front of the dispersing crowd with milking pails for donations.

After the couple loaded their bikes into a large white van and pulled off their hard hats, long hair tumbled from one of them. The guy and gal backed the van up to the teardrop trailer and attached it behind.

Reba waved at Tucker Paddy and his two sons, Amos and Pico, and Cecily Bowers in black spiked heels and apple green pants and blouse, white upswept hair tucked into an apple green straw hat. She spied Tim with his son, William, and daughter, Kaitlyn, hustling to his pickup, with wife Sue Anne lagging behind, shoulders sagging, and neck bent.

But still no sign of Grandma Pearl.

Beatrice Mathwig greeted them with a round of hugs. "I don't know where Pearl is," she said, "but she had something important to do ... before you and Hanna Jo got home. 'A task I've left undone' were her exact words. This really frosts my cookies, but she insisted on not telling us the details. She didn't want to worry us, she said. I think Seth and Hester went with her." She frowned in an obvious snit. "And Vincent, too."

After a pause, Beatrice continued, "Even he wouldn't divulge anything. However, I thought they'd be here by tonight, for the circus act and ... your homecoming."

"Who is that couple?" Reba pointed to the white van with magnetic plates.

"A brother and sister act traveling across the country. They've been here all week. Everyone's enamored with them. Sure have enjoyed them at the hotel. They've got the most charming accents. Thick Scottish burrs. Started in New York, they said, and they're headed for western Canada. Then they'll journey east and return to Scotland. They're on holiday, as they put it, a gap year from their universities."

"Where in Scotland?"

"They mentioned both Glasgow and Edinburgh Universities, I believe."

Reba pressed her lips together, trying to assess all the news. She started to ask more, but Beatrice scooted away before she could.

After a greeting from Tucker's wife, Ida, Reba blurted out, "What's going on over there?"

"The new church. Isn't it exciting?"

"But who ...?"

"Champ Runcie. He's got everything up and going. They aim to start on it soon. Quite a few signed on to help, including my Tucker. They're waiting for a building permit."

Other folks hugged them or held out their hands to Reba, Hanna Jo, Jace, and even Abel.

Cicely Bowers offered to Hanna Jo, "Remember this and you'll survive fine—the people of Road's End don't like to gossip. They *love* to gossip. That's their problem, not yours." She hugged Hanna Jo a second time. "You remind me so much of my niece, Trish. Please come visit."

After that, the field vacated quickly.

"Who is Cicely?" Hanna Jo asked.

"She's new in town. Been here a couple years. From Seattle. She's become a good friend of the Mathwig triplets. She's known for loving hats of all kinds. She bought that big old, rambling Stroud house from Seth and converted it into a Bed and Breakfast."

She looked around for the traveling couple and noticed Abel peering in the van and peppering them with questions. She hurried over to whisk the boy away and thought she detected a quick, furtive glance between the two strangers when she mentioned her name.

The young woman wound her tawny hair, longer, thicker, and curlier than Reba ever dreamed of having, even with a Curly Cue treatment, into a careless knot. "So, you belong to Pearl Cahill. We thought you weren't arriving until tomorrow or later." The burr on the r's didn't soften the obvious disappointment.

"I'm Archie," the young man inserted. "This is my twin sister, Wynda. Pearl invited us to stay at her place. We've been doing a few chores for her. But, of course, since you're here ..." His flat voice trailed off. The statement hung heavy in the air, a dangling question attached.

"Do you know where Grandma Pearl went?"

"Sorry, no. We told her we'd look after the place, until she returned

or you arrived."

Hanna Jo stomped to the Chevy, face flushed, shoulders arched. Reba sensed her flinch of rejection.

"We meant no harm," Archie replied. "We try to help out wherever we go, as well as entertain. And we *ken* a thing or two about horses and *coos*."

"*Coos*?" Reba repeated.

"The beef. Your animals. As mentioned, we've been helping a wee bit."

She wondered if he'd washed her pickup.

"Great riding," Jace interrupted. "How'd you learn to do that?"

"Lots of practice." Wynda splashed an awesome smile all over him. Flaxen hair, rosy cheeks, energetic, slender with dark, snapping eyes, and rich, warm voice. The tantalizing accent could charm a viper. "We learned from a man in Edinburgh. We're not half as good as he is though."

"Really?" Jace plied his best grin.

"Would you teach me?" Abel tried to peer in the van. "I'm almost eleven."

"Maybe we could show you a thing or two." Archie side-glanced Reba. She wondered if she should encourage them to stay another night. Typical Road's End hospitality. Only she didn't feel up to it.

"You know, I wore Oshkosh dungarees at your age," Archie said to Abel.

"And you hated them," Wynda reminded him.

Abel scrunched his nose. "I don't know what that is."

Archie tapped the boy's shoulder. "That's a good thing."

Coming from behind, recently returned Gulf War veteran, Sergeant Elliot Laws, and his father, Nez Perce Indian elder, Thomas Hawk, appeared beside them and introduced themselves to the Scottish pair.

"I've met a few of your countrymen," Elliot said. "I heard the Scottish regiment play the pipes in the Gulf War."

"Aye, a bagpipe is meant to inspire fighters and provoke enemies." Archie reached into the van, pulled out a bagpipe, and on the spot played a few bars from "Danny Boy." His small audience grew to a few more passing by on the road who stopped, so he expanded the song. All applauded when he finished.

"Incredible bike and bagpipe performance," Jace remarked as the two eased into their van.

"Great to see you, Elliot," Reba said. "How was your journey to Canada with your grandfather?" She nodded at Thomas.

"Great. Lots of Chief Joseph Trail stories to tell my kids someday. And I think it helped ease my headaches, since I returned home."

"We'd like to hear all about it, when you get a chance."

"Come to the next powwow," he offered. "I'll be doing several presentations."

Archie started to close up his van. They all returned to their rigs and the Jace car stragglers soon rolled down the road toward the stop sign. The van kept going straight to town and the Chevy turned left.

Reba hoped the Scottish twins could stay at the Road's End Hotel and prepared for a full-blown Hanna Jo meltdown. Instead, her mother heaved a sigh and said, "Actually, it's better this way. I didn't want a fuss, with a welcome home party and all. We can go about our business in private and figure out our next steps."

Reba let go the gust of breath she held. But they both expected Pearl to at least be here and waiting for them.

Jace braked the car, pulled over, and turned off the lights. "Look up at the sky."

Bursts of beams shot across like a fanned out tail. A shimmer of heavenly fingers reaching, stretching, scattering beyond stars and planets.

"Shooting stars?" Hanna Jo nudged Abel who rolled down his window for a clearer view.

"No, the Perseids," Jace replied. "Meteor showers. They're just getting started. Here comes some more! Hundreds per hour this year expected, they say. The dust particles will remain almost forever."

They all piled out of the car.

"Watch for them every night you can," Jace added. "They'll keep increasing the next week or longer."

They gawked at the heavenly lights in awe. Was it a sign of good things ahead? Or a sort of omen? Either way, Reba valued viewing the display right here, right now, with these people.

"How do you know so much about it?" she asked Jace.

"Hobby of mine."

Reba loved learning new things about her future rancher hus-band. She leaned in tight. "Thank you," she whispered.

"For what?" he whispered.

"For being here. For being mine. For loving me." She squeezed his firm shoulder, snuggled tight, and inwardly embraced his support and nearness. For a moment she set aside the perplexing situation ahead.

They lingered at the spot as the universe seemed to put on a production solely for them. A shared, comfortable hum of silence stretched between them. With great reluctance, they eased back into the car and Jace turned on the engine. They cruised down the road to the ranch house.

Jace pecked Reba's cheek before she got out. "Call me if you hear from Pearl," he said. "I'll see you in the morning."

He and Abel headed to town and the apartment they shared with Norden.

Chapter Three

After Reba unpacked, she peeked again into Pearl's room. No clues.

She tapped on her mother's door. Her bedroom looked like a bomb detonated. Contents of drawers tossed on the bed. Closet emptied out. High school memorabilia scattered. She noticed something new already added ... posters of singers from the sixties on the wall with masking tape, of Bob Dylan, Glenn Campbell, and the Fab Four Beatles.

"Where did you get those?" Reba asked.

"Obviously you haven't cleaned behind the dresser. I hid them there long ago."

"You need to frame them and hang them proper."

The turquoise and gold squash blossom necklace inherited from Maidie Fortress spread on top the dresser out of the open velvet lined wooden case.

"You need to store that necklace in a secure place."

Her mother looked up from a stack of photos. "Uh huh."

"You okay?"

"I've come to the conclusion, I think I could live here again and survive. At least, I'd like to prove it to myself. And to you and Mom." Her mother pulled her senior picture off the wall. "Did you know I was a cheerleader?"

"Yep."

"I was a happy kid and teen too, until ..."

Reba turned icy as she flinched. *Until I was born?*

"When I found out I was pregnant, I headed to Boise, to stay with Vincent and his wife. You never knew her. She died soon after of cancer. A wonderful woman." Hanna Jo pushed against her temples with a palm. "Don't know if it makes any difference to you, but I suffered post-partum depression. With Michael too. That's when I found out what to call it. I lived like a recluse. I felt so chained ... so weighted down. After Griff left me, I headed to the Nevada desert. That's where I became known as Wild Horse Hanna by the locals."

Reba listened to her mother ramble, as she pushed away thigh-high panty hose, green eye shadow, and vinyl records including "Yellow Submarine" by the Beatles, so she could ease onto the bed. She didn't want to interrupt this rare moment of open sharing.

"Don't think Mom knew this," Hanna Jo continued, "but Papa Cole found me once. Through Vincent, I think. He made sure I was okay. He tried to get me to come home. Maybe if I had ..." Her eyes squinted. With her mouth pulled down, she looked years older. "I attended a party of sorts. Out in the desert. Had only a few drinks but got crazy drunk. I wandered away and flung myself on one of my favorite wild horses. I fell off and suffered a concussion. Did strange things, I'm told. That was the first time I was taken to the mental institute."

Questions ripped through Reba's head. She ventured one. "How did you take care of yourself, pay for all of that?"

"Well, I admit I'm not good at saving money. If I have it, I spend it. Griff certainly knows that about me. But I never went into debt and do have a few dollars left. All those odd jobs I talk about—that's real. But none lasted long, especially the truck driving. I'm not the best driver. Had plenty of fender benders." She faked a grin.

That reminded Reba of her mother's crash in Reno on McCarren Boulevard, shortly after running off with Pearl's rig, and right after they rescued her from the mental institute.

"Papa Cole gave me money a few times." Hanna Jo rattled a groan. "I'm going to need to get a job."

"Hey, you're back at the ranch. Grandma pays me wages plus room and board, of course."

"But can she afford us both full-time?"

Jace too. And whoever he'd need to hire for the farming of crops.

"We'll figure it out," Reba insisted. She fully believed Jace could come through for them, one way or another.

"Shall we check the animals?"

"I'm bushed. Let's wait till morning. First dibs on the bathroom."

At 5:00 a.m., Reba poked around in the cupboards and fridge to prepare a breakfast of strong coffee and buttermilk pancakes with huckleberry syrup. She added bacon to her stack of pancakes and ate a plate full. She scanned the county newspaper, read through a stack of unpaid bills, and contemplated the first day of riding the ranch with her future husband and what happened to Grandma Pearl.

Her mother appeared in sunglasses, Wranglers, tank top, and old boots, ready to work. "What's on the schedule?"

Reba smiled, encouraged by her enthusiasm. "First, head to the barn, manage the horses, and then off to the main pastures to check the cattle. Not sure what all has been going on, but, as usual, there should be plenty to do."

"You ride out to the pastures with Jace. I'll stick with the horses."

"Aren't you interested in the cows at all?"

"Not really. Have at 'em."

While Hanna Jo ate, Reba packed roast beef sandwiches and potato chips in brown paper bags and filled a couple thermoses with coffee and punch Kool-Aid. Hanna Jo strolled outside and Reba followed through the overgrown, surrounding lawn. Grandma Pearl had neglected yard duty.

"This ranch used to be my safe haven from so many things," Hanna Jo said. "Now it spooks me."

"Only if you let it." Reba tried to keep up with her mother's longer stride. "My friend Ginny George and I liked to hunker around here more than any other place."

"Funny, I had a lot of friends, but no one special person or any very close. Even those I thought were friends have moved away, last time I heard."

Reba mused about that. Everyone in town talked about her mother so much, she presumed she was very popular. Didn't mean she couldn't also be lonely.

"Actually, my best friends were the Runcie brothers," Hanna Jo continued.

Reba took in a sharp intake of breath. She wondered whether to encourage a sore subject. "Don too?"

Hanna Jo closed her eyes. "Oh, yeah. He was the worst tease. Liked to call me spitfire." She peered around and inhaled. "Love the perfume of mountain air and the pungent, earthy smell of a barn."

"I so agree with that."

"The horses are shedding and the hooves could use a trim," her mother commented.

They fed and brushed down the horses until Jace and Abel showed up. Jace immediately picked out one of Pearl's mares. He took her to the water trough. "She looked a bit thirsty," Jace said.

Abel climbed with ease behind Jace after he saddled the mare, like he'd done many times on Arabians at the McKane Riding Company in California.

"We need a kid horse," Hanna Jo announced. "In fact, lots more horses of all kinds."

"Hold that thought," Reba replied. "We'll talk to Grandma about it." Reba mounted Pearl's favorite mare with a press of rising excitement. "Be back in a couple hours." Now began Jace's first official training lesson in becoming her rancher husband.

She noticed a cloud cover blowing in from the north. Partly cloudy? Or summer shower? Nothing would dampen her mood. She turned to her riding partner. "You set a nice seat, cowboy."

He tipped his hat. "Why, thank you, Ma'am, and so do you."

Living her dream, Reba rode beside her man out on the Cahill property, inhaling Cahill air, viewing the spread of a Cahill landscape. They followed one of the wood post and barbed wire fences several miles before Reba scouted for the first sign of cows in the pastures. She'd expected to see them before now.

For Lesson One, she began with stats. "We've got about ten miles of fence."

"That's nice. Your eyes ... they're so green this morning."

Reba blinked. "They're hazel, according to my driver's license."

"Not really. Despite the fact they sparkle at times, they're a disturbing shade of emerald green."

"What's disturbing about them?"

"A guy could drown in them. They made me fall in love with you. That and the dusting of freckles on your ..."

"On my what?"

"Your neck."

She snickered. "And what about my Curly Cue hair?"

Jace lightly slapped at the reins. "Everything about you. Your smile. Your blushes. Your charm. Reba Mae, you're good for me."

Abel gagged. "You guys are grossing me out."

"Listen and learn, Buddy," Jace said.

Reba got serious. "No, you listen and learn. You, sir, are trying to divert me from an important matter. Pay attention. Now, how much fence do we have?"

"Ten miles," Abel replied.

"Good for you." She turned to Jace. "And the Cahill Ranch covers 1200 acres."

"How tall are you, anyway?"

Reba scowled. "5' 3 ½". Born 1966. I play guitar and sing at church when Grandma insists. I've been known to cook a mean beef stew. Anything else you want to know?"

"Your greatest fear."

The sudden question rocked her, almost marring this near-perfect moment. Floating words tumbled around her. She could fill a list.

Losing Jace.

Losing Grandma Pearl.

Her mom returning to the institute.

Learning more terrible family secrets.

Quigley escaping from prison.

Her life's purpose shattered.

Being abandoned again.

Losing ... herself.

Reba looked all around. "Losing this ranch." Her grandma's ranch, that is.

"And ..." Jace continued.

A pause prickled between them.

"And what?"

"Being like your mom."

Reba flinched, her jaw flexing, and shuttered her response. He pulled that observation from the core of her. She needed to change the subject quick. "Moving on, we care for sixty head of cattle."

"Let's see, that's at least two bulls."

"Good! That's right, one for every twenty-five or so. And we pack elk hunters on weekends in the fall. It brings in extra funds."

"You look so comfortable on a horse," Jace continued, "like it's an extension of you."

"Yeah. Riding exhilarates me, as well as helps me forget things I don't want to remember." Such as her sad family history. "No hour is wasted that is spent in the saddle." A thunderhead towered in the distance. She thought she heard rumbling far away. "I'd better finish this quick."

"Finish what?"

"Lesson One of the ranch training of Jace McKane."

"Okay, go for it." He shifted in his saddle and rode a bit closer.

"*If* we'd seeded any crops this year, we'd have to harvest, clean, and service combines and trucks right about now."

"Maybe next year?"

She nodded in delight. "We've basically been letting the ground go fallow since we lost Grandpa two years ago. It's long enough."

"What crops do best here?"

"Bluegrass and wheat, canola and barley. Also, peas and clover. And August is a good month to hire a crew to pick up rocks in the fields before seeding. We need to do that every year."

"Why? Don't you get rid of them?"

"Not really. Frost and freeze expands them, pushes up another reservoir of them from down deep. Plus, the ground dirt settles."

He jerked to another subject. "Ever thought about adding pigs?"

She frowned. "Pigs! Had several for 4-H projects. That was enough for me. They're ornery and sneaky."

"And smart, I hear, as well as very tasty. Or how about llamas?"

She shrugged and pointed down a draw. "There are some of our *coos*." Using the Scottish term made her wonder if they'd see Wynda and Archie ever again.

She started right in on Lesson Two. "We vaccinate cows in spring for various diseases, castrate the bull calves, and brand them with a red-hot iron."

"Does it hurt them?" Abel asked.

"Not really. Then we pair up cows and calves and haul or drive them by four wheelers out to these pastures. After that, we check for horn flies, porcupine quills, rattlesnake bites, poisonous plants, and their water source. We also supply them salt blocks or loose salt in the feeder—about a ton a year."

Jace snickered. "And the bulls just do their thing."

"Gotta pay close attention to the bulls. They're notorious for getting injured—feet go bad, they break legs, get cut up fighting near barbed wire fence, infections or injuries ... in private places." She avoided looking at Abel or Jace.

"Well, they are very active," Jace remarked. "Where do you get your bulls?"

"Private treaty or bull sales. They're expensive ... $2500 or more for a range bull. Trouble is, the better the bull, the more likely he is to go bad. Cahill's Law. Anyway, sure seems like it."

Jace surveyed the terrain. "Not much good eating left in this pasture."

"We supplement, feed them with grass hay—35-40 pounds per cow per day—and protein tubs."

"Spendy."

"Yep. Another reason to get our field crops going again soon."

"Any predators?"

"Not so much in summer. In winter, coyotes. An occasional bear or wolf. It's rare though."

A flash of light streaked and thunder roared closer, deep in the canyon. "And they occasionally get hit by lightning," she added. Charcoal clouds hovered overhead and released a splat of sprinkles. "Maybe we'd better turn around ..." she began and stopped.

A rig headed their way, fast and furious. As it got closer, she shivered, like a frigid wind blew in the sultry, late morning heavy humidity. Surely she wouldn't have to face the Runcies so soon. She was so not ready.

She needed more time to figure a way to co-exist, as one of a dozen surrounding area ranchers in this close-knit community. However, not right away. Certainly, not this moment.

But there they loomed, big as strife.

Chapter Four

*D*river and passenger piled out of the pickup, slamming the doors.

Tim Runcie held back, while his father, Don, stomped forward with a greeting. "Reba, Jace, nice to have you in Road's End again. Mom said she saw you last night."

Reba fought for control of herself and the mare that reared and circled at this unexpected encounter. They stood so close, while hidden secrets enclosed them in steel barriers, like separate prison walls.

A wall towered between them.

High.

Impenetrable.

She tried not to let the knowledge pounding her mind so loud look too obvious. Surely they could hear it, sense it.

Don with the strong, sun bronzed stubbled jaw and Tim with the sun-streaked dark hair owned a part of the genetic code coursing through her. She presumed they didn't know that fact. She hoped they never would. With a start, she realized Jace probably didn't either.

Should she keep knowledge like that from a fiancé, from a husband? She suspected marriage might be the ultimate invasion of privacy. No secrets allowed. But how could she begin to broach the subject?

"What's up?" she said.

Don began coughing and quickly pulled up the bandanna around his neck over his nose and mouth, his notorious allergies acting up. "Nothing, really. We were looking for that last herd of cows. We thought they might be down here." He held out a grimy, calloused hand used to hard, heavy work, to both of them.

Reba marveled again how this man, and others like him, stuck to farming with all their related miseries. Allergic to his job, what irony and agony.

"I don't understand. This is our pasture." She looked down the draw again as thunder rumbled louder. "And our cows. Look for yourself. They're red with Cahill brands."

Their trademark fat Hereford cows auburn and magenta starkly contrasted with black Runcie Ranch cows.

He sneezed more than once, stared at her, and cleared his throat several times. "You don't know, do you?"

"Know what?" That chill again.

He slammed his eyes shut, his forehead creased with anxiety. "Reba, I had no idea ..." He hunched over as if in pain. "I didn't expect to be the one telling you. I thought Pearl ... you see, actually, Cahill Ranch is Runcie pasture now, including all the cattle."

His words slithered in her mind, flicking like a deadly snake's tongue. She couldn't bear to look at Jace. "Don, are you crazy? This is Cahill land and you know it."

He looked down, shifted from one leg to another, his hat crooked on his head. "No, it's not. Dad and Pearl signed the papers days ago."

"Days ago?" Jace retorted. "Even if that was so, you can't take immediate possession. Those things take time."

"Pearl insisted. She gave us permission. She told us to get right on the land and take it over." Don looked around and hacked again, this time deeper. He turned red stained eyes toward her, and then averted his glance. His obvious misery revealed he realized an absolutely good thing for him, translated to the worst news ever for her.

He straightened his shoulders, as though to try a re-set. "Way too much star thistle here. We'll have to remedy that."

Reba too stunned for a snippy comeback, Don continued, "We're looking for extra help, if you know of anyone." He squinted at Reba, then Jace with both apology and hint of loaded question. "Gotta run. Big day of harvest."

He gaped at the storm brewing sky. "Well, maybe not." He marched to his truck.

He and Tim jumped back in their pickup and retreated over a rise as quickly as they arrived.

Don might as well have beaten Reba with a tire iron and left her for dead. The effect wrenched the same. Her joy wadded up in a bloody rag at her feet.

"Reba Mae," Jace began and stopped.

A gust of wind dashed over them, whipping Reba's hair and spinning ground debris like devil dust. She swiveled her shoulder into it as a loud crack and crash thundered directly overhead and zigzags of light splayed.

Jace muttered something.

Reba turned the mare, tried to ignore him, and shut out the whole world.

Jace shouted through the storm. "I think we just got offered a job."

"On our own ranch." Reba spit the words out. Growing rage tromped up her spine like steel. "I should have asked him where Grandma Pearl is. He seems to know much more than anyone what's going on around here."

She tried to settle the mare as lightning snapped again over the canyon. She clutched the horse's mane as hard, muddy raindrops pelted her face. The storm flare outside matched her inward churn.

"Shouldn't we head home?" Jace hollered into the downpour.

Home?

Where was home?

Reba, Jace, and Abel rode back to the house as wind howled and rain dumped over them in sheets. Drenched in the downpour, the storm eventually quit as quickly as it started.

Jace attempted conversation. "They've got to have proof, a properly signed bill of sale, signed by Pearl."

Reba held up her hand to stop him. Too devastated to respond, her earlier clueless ramblings of ranch training now mocked her, as did her long-time desire for a rancher husband.

Everything seemed so good and then ... *whack!* ... blindsided and gut-kicked. A rock of dread eeled its way into the pit of her stomach.

If Don was right, Cahill Ranch no longer existed, swallowed up with Runcie land. What did this mean for her? For Hanna Jo? For her relationship with Jace? Everything seemed so right with the two of them a week ago when he announced he wanted to learn to be a rancher, when they expressed love for each other.

But now what?

The loss of the ranch threatened the core of everything she was or aspired to be. Pain flowed through her like a rogue wave. Grief wrapped tight around her, burrowing into her bones. Would this rip apart the fragile, recent coming together of their family?

And what did the deal between Grandma Pearl and Champ include? The barns and corrals? The horses? The house? Perhaps she and Hanna Jo were now squatters. Why hadn't Grandma Pearl told them, at least discussed it with them ahead of time?

And why wasn't she here?

As a rule, Grandma Pearl didn't make big decisions on the spur of the moment. She thought things through. But once she made up her mind, she acted. And she'd presume others agreed with her, convinced by her reason and logic. Like when she encouraged Reba's best friend, Sue Anne, to date her high school sweetheart, Tim Runcie. That supposed act of betrayal turned out to be very wise, in the long run.

However, this time, she had lots more explaining to do.

Head throbbing, confused, Reba blurted out, "Maybe Mom and

I have to start paying rent to the Runcies."

Jace shouted in the storm. "We'll figure this out." He countered the jagged, apprehensive lines etched across his forehead in a semblance of a smile.

So, Champ finally won his long-coveted prize: combining his ranch with the Cahill and Stroud land. He believed they owed it to him, that the land should have been his family's from the beginning. And more than once he made snarky comments about women not able to manage a ranch on their own.

Reba admitted she couldn't do it by herself. And Grandma Pearl with knees and hips buckling didn't pull her full physical share anymore. However, they'd still been partners.

"The Dynamic Dudettes," half-brother Michael called them.

But with Jace and Hanna Jo, they increased the chance at a workable crew, with farming crops added again. Now they'd never know if the Cahill Ranch could succeed on its own or not. They'd lost the race before the first shot fired.

While they walked the horses to the barn, squishing in soaked boots and socks, Reba spotted Pearl's rig in front of the house. Seth's purple Model T parked close behind. "Looks like Grandma is here. You better get Abel home and into dry clothes."

"I've got extras in the Chevy," Jace said. "I'm staying here until we find out what's going on." As she pulled the uneaten sack lunches out of the saddle bags, Jace hugged her close from behind. "We're in this together," he affirmed.

Despite his assurance, Reba feared this would rip them apart.

What did they now have in common?

Jace and Abel sprinted to the Chevy for a clothes change while Reba snuck around to the back door. She scurried into the laundry room piled with several plastic bags filled with clothes, plunging through to find her cleanest shirt and jeans, then headed to the bathroom to change and get out of her wet clothes.

She took her time, trying to calm her frantic mind, compose her bursting heart. She heard male voices from the living room and recognized raspy Seth and Vincent Quaid.

Heart hammering against her ribs, throat dry and taut, she

slapped on a smile, thinking, *I don't want to be here!*

As she stole down the hall, she viewed more of those gathered. Seth's bride, Hester. Jace and Abel already in dry clothes. And Grandma Pearl sitting next to Vincent in her best gray polyester pantsuit, salt-and-pepper hair curly tight against her head like a fuzzy swim cap.

As Reba prepared to greet them, Hanna Jo banged through the front door, flushed, hair wild, flinging a straw cowgirl hat on a wall peg. Pearl rushed to her with open arms.

Reba studied her mother's reaction. Hanna Jo's gaze steadied on Pearl, gave her a quick hug, but as soon as she loosed her grip, she flew to Seth. She tousled his silver hair to flop over his forehead and kissed him on the cheek.

"I've got lunch about ready," Pearl said. She almost bumped into Reba. "And here's our other girl." She squeezed her. "The homecoming's a bit late, but we finally made it. You all stay here. Reba can help me while you visit." She marched into the kitchen, swirled with fruity and herbed fragrances.

On the dining room table spread two bowls of sliced watermelon and pineapple, potato salad, and several big paper buckets from Kentucky Fried Chicken. "Grandma, where have you been?"

"Now, don't you girls worry. The surgery rates high for success."

Reba stared at her. "What surgery? On your knees?"

"No, for the colon tumor. I've spent a couple days in the hospital, but I'm fine. They took a biopsy when they removed it."

Reba's glance drifted to the circled date on the calendar. A doctor appointment? "When will you know results?"

"By next week."

"Have you been in pain?"

"I've had some discomfort. Just need to lay low a while."

Reba leaned on the counter. Her grandmother seemed tired and a bit sluggish. What if it was cancer? A sharp twinge knifed through her. "What made you go to the doctor?"

Pearl handed her white paper plates and red and white checkered napkins. "Ursula Younger urged me. She and her boys have been helping on the ranch. She said I acted strange, like staring at books

without reading and gazing at the TV, but not paying much attention. She'd tell me things, but I wouldn't remember. I took longer naps than usual. I told her aging did that to you. Maybe I was getting senile. Finally, she talked to Seth and Hester about it. They forced me to the doc in Lewiston, who sent me to the specialist in Spokane."

Reba pried open a drawer to grab forks. "Where are the Younger boys? Haven't seen them since we arrived." Even at the bicycle trick act on Summer Camp Road.

"Football tryouts. Several of the prairie high schools joined together to form a team."

Did the surgery factor into turning the ranch over to Champ, unnerved by a cancer scare? Reba could hardly breathe as she broached the subject. "I saw Don Runcie out in the pasture today. He told me ..." She let the words dangle.

"Oh!" Pearl gasped in a kind of convulsion. She jerked around to holler toward the living room. "Time to eat!" Her face flushed as she frantically rubbed hands on her apron, like scratching an unbearable itch.

A bustle of commotion included Hanna Jo pushing toward them in the kitchen. "Don told you what?" She must have been standing at the doorway.

Reba flailed in a coil of panic, not knowing what to say. She dreaded her mom might shatter like crystal.

"I sold the ranch ... to Champ," Pearl blustered.

The moment turned surreal. Voices, movement faded away as Pearl, Reba, and Hanna Jo entered the grip of festering, unspoken accusations. Roaring beasts of the past threatened to erupt to a breaking point.

Help us, Lord.

Chapter Five

Reba braced for a blow-out in front of their guests. She sensed her mother set to explode. Reba tried to stretch her taut, wooden neck muscles, detected her mother's lips moving, and wondered if she prayed too.

Instead, Hanna Jo squeezed her eyes shut. A shaky, halting voice wheezed out, "Why now?" before she rushed out.

Pearl spread her fingers like a fan against her chest as she joined the nine gathered around the table.

Reba scooted next to Jace. She trembled as she reached out for his firm, assuring hand.

"Have you talked about the ranch with Pearl yet?" he whispered.

"A little. Don't know much. Where did Mom go?"

"To wash up, she said."

While they waited for Hanna Jo, they passed around the food. After a knock at the door, the Scottish twins entered with a "*Yoo-hoo.* So sorry to intrude. We'll come back later."

"No, you won't." Pearl reached for extra folding chairs against the wall and insisted they join the group at the table. She introduced Archie and Wynda as "hard workers used to ranching. You should see how they got Paunch and Aussie to work the cattle. Beautiful."

"Very impressive," Hester agreed.

Reba stuffed a retort. The cattle didn't belong to them anymore. And she did consider these strangers as intruders with all the tension of the unspoken needing to be aired.

"Wynda, Seth tells me you play the flute," Pearl said.

"Yes, and Archie plays trumpet and bagpipes."

"You ought to get with Seth sometime for a little jamming."

"Oh, we already have ... last night."

"They had checked out of the hotel," Hester explained. "They didn't realize ... that is, you told them ... anyway, the hotel's full. They parked their van at our place and slept there."

"Oh!" Pearl said. "I'm afraid that was my fault. I should have informed Reba and Hanna Jo. The bunkhouse is still available."

"We left our bags there," Archie said.

Reba excused herself to check on her mother. She cringed she hadn't offered the bunkhouse to this couple herself. But she'd been caught by surprise. And disoriented by their first night home. And now she felt more out of sorts than ever.

She tapped at Hanna Jo's door. After she rapped again, she slowly peered in. "Mom?" She entered the still chaotic room. She glimpsed into the bathroom and looked out at the back porch and yard. She sauntered back to the table and whispered to Jace, "She's gone."

"Where to?"

"Don't know." Was this the way it would always be? Never knowing when her mother would take off? "She should have told us she was leaving," she added.

A mutiny of emotions invaded Reba, all mixed together, like some mad fiddler played them. She tried to enjoy Wynda and Archie and their fascinating accents and captivating personalities as they chattered about life in Scotland. They reminded her of Grandpa Cole and his stories of Scottish myths, the seal people, and water horses. But she had no hankering for chitchat.

Her brief honeymoon with joy imploded.

How ironic those foreign strangers on a lark away from college, bent on their own youthful adventures, overshadowed the finale to the Cahill women's own arduous trials. And triumphs.

Her engagement.

The homecoming.

On top of it all, devastating reality now darkened everything: the loss of the ranch.

The cocoon of brief well-being she felt on the road cracked and the only butterflies to escape fluttered in a frenzy in her stomach. She prayed to hold on, to control herself in a growing, untenable situation.

"Mother, don't you disappear on me," she whispered.

Had she checked out for good? Again?

Only this time, Reba could understand Hanna Jo's rebellion and despair. Perhaps she fled to the hills, like Reba often did, to assess things, to be renewed, to face hard facts.

"What was he like, your grandpa?" she faintly heard.

"What?" She looked up, trying to focus on those present. Wynda was talking to her.

"I'm sorry, I didn't mean to intrude. I was curious about the Cole Cahill I hear mentioned a lot."

"Well, I always knew he loved me and was on my side." She smiled in spite of her noxious mood at the mental image of the tranquil, gentle man. "He was kind, but he did have stretches now and then when he got riled. He'd ride to town like Gary Cooper in High Noon, to face down the brutes, so to speak, if he thought anyone got treated unfair."

For instance, he'd never abide the way Champ treated them lately. And she knew for certain, he'd never agree to hand over the ranch to that man. "You do know Grandma recently sold the ranch," Reba said to Archie, spite in her heart as she glared at Pearl.

"Well, that's a fine how do ya do," Archie replied. "Who's got it now?"

"Our neighbors, the Runcies."

"Did you get a fair deal?"

"Well ..."

Reba's hesitation elicited a strong response.

"What do you expect then? The name's Runcie. He's an Englishman." Archie spit into his hand and wiped it with a napkin. "He's a jumped-up little jerk."

A bit of spite between the Scots and Brits? Whatever, the young man endeared himself to Reba with that slight.

After lunch, Jace caressed Reba's hair. "We'll work through this," he assured her.

She shrugged, too numb to speak.

"Find out if Pearl will let me look at the papers for the ranch sale."

"Hoping for a loophole?"

"I don't know. I'd like to read them over, to know where we stand."

Abel asked permission to feed the bowl of watermelon rind in the kitchen to the horses. Jace went with him and then they left for the Outfitters Shop to help Norden stock shelves since he recently lost an employee.

"And you need time with your family," he told Reba.

Clutching pinky fingers, Seth and Hester headed home for naps.

"Let us know if you need us to do anything, anything at all," the MacKenzie twins said and excused themselves to set up in the bunkhouse and bike down the Old Grade.

Reba and Vincent washed dishes and cleaned up the kitchen still smelling of lingering greasy chicken, while Pearl changed her gray pantsuit for a pair of denim overalls. When she returned, she fixed steely, blue eyes on Reba.

"Grandma, why?" Reba twisted and unwound a damp white muslin towel embroidered with sunflowers.

Pearl peeped at Vincent. Now her eyes glistened, turned watery.

He held up his hands. "I knew nothing about it until afterward. I wouldn't be here now, except Seth and Hester told me about her going to the doc and it sounded serious. I was concerned."

Reba wondered if he and Beatrice Mathwig ... earlier in the summer they seemed chummy, especially when Grandma Pearl kept him at a distance.

Pearl plopped her hands on her hips. "Okay, none of you is pleased, but there were so many reasons. To begin with, you haven't been here to help out and ... I didn't know *for sure* when or if you'd return."

When Reba began to protest, Pearl held up her hand. "Let me finish. I know most of your being gone had to do with Hanna Jo. However, I wasn't feeling well, kept getting sicker, weaker ... troubled by my poor health ... rheumatism and bad eyesight, for starters. On and on. And Champ threatened eminent domain again—for the whole ranch. He claimed he could prove suspicion our property was involved in some sort of criminal activity. At the least, he'd cut off our utilities."

"What criminal activity?"

"Cattle rustling. Tax evasion. Animal abuse."

"What? He couldn't get away with that, any of it. Why didn't you tell me?" Reba implored.

"Or me?" Vincent's face blotched with irritation.

"I tried calling, but when I'd reach you, the timing seemed wrong. You seemed hurried or in a quandary. And I'm sure Champ could somehow make it stick or smear us in the trying. Besides, I didn't want you bothered about it. And I could see old age creeping up on me. And then, our property tax raised ... a lot."

"Champ's finagling?" Reba asked.

Pearl shrugged. "Maybe. I already owed a sum in other back taxes. Add to that all the worry about Hanna Jo. It weighed on me. Then, I found one of our bulls shot dead."

Reba snapped the towel over a hanger. "Who did it?"

"Don't know. Could have been a careless hunter. Unfortunately, he was too old and tough to butcher."

"The hunter?" Vincent kept a straight face.

Reba gave a glimmer of a small smile with taut muscles. "If only we could have talked it through ... all of us, including Mom and Jace. And Seth. This used to be a part of his ranch. There's family history here for him too."

"There's more." Pearl shuffled to the couch and stretched her legs prone on top of moose and wolf print brown pillows. "Champ offered to drop the lawsuit in the bargain, *if* I decided before you got home. *And* ... he'd release the building of the new church to me, including the property he confiscated from us, plus all the supplies and equipment already purchased."

A frown crouched between Vincent's eyes. "So, he sweetened the pot."

"Considerably. Can't you see how tempting that was?"

"Exactly what does Champ get?" Reba asked.

"The pasture, fields, cows, outbuildings, and most all the machinery. We keep the house, main barn, corrals, and mares."

"But what about me and mom? And Jace? We arrived home fully expecting to help you out, to take over, to begin running the ranch. Did you really think all that through?"

Pearl's eyes welled up again and Vincent rubbed her shoulder. She leaned against him, shrinking in size. "Of course I did. But everything seemed hazy on your end. And I knew about the money I owed. Vincent ..." She looked down. "He offered to help several times, but I couldn't let him do it. I just couldn't. Then add the lawsuit, all those long years of litigation ahead of us. That's what I'd bequeath you. I didn't want you or Hanna Jo to feel tied down to this place, like you had to keep it up, and take on the debt and hassles. I wanted you both to have choices."

Reba squeezed her clammy palms hard, fighting a burst of hysterics. "This gives me and Mom no choice at all. There's nothing here in Road's End for either of us. And this thwarts any prospect of becoming a family again." Or her and Jace to remain a couple. Practically her whole life she'd been searching for a rancher husband.

Now what?

However, she couldn't help agonizing for her grandmother too. She dearly loved Grandma Pearl and finally understood her conflict, how old and tired, worn-out and sick she felt. And the debt must have overwhelmed her.

She dropped her head. She couldn't bear for her grandmother to perceive the signs of fury rumbling around inside.

"I wanted you to discover a life away from Road's End ... and from Champ. I thought it the best solution for everyone."

That reason sounded lame to Reba. "But ranching is all I know, the one career that fits. You taught me everything about the job from the day I hid in the root cellar. Now you've taken it away." Her mind fisted in a ball of broken strands so tight she could scarcely breathe. Certainly little other opportunity existed for making a decent living in Road's End. Where would she go? What would she do? "The papers you signed, could we look at them, me and Jace?"

Pearl seemed relieved, like this was a sign of acceptance. "Sure. Why not? Meanwhile, you should know you can live here for as long as you want."

She meant to be generous, yet it seemed so inadequate, so … final.

Reba longed for Jace to be here, to hold her, comfort her, and come up with an instant miracle solution. She also dreaded the discussion she knew they must have. Where did they go from here? What did this turn of events bode for their future?

Then, she remembered something else. "You told me the prime reason you left me and Mom on the road there in Nevada was to return home to fight for the ranch. You had to get back to do that," she charged.

She'd witnessed Pearl contend for justice and rights many times before. At the Idaho state legislature to speak out for tax relief for farmers and home schools. To mediate peace with Nez Perce tribal councils over reservation issues. To debate Washington D.C. bigwigs about wilderness boundaries. Now this once strong woman floundered in defeat without so much as a whimper.

"I did try. Vincent knows. He was my accomplice. I managed to make Champ so angry, he threatened a second lawsuit, for harassment." Pearl plodded to her bedroom and returned with a manila envelope packet. "Should be all there."

"Could we make a copy? I'll return the originals."

Pearl nodded and Vincent suggested she use the Xerox machine at the hotel. "I'd like a copy too," he said.

Pearl spread out on the couch again and Vincent adjusted the pillows under her head and quick-rubbed her calves and feet. How comfortable they seemed with each other.

"Reba, I may have had to sell the ranch to pay for court costs anyway. And there's more." Pearl let out a moan. "My failure ... as a parent. I've had to admit I'm not the best mom in the world. Even as a young girl, Hanna Jo could be on top of the world one day, on the bottom of the heap the next. Sometimes we ordered our existence around her moods. Not a good idea. I know it now, too late. I tried to make up for it by being tougher with you. Guess I was a poor grandparent too."

"That's not true, not a word of it." Reba glanced at Vincent for further affirmation.

"I agree," he said.

"But what has that to do with selling the ranch?" Reba prompted.

Pearl closed her eyes. "I couldn't put you both through this. I've fought Champ so long, so many decades. The lawsuit ... that was the last straw."

"But we fully expected to face the challenge together." She looked again at Vincent who nodded.

Pearl kept on as though she hadn't heard her. "You know, I considered running for mayor against Champ."

"You'd make a great one," Vincent said.

"So I've been told ... by many. However, I finally realized I had no *oomph* for it. No stamina. I'm done." She opened her eyes and shook a knobby finger at Reba. "I never want to go to an old folk's home. I boarded at one once in college. A man died at the dinner table. They had to close it down since it was so poorly run. I'd rather hire someone when and if I ..." She paused as they filled in the obvious.

They heard a squeal of brakes and a bang. Reba pried open the window blinds. "It's Soren. And Valery."

They slipped out on the porch after Reba and Vincent helped Pearl up.

"Howdy." Tall, thirties, muscular, handsome Soren tipped his cowboy hat, revealing dark but silver streaked hair. Determined eyes, sturdy, muscled arms, the one that got away. The one Reba never had in the first place. "We brought Banner to you."

Valery hugged Reba and Pearl hobbled over with her walking

stick to shake their hands.

The buckskin popped from the trailer like a skittish colt, though she was full grown. No longer on her home turf, she confronted foreign sights, smells, and sounds and let her general disapproval about everything be known.

"I was told she can be reckless," Valery said. "But she's got stamina and sound body with a strong heart and lungs. She's intelligent too. And, I believe, still teachable."

"Do you know what happened to her in the Gulf War?" Reba asked.

"She was made battle ready by being taught to carry ammunition and injured soldiers to safety, before she got wounded in her flank."

"A hero," Reba said.

But right now the buckskin shied from the slightest movement or noise. A twig snapping. A branch swaying in the wind. She trusted none of them, including Reba, despite their bonding at Soren's corral the month before. Not even Soren or Valery could control her. She kicked and reared as wild as could be.

"She can be bothered by smells," Valery hollered after a milder kick. "I found out she prefers jasmine and lavender rather than peppermint."

"Lavender is supposed to be calming," Reba mentioned.

All three of them maneuvering her, Pearl coached from the sidelines. They finally finessed Banner into the empty corral. The beautiful animal responded to every movement in a state of agitation, ready to flee. Hard to imagine she once exhibited the pluck and willpower to perform great deeds.

As the buckskin cowered in a corner, Valery announced, "We're officially on our honeymoon."

"We tied the knot before we left Vegas," Soren said.

"Who's minding the New Meadows ranch?" Reba asked.

"My former boss and neighbor, but we've got to get back soon." Soren clamped onto Valery's arm.

Reba noticed the cross around his bride's neck made out of nails, a symbol of her newfound faith.

"When's *your* big day?" Valery asked.

Reba bit her bottom lip and shrugged. "Nothing's decided. I'll, uh, let you know."

The happy couple didn't inquire further. They left soon after, to visit with Seth and Hester on their way to Coeur d'Alene and Valery's family in Spokane. Meanwhile, smoke billowed to gain a chokehold over distant charred fields.

"I see swirls both north and south of us," Pearl remarked. "You want to come with me to see if any of our neighbors need help with lightning fires?" She poked her stick toward Vincent.

"I can come, too," Reba said.

"No, you stay here and get acquainted with your new charge." Pearl waved as a rider charged toward them. "Maybe Wild Horse Hanna has some suggestions."

Her mother returned from the hills, but didn't pause long enough to issue greetings, offer where she'd been or why, or to acknowledge Banner's arrival. She tore off to the barn and rushed to the rear of the house. At least, she didn't slam the door.

New clouds formed as growing mushrooms.

More lightning likely to explode.

Chapter Six

After the thunderstorm, smoke clogged the mottled sky with a brown fog of haze. Reba ministered soothing drops to her irritated eyes, rough and dry like sandpaper, and edged toward the corral. The gate creaked open as she confronted her new charge.

Shadowed by thick despair and betrayal, Reba stewed about what to do with the rest of her life.

With Jace.

Or without him.

Banner continued to act like she'd never had any previous connection with Reba. Back to square one. The mare reverted to terror-stricken rebellion.

Reba spent the first hour or two trying to engage the buckskin from a non-threatening distance across the corral. She followed the routine she developed as a sixteen-year-old when she got a chance to break a high-strung Johnny Poe.

First, connect with Banner's eyes, as soon as possible.

She inched closer, while they got used to each other, one careful, cautious step at a time. Building trust. Repetition, repetition, repetition, hoping for a breakthrough. She even dabbed herself with Grandma Pearl's lavender cologne and stuck a wet jasmine tea bag in her pocket.

She finally risked talking to the mare and held out her hand. "Trust me. You can trust me, girl."

A tiny step forward.

"Banner, trust me one more time. Good girl."

At the right moment, she would slowly rope and un-rope her neck, all the while crooning to her, with the aim to eventually rub her all over. Reba plotted her strategy as the pale pink western sun lowered, turning deep rose and finally a shade of burnt orange. What a dramatic change in minutes, in the sky, in a life, like the stroke of a heavenly pen.

"Three field fires burned hundreds of acres of crops, threatened livestock, and edged close to several homes," Grandma Pearl reported back at the house.

Neighbors and volunteer rural firefighters put them out.

The next day, striated pink and orange still streaked across the expanse above.

Reba peered into Banner's cautious gaze again. While she tried to connect with the mare, an invasion of thoughts pinged back and forth, scurried like rats. She tried to let it sink in, what it all meant, the loss of her identity and security. She felt kicked out of her own pasture.

Maybe she and Banner shared emotions in common.

When Banner turned her back, Reba gazed bleary-eyed around the ranch, the fields, and the hills beyond, her former place of belonging. Then she scanned the old house, the one that still belonged to Pearl. In need of fresh paint, long overdue for roof and shutter repair, she wanted to hug every inch, hold it close.

In high school, Tim Runcie sprawled on the living room's worn and frayed carpet and told her, "This house groans."

"Why do you say that?" she asked.

"Because it has come through hell and high water, but still tries so hard to be friendly and welcoming."

Tim surprised her sometimes with bursts of insight like that, through all the flirting and teasing. And deceit.

She tried to remember why she left Cahill Ranch. College, of course. But she also wanted to see a bit of the world, experience something other than pines. And clear her senses of Tim Runcie. And, later, Enoch James. So, she registered at Santa Barbara University, to stick her feet in the Pacific Ocean and study public relations.

To get away from Road's End.

Like her mother did.

Except ... Reba returned.

She discarded beach shorts and tank tops and tossed on ragged Wranglers, this time for good. She roamed the pastures once more and put into practice everything she learned from her veteran cowgirl grandma. Reba believed she discerned, at times, what cows and horses thought. But she'd be the first to confess, she didn't understand what made a man tick, what he wanted, what he needed.

Until Jace.

For several days, they avoided the crucial conversation they needed to address while she fussed with Banner. Jace and Abel worked with Norden at the store, listening to his own complaints against Champ Runcie and Norden's mission for justice against the threat of exorbitant city taxes on the town's businesses, and how he could protect his store.

When Hanna Jo heard this, she rushed to Norden, ready to organize a protest. "That's not right!" she blasted.

Reba expected signboards to show up at Champ's house any day. Instead, Hanna Jo departed each morning, riding north, silent and sulking.

Biding their time, she and Jace ignored the obvious.

Finally, Reba asked him about the sale papers she'd read several times. "Interesting," was his vague reply.

Reba kept working Banner through a heat spell of eighties and nineties on their high mountain perch. They needed another thunder storm to cool off again, as long as no more fires started.

One day, she wanted to retch under all the uncertainty. While sweat burned Reba's eyes, her stomach clamped tight. She pushed the palm of her hand on her stomach and breathed slowly, deeply a dozen times, until she finally relaxed.

"Reba?"

She turned around. Despite the swelter, Pearl sat on top the corral fence in long-sleeved, red flannel shirt and Wranglers, bandanna tucked around the neck, brown felt hat in hand. Reba sauntered over and climbed up next to her, attentive to the buckskin hunkered against the far fence, munching a flake of hay.

"It's gotten so complex, it's overwhelming," her grandmother began. "I was losing myself, my sense of direction. Doing countless activities on the ranch started to zap my energy. I guess I wasn't thinking too clearly." An attempt at apology.

Reba inhaled and held her breath as long as she could. She said a quick prayer for self-control, for grace under the pressure to keep from lashing out. "Well, it's too late now. What are you going to do?"

"Quit trying to fix things, for one."

"So, we let things fall apart?"

Pearl grimaced, stretched her jiggling right leg and patted her hat against a knee. "When they lowered Cole into that deep grave at the cemetery next to the Grange Hall and I said good-bye to my dearest friend in the world, all I could think was, 'Why aren't you here, Hanna Jo?' And now that she's back, my mind rumbles around with worry. Robs me of sleep, like a monster propped on me, suffocating me. The less I sleep, the more that monster bullies me."

Reba began to relax. No wonder her grandmother's thinking had been so foggy lately.

"Know what my life's been about?" Pearl continued. "Cattle, horses, wheat fields, except those few years I taught school."

"You graduated from college in Missouri, didn't you?"

"Yep. Stephens College in Columbia. My family was all from Missouri originally. I was born in St. Joseph. Many of the early pioneers began their trek west from there, you know."

Banner whinnied, as though to tell them to stop bothering her, to keep quiet.

"It's okay, girl. We'll be leaving soon," Reba said.

Banner's head dropped and she kept eating.

"That's right, girl, you hang on."

"You're going to train her just fine," Pearl said. "Of course, I've gotten bucked off horses after I trained them, even by one I'd ridden hundreds of times. And got kicked in the head. Johnny Poe's the only horse I never could ride. No one could except you and Seth. I know he tried to warn Champ, without success. That day on Worthy Mountain in Nevada ... the ride too close to the cliff's edge."

Which confined the foolish, stubborn man to a wheelchair for life.

"About Champ ..." Reba began. What about him? Where did they begin?

Pearl hugged her arm. "I want to help however I can." She tugged tighter. "Mending fences ... that's what I do."

However, this time she gave away all the fences. And the break between Reba and Hanna Jo and Champ had all the markers of permanence.

"Really, what do *you* want to do now, Grandma?"

A pleading kind of pain filled her eyes. "I guess I'll become a useless speck of humanity."

Reba steeled herself against pity as she had to ask, "Grandma, don't take this wrong, but did you consider what Grandpa would think about giving the ranch to Champ?"

"Yesss ..." She straightened her back, twirled her hat, and crunched it on her head.

"And?"

"He'd never agree to it. So, I'm pretty much all alone in this decision."

"I never recall the two of you ever arguing about anything. He called you his 'Pearl of great price.'"

Pearl fingered a tear. "He claimed he'd do anything to get me and to keep me. And I wanted him happy, so it was a fair trade."

Reba recalled an incident at the funeral. "What was that paper you tucked in Grandpa's casket?"

"My last love letter to a dear old man. Now I shall go prepare dinner for us. Are we to expect Jace and Abel to join us?"

"I think so. Depends on how long Norden needs them."

"Won't matter. I'll fix plenty, just in case. I'll ask Wynda and Archie too."

Reba offered a tight, close-lipped smile. Why hadn't their foreign guests moved on yet?

She headed to the house behind Pearl and tapped at Hanna Jo's door, with no response.

Jace arrived with video games and Abel plunked down in front of the TV, pulled off his shoes, and curled bare feet into the carpet.

Wynda brought a vase with an arrangement of daffodils, lilacs, and fireweed. "Makes me think of home," she remarked as she placed it in the center of the dining room table with a dazzling smile aimed at Jace.

The Scottish girl's eyes shaded violet. She wore white sandals and white jumpsuit, her toenails painted purple. "By any chance, would you mind if we stayed a couple more days, maybe longer?" she asked Pearl.

"Why, sure, I don't see why not."

"I'm curious ... how did you ever wind up in our town?" Reba added silently, *and stay so long.* "We're so out of the way from anywhere."

"Well, for one thing," Wynda began, "This part of Idaho reminds us of the Scottish landscape where we come from. You've got robins and that's our national bird. You've got purple thistle, our national flower. And we have Camperdown elms. In fact, the first mutant was discovered in Scotland at the Camperdown Estate. However, our *coos* are a bit different. They're beasties, enormous creatures with

shaggy, orange red coats and sharp horns poking out at dangerous angles. And our sheep tend to be black faces."

"On our twenty-first birthdays," Archie replied, "we determined to see how the world looks and works. 'I travel not to go anywhere, but to go. I travel for travel's sake. The great affair is to move.' Robert Louis Stevenson said that. We landed here and liked it so much, we decided to stay a spell."

"And your family doesn't mind?"

"Not really. Our *faither's* a laird, a minor one," Wynda quickly added. "He's a comfortable farmer and we grew up in a two-story granite house with a wonderful view of the farming land. It's got a lodge, too, and the house has a verandah which runs around two sides."

"And a huge garden all around." Archie said.

"Charming," Reba said. "I assume he has plenty of workers."

Archie and Wynda exchanged a look.

"Yes, he does," Wynda said. "We have an older brother who is mainly in charge."

Archie changed the subject. "Do you happen to know anyone who's pro at handling a video camera? We talked with the local park ranger about biking around the lake. If we could get a recording, that would make a fantastic souvenir to bring home. Could get lots of beautiful shots to sample our trick biking, perhaps for an agent."

"Check with my brother, Norden," Jace replied. "He talks with all kinds of people in the area."

When Vincent appeared at the door, Reba asked Pearl, "Should we wait for Mom?"

"She's an adult. She can come and go as she pleases."

Reba bristled with objection. She forced strength in her words. "We shouldn't excuse her rude behavior."

Abel slapped bare feet against the linoleum kitchen floor and peered at Reba.

"You hungry?" she asked.

He nodded and Reba fought against her foul mood as she and the dignified and commanding Pearl, like in former days, served the six of them broiled steak and fresh green beans with cheesy jalapeno cornbread muffins and rhubarb-apple pie.

"I confess I did not bake the pie," Pearl said. "Charlotta Mathwig brought it."

"She should open a bakery or restaurant," Jace commented.

"She does do catering at times." Pearl cut him another piece.

He shared half of it with Abel.

Reba considered lingering questions she had for the Scottish twins, but before they could be asked, Wynda and Archie headed to the Outfitters Shop to talk to Norden.

After dinner, they all attended a lawn party at Seth and Hester's. On this pleasant summer evening, Seth played his fiddle and neighbors stopped by to listen or dance on the lawn or cement garage floor. The Younger and Paddy kids chased each other, climbed Seth's Camperdown Elm, or hit croquet balls through wickets.

Others played games on card tables and folding chairs they brought. At Hester's table, she concentrated on a diamond shaped crossword puzzle while Pearl and Reba played Scrabble.

Abel hiked up the incline to Seth's place from the Outfitters Store. He sneaked up behind Reba. "Hey, Ranch Boss, where is the center of the world?"

Hester answered for Reba. "That's easy. Right here in Maidie's garden, where I spend most of my time."

"Oh, yeah? Jace says it's anywhere Reba Mae stands."

Reba perked up. Maybe Jace still envisioned a future for them.

Abel revealed a Rubik's cube from behind his back. "And here's another puzzle I figured out, with Jace's help." He twisted the block until the colors scrambled. "Here. There's only one correct answer and billions of wrong ones. Clue: start with the corners and they can only be corner pieces." He rushed off to join the other kids.

They handed the cube around like a hot potato until Archie caught the plastic missile and started a series of furious twists, gave up, and tossed it to Abel.

After the Scrabble game, Reba, Pearl, Hester and Seth sauntered to Maidie's garden. Hester had nursed it back to health again. Vegetables and flowers thrived—daffodils and tulips, irises and petunias on raised beds. "Took quite a bit more trouble than it should," Hester said. "Someone spread everything with such a strong herbicide. It not only killed the weeds, but everything else too."

Pearl shook her head. "Who on earth would do such a thing?"

Hester sighed. "We think it was Maidie. There toward the end, she didn't always realize what she was doing. She probably mistook it for fertilizer."

Seth repeated the family history they all knew. "After fiancé Zeke died falling off that Runcie oiled roof and ..." He paused. "After the birth of the twin babies, Maidie holed up in the cabin and screamed herself into raging fits."

Reba recalled the crude gravestone on Coyote Hill with David Daniel's name on it, her mother's suspected twin brother.

"Of course, that was before Seth helped her discover gardening," Hester said.

"Yeah, that soothed her." His eyes squinted into soft sadness.

A moment later, Seth motioned to Reba to come with him to the shed. When he opened the door, a splay of summer evening light crowned a castle dollhouse. "Maidie made the blueprint. Adrienne helped build it."

Reba admired the painted, white, four-foot-tall castle with three levels, balconies and winding staircase with railings, four rooms, turrets, and wooden furnishings including two thrones.

"I thought you might like it ... a Welcome Home gift ... and for your future daughter."

A sudden heaviness fell over her like a thick wool, black veil and weighed her down.

Children? With her family history? Could that ... should that ... ever be?

Chapter Seven

*H*anna Jo cracked a bathroom window an inch or two the next morning, to rid the room of a musty smell, and lit a joss stick with a sharp sandalwood scent. Then she bathed in cloves, smoothed on body butter, and a few drops of Pearl's Estée Lauder she'd found in the medicine cabinet.

She'd paced in her room like a caged tiger the night before, sizzling with emotion. Although she braced for hurt when she returned to Road's End, prepared the best she could, the ranch sale announcement stunned her.

She dressed and stole out again to Coyote Hill. Riding the perimeter, she viewed a panorama of fields all around—wheat and barley, oats and canola. Combines harvested at a snail's pace on flatlands and sloping hills, the culmination of a year's worth of effort. She admired the smooth teamwork of grain cart tractors and grain trucks pulling into the fields, unloading the combines on the go, and transferring grain to the trucks to be hauled out.

She searched for the Runcies' black peas and white clover too, mainly for feed or cover. She studied all the fields, trying to sort out the crops by color, and straining to rationalize why she left all of this behind. Certainly not because she aspired to a nine-to-five office job of any sort.

A shimmering image of Papa Cole emerged ... soft voice, country to the core, yet a man of the world in all the topics that caught his interest.

He kept Wall Street Journals in his bathroom magazine stand and read every word.

He could converse on the Soviets in Afghanistan, the Vietnamese in Cambodia, and the Cubans everywhere else.

Meanwhile, he worried about each aspect of farming. The weather. Road conditions. Machine breakdowns. Commodity markets and prices. Flooding or drought. Trying to guess which way the markets would go was often as difficult as forecasting rain and snow patterns.

For a brief moment, she wished she'd stayed and learned from him, mentored day by day at his side on this mountain top prairie land. Maybe she'd have made a decent farm hand. Now, it was forever too late. She'd never know.

After returning from her ride up Coyote Hill, and with no sighting of beasts of any kind, Hanna Jo sprawled on her bed. Her mind riddled with the complications of her relationships and the trauma of tragedy over the years. She inwardly cowered, petrified to risk her crimped heart—with people ... or with God.

Was it because she was mentally unstable, like her biological mother? Perhaps a mix of factors complicated her makeup. Whatever, she certainly needed a purpose to keep going. She hated to admit how much returning to Road's End unnerved her.

Road's End, the place she long ago called home. This town surrounded her with people who *belonged*. The single spot on earth that stayed the same, with no hint of change. Yet everything had altered inside her, gotten distorted. Her balance upset, she felt thrown off kilter. She felt separated from these people by a chasm, a swell of knocks and bruises, still coated yellow, like a sepia history.

"Come visit me," Maidie urged when Hanna Jo turned eighteen. Then she started to utter nonsense about being her mother.

"Maidie, you know Pearl Cahill is my mom."

Maidie paid no attention to her protest. "I want you to have this," she said and slowly handed her the gold and turquoise squash blossom necklace as she blurted another outrageous assertion. "Champ Runcie was your father. He gave it to me."

At first, she didn't believe it. Pearl and Cole Cahill were the only family she knew. No one told her any different. But when the awful truth she was adopted seemed plausible, she couldn't deal with it and the facts of her true parentage. The news left her bent, broken, like a wind-battered sapling.

The worst decision she ever made: an affair with Don Runcie, a married man, just sank her lower. So wrong on many levels. She knew better from the most basic tenets of morals out of the Christian faith Pearl preached. Now, she must endure the consequences that made a royal mess of her life. And Reba's.

She dreaded even more a memory at the Camperdown Elm, her father's death bed. He became a wisp that sallow day as he withered beneath the tree.

Then the escape from her father's dying side blurred for days until her vision cleared on familiar break-away turf. Fine, wet sand on the California coast merged sky, water, and earth to tawny shades, like light through frosted glass.

How difficult to communicate to another human exactly what transpired then, how she processed things. Her mind swelled at the moment Papa Cole clutched his chest, when he saw her. She reasoned herself into running away to survive the ugly truth, about herself and her family. She could never explain its rightness or logic to her adoptive mother Pearl or to her little girl, Reba, now all grown up. She didn't even try until ... until she at long last returned home.

She used to wonder what it would be like to be somebody else, tried to imagine being inside another's skin, their thinking and view of the world. However, in Road's End that attempt at empathy stunted. Too much humiliation and shame. What was done to her, and what she did to her own self, jaundiced her mind.

She bolted—gone like the wind--ran away from everything that hurt so bad. She tried hard to forget. But now her world choked smaller, tighter, the longer she lingered in Road's End.

She needed help. She should pray, like she did as a child. She could ask God for courage to try to understand why a simple country town brought her only despair.

Hanna Jo, what do you want?

The unexpected question resonated like a thrum of echoes in her childhood room.

She wanted ... what? Purpose? Love? The devotion of a man again, like she had with Griff?

She'd never accepted the constraints of marriage before. Yet, she wanted the closeness, the intimacy, a kindred spirit companion.

Griff!

He thought of her as fickle and unstable. And he knew what a brimstone of a creature she was behind all that beautiful amiability. She'd read that phrase somewhere, recognized the personal application, and wrote it down. When she told Griff, he roared with laughter. She adored his laugh. He left anyway, without looking back. She wrote to him several times and attempted calls. She got ready to go wherever he wanted.

Finally, he returned.

However, she pushed him away again, in a quicksand of words she wished she hadn't uttered. Her heart nearly burst. "I want him so much," she told herself. "I've got to connect with him again. Gain his trust."

If only she had another chance. How could she make him believe she'd changed, after all she'd done? At the same time, she despaired, had she truly changed? She wasn't even sure herself if she'd run again, so how could he possibly trust her?

The world inside her mind ... much of it hued by her growing-up years in Road's End. But now, nothing changed. Everything changed. Her mother sold the ranch, the main reason for her return, the possibilities it held. What did she do now?

God, please help me.

She dumped the contents of her purse on the bed. There it was, the crumpled slip of paper where she'd written down the last phone number Griff had given her. Would he still be there?

She jabbed in the digits and almost plunked the receiver down as soon as it started ringing. But she forced herself to hold on.

"Hello."

She melted in relief. "Michael! This is Mom. How are you doing?"

"Hey, good to hear your voice. I'm enjoying twenty-four hour sunlight and riding under a midnight sun. Dad and I go out again in the morning. Fishing, of course. Where are you?"

"Would you believe? I'm in Road's End." She stopped to pull the receiver away and stifle a hiccupped sob. She eased her head close again. "I miss you." And Griff. How she longed for that man, even after all these years apart.

"You want to talk to Dad?"

Hanna Jo turned into gel-filled anxiety. A rush of options assailed her. What if he didn't want to talk, had enough of her lunacy, didn't want her? Surely he'd moved on and loved someone else. No point in talking to him, no point at all.

"Maybe another time."

Michael took this rebuff in stride. "I've been painting Alaskan scenery and wildlife. Lots of time for it when we're on land."

"Oh. Good for you. No pretty girls on horses?"

He snickered. "Some of that too."

"Playing the drums?"

"Nah, but I'd like to. There's this guy wanting to start a band."

"Got a girlfriend?"

"Not here. Have you seen Nina Oscar since you arrived? Pretty. Friendly. And very blonde!"

"Not yet, that I know of." She'd ask Reba about her.

"She's studying to be a pediatrician, like her mother."

"Impressive."

"Well, gotta go. Love you, Mom."

"Love you too." She cradled the receiver and her heart.

Hanna Jo, what do you want?

Quiet words. Thunderous authority. She didn't move. Every nerve bristled. This time, she recognized the divine voice.

What did she want? Not much. Hearing "I'm proud of you!" from her mother, Pearl. Forgiveness from her daughter. And to hear

Griff's voice again. To coax an "I love you forever" once more from him.

Lord, thanks for asking. Thanks for caring.

She sighed and considered abandoning the whole out-of-reach, flitting butterfly idea of Griff back in her life. Besides, she didn't relish the emotional quicksand. Meanwhile, she'd chase and corral wild horses, a challenge she knew how to do. She'd seen evidence they roamed these hills.

If any existed out there, she'd find them.

Chapter Eight

Hanna Jo took Pearl's list off the fridge that afternoon. "We've got to do our share," she told Reba. "Let's help buy groceries at Whitlow's."

Monroe 'Buckhead' Whitlow, Sue Anne's father, greeted them with his southern twang. As usual, he wore a long-sleeved shirt with starched collar and polished shoes because the attire "makes me mind my manners," he claimed. He smelled of mint and a flower like magnolias and was telling a couple who looked like campers from the park, "Two rights don't make a left."

Hanna Jo heard the clicking of dentures before she and Champ literally bumped into each other as she turned their cart against his wheelchair in the boxed cereal aisle. A first face-to-face meeting since she returned home, she was struck by the same beady, black, and almost deranged eyes.

"Oh, Champ, so sorry," she said.

"Heh," he grunted, with a dismissive kind of wave. "I heard you were in town."

She offered him a sharp, quick nod and tried not to draw back in shock. What age was he now? Late eighties? Such a striking change. He'd gained a lot of weight with stomach protruding and obese jowls. Of course, he couldn't exercise much.

"I expect you won't stay long?" His bushy eyebrows raised.

Stifling a snide rebuke, she glanced at Blair Runcie—lack of eye contact, burning cheeks, sagging posture. As Blair muttered a stiff greeting, the woman stumbled under Hanna Jo's gaze, knees hitched. She recognized that stance, seen often in many other abused women over the years.

For a moment, Hanna Jo flushed with sadness for the both of them, no matter what wrongs they'd done. A veil lifted, a curtain parted. Rustles of unhappiness and depression lived here. She could smell the putrid essence a mile away.

She understood why despair could attack Blair, but Champ? Despite his disability, he seemed to have everything in life he ever wanted. The Cahill and Runcie ranches combined under his ownership. He ruled the whole town of Road's End.

Reba sharply inhaled. Hanna Jo quickly replied, "Not sure yet." She looked at Blair again, ignored Reba, and said as sincerely as she could, "Let me know ... if ... there's anything, anything at all I could do for you."

Champ started to wheel by them both. "I think you've all done quite enough." He glared at Reba and slammed the side of his wheelchair with one stiff arm. Misery and disgust rolled across his face and registered in every pore. "What if it were reversed? How would you feel?" The man still showed swagger, even without his legs.

She tried to mentally shut Reba into silence. Meanwhile, she didn't know how she'd respond to such a calamity. In an instant of a rash, reckless action, to be severely handicapped, when used to the demeanor of robust and in charge. She breathed a brittle relief when Champ wheeled away, stiff and unsmiling, with docile Blair trailing behind. Hanna Jo reached out and touched the woman's shoulder as she passed by, but got no response.

At least Blair no longer displayed perpetual, unexplained bruises on her face and arms.

For the first time in her life, Hanna Jo felt like her very soul burned, bare before the world. This confrontation clinched it. Champ was right. Why stick around here? Without the ranch, she had no reason to stay in Road's End. She might as well get out of everyone's way.

She made a quick resolution. She'd stay in Road's End as a trial run for the rest of the month, counting down the hours to the end of August. After all, wild horses still roamed out there for her to catch.

That evening a cozy crowd gathered in the Cahill living room. Reba stared as her mother flounced toward them from the hall in mule shoes, yellow and red bermuda shorts with an orange and pink top, and jaunty yellow polyester hat like Cicely might wear. She'd painted her nails in multi-colors: blue, yellow, purple. "I dare you to comment."

"The definition of sanity in a court trial is that you know right from wrong," Reba said. "And that is so wrong."

"It's no big deal," Pearl said. "She did stuff like that often in high school."

"The key phrase being 'high school.'" Reba glared at both of them.

"I call it shabby chic." Hanna Jo's bobbed haircut might be short in length, but she was long in attitude. "I did find all this in the back of my closet. Besides," Hanna Jo positioned her hands recitation style. "My truth is what I see with my own eyes, what I touch with my hands, and what I think with my brain. My truth starts here with me and ends with me." She twirled around in the slide-in, pointy toed shoes in two spurts, a full circle.

"Mom, you're acting weird. Really bonkers."

"I call it pluck and taking charge of my life. Besides, half the town of Road's End is a little crazy. And they sure *expect* me to be. I fit right in."

"You're having an episode."

"At the institute, we called them 'situations.' You see, after this, anything I do will seem way more normal."

"By the way, we got a phone call from Reno," Pearl said. "We may get a visit from a case worker or counselor soon, to check on you."

Now Hanna Jo glared. "I refuse to go back there."

"I told them you were doing just fine."

"I'm not mentally ill. I had a temporary breakdown by doing something stupid, like taking that peyote. However, even if I was, I'd be in good company. Many great achievers dealt with mental and emotional challenges and some still do."

"Like who?" Reba asked.

"Vincent Van Gogh, Isaac Newton, the Marquis de Sade."

"The sadist?"

"Okay, not the best example, but there are plenty of others."

Reba studied her eyes, alert, alive, energy crackled around her. "You know something. What have you been up to?"

"There are wild horses in Coyote Canyon," she blurted out. "At least one's a black stallion."

Abel popped up from being glued to the TV. An assortment of Nintendo video games around him—Donkey Kong, Mario Brothers, and Tetris. "Can I see them?"

"No, because there aren't any," Reba insisted. "We've never noticed wild horses here. Not herds of them, anyway."

Hanna Jo smirked. "Maybe because you never looked for them. I can tell you don't believe me."

"You're having hallucinations again."

Her mother's silly grin evaporated as she put on a serious tone. "It's not like that. I saw them for real. I think it's because either a cougar or black bear chased them out of their secluded stomping grounds. I recognized signs for them both."

Pearl leaned forward. "It's not impossible. We've had horses run off over the years and never found them. So have other ranchers."

"But that's not the same," Reba protested.

"Sure it is," Hanna Jo said. "Doesn't take them long to revert to their wild roots. I'm going to bring those horses here myself tomorrow. At daybreak." She turned to leave the room.

Abel bounced out of his chair and sprinted after her.

Jace called out, "Abel, you can't go, so don't even ask."

The boy returned in a pout and Jace offered to take him to the corral to see Banner. He brightened and after Jace gave Reba a quick hug, they slipped out the back.

Pearl eyed Reba. "She'll need help."

"Who? Mom? She definitely needs help, but she says she can get the horses herself."

"Well, she probably could ... eventually. But if wild horses really roam around Coyote Canyon, the three of us could round them up much easier and faster."

"Grandma, you shouldn't overdo. You said you have no strength."

She rose to her feet and straightened her stance. "I've never been more convinced of anything in my life. I need to do this. For Hanna Jo. For me. You coming?" A blush of vim and vigor glowed in the older woman's face.

Reba, Pearl, and Hanna Jo left early the next morning to go after the supposed wild horses on Pearl's mares, after ignoring Hanna Jo's vigorous protests.

She demanded, "Here's the deal. I'm the boss." She stared down her daughter and mother until both agreed.

They wore cotton gloves and brought whips and ropes "although most likely we won't need them," Hanna Jo said. After the trio plodded down a dirt road for a mile, she told them, "Did I tell you I'm being followed?"

Reba inwardly groaned. A delusion or the truth? How could she ever know with her mom? They'd have to figure these claims out, one event at a time. "No. By who?"

"Don't know. I also saw someone skulking around the Camperdown Elm last night."

Reba whipped around. "Skulking?"

"That's what I'd call it. I snuck out with a big, heavy flashlight to check him out. But he ran off."

"You know what?" Pearl said. "I saw someone messing around that tree too."

Hanna Jo crowed. "Aha! And I thought the guy resembled Quigley."

The name struck alarm and revulsion in Reba's chest. Quigley Dalton, the thief, the nightmare of a stalker, the killer. He resided locked tight in a California prison, awaiting trial for two murders. One major life hassle removed. "Can't be. He's in jail."

Hanna Jo planted her feet in a wide stance. "I'm not sayin' it was Quigley. Just made me do a double-take. Meanwhile, don't walk down any dark alleys. Or dark anything. I'm sure not going to."

A phrase from Edgar Allen Poe's "The Raven" preyed on Reba: ... *whose foot-falls tinkled on the tufted floor ... And the lamp-light o'er him streaming throws his shadow on the floor.*

Reba wondered if she and Pearl should have come along on this wild horse venture after all. What if they saw no wild horses? Besides, if there were any, one experienced rider like her mom could do a better job. "How do you want to capture the horses?"

"Well, it would be easier with a helicopter."

"Is that how you did it in the desert?" Pearl asked.

"Nope, not me, but others did. We have to be careful not to run them. Nudge and follow them instead."

"Really? How do we do that?"

"Very carefully. Try to herd them along like you do cattle. If the stallion or one of the mares tries to run off, we'll corral them back to the herd."

"Okay, I get that." *I think.* Sounded much easier said than done.

"All the way to our corrals?" Pearl repeated.

"Of course not. Too far. Too hard. I scouted their natural route and fashioned a kind of capture trap, about halfway to the corrals, close enough to trailer them on in. I'll show you where when we get there."

After they rode awhile, Reba followed behind Hanna Jo and Pearl as they took a sharp turn north. "You did say these horses are beyond

Coyote Hill?" Reba called out.

"Yes, but ..."

"We're headed toward Runcie land."

"I've got it figured out. We wait until the horses get off Runcie property, or we encourage them a bit."

Reba looked around and hoped anyone with a connection to a Runcie rancher was busy far away from here. She did not want to provoke a confrontation. Pearl's nervous gaze indicated she thought the same.

"I know what you're thinking," Hanna Jo said. "We can do it."

They rode up to a round capture pen which consisted of pieces of broken fencing propped up with fallen tree branches and logs beside a row of stubby, bushy blue spruces. Reba scrutinized the catch setup closely as she rode around. Then, she dismounted and rattled each section. Surely they could be pushed through by frantic horse-flesh or jumped over.

"I know it's not the best," Hanna Jo said, "but with you two along, I can stay here for guard duty while you go get the trailer."

Reba chose her words with care. "I am impressed with how well you used the available resources."

"But you're not certain if it will hold. Once we get them here, I'm betting the stallion won't leave the mares. And the mares won't leave the colts."

Reba frowned and crinkled her nose.

"Well, at least we can try," Hanna Jo said. "The worst that can happen is they get loose."

No, the worst that could happen—one of them or the horses got injured or killed.

Her mother circled the catch pen herself as direct rays of sunlight splayed over the mountain tops. "Let's take it slow now to conserve for the chase later."

Reba and Pearl followed close behind her to get to Coyote Hill, past the north pasture. They topped another hill high enough to view the whole region. Fenced fields of browning wheat swirled in swaths around and over the swells and valleys. Dozens of cow trails criss-crossed everywhere in between clumps of purple thistle, pink and fuchsia wild rose bushes. Bald eagles perched high on cottonwood tree branches as lookouts over the riders.

Soon they reached beyond Coyote Canyon.

Hanna Jo motioned them to stop. "They're over in that open area," she whispered. "Don't make any sudden moves or sounds. Follow me and my directions."

As slowly and quietly as they could they circled a small forest, staying behind boulders and stumps, ducking to get a better view among the pines and firs.

Then Hanna Jo waved them close to her. "We watch and wait," she whispered.

Within a half hour, neck and shoulders aching with the strain, Reba spied a majestic black stallion in the center of the trees raise his head and turn his ears toward them.

Suddenly, the air shrilled with neigh and whinny alerts. Their own mares answered back and pranced around. While the riders gained control, the stallion disappeared.

They made a wide berth around the small herd of three mares and two colts that gathered closer to each other. Reba caught a flash of black to the far left. She knew enough about wild stallions to realize his jealous possessiveness of his mares could turn him to a vicious fighter, as fierce as a raging grizzly. When he made a charge toward them, Reba noted the striking resemblance to her former horse, Johnny Poe—the stance, the gallop, the white markings, the build.

"Stay calm," Hanna Jo coaxed. "Mom, stay by that largest boulder until we get the mares and colts moving."

Hanna Jo tried to nudge the black stallion toward the mares as he maneuvered like a spirit horse, fading, appearing, and vanishing from sight among the pines. They snail-paced behind him with a pattern of stopping and waiting before a steady forward movement, Reba to the far right and Hanna Jo to the left.

The next time they plodded ahead, Reba noticed a sweet and cloying smell like rotting vegetables that kinked her stomach. She peered around until she discovered a dead cougar in the brush. A huge one. Something big and powerful brought the beast down.

Was it attacked by a black mamma bear protecting a cub? Or by that wild, black stallion?

She chilled at either possibility and tried to get her mother's attention to warn her off this whole venture. However, Hanna Jo forged on without a look her way.

Then the stallion turned and cantered toward Hanna Jo, looking friendly enough to be asking for a nose rub. Reba held her breath as her mother eyed the black horse. He sauntered closer.

And closer.

Right in front of her, the two stared each other down. Then the horse's ears twitched. In an instant, the stallion lunged, towering over Hanna Jo with hooves and gaping mouth.

Reba screamed and kicked her mare into a gallop as tree branch needles slapped her face. She got near enough to try to draw his attention away. Hanna Jo slammed to the forest floor and did a quick roll behind a stand of aspens. Reba wondered if she should stop and stand still or keep running. The mare decided for her. With a quick halt, Reba tumbled over the horse's head. With both mother and daughter down, the stallion wheeled around in a threatening charge toward Pearl.

Hanna Jo screamed, "Stay still, Mom. Don't run!"

The stallion galloped within feet of Pearl and stopped.

"Keep your eyes on him. Don't turn away," Hanna Jo urged.

He soon turned from Pearl and trotted toward Reba. She noted her horse stayed and didn't run. Neither did the other mares.

She grabbed hard at her mare's reins and ogled the stallion as moments seared between them. Then she carefully rose into the mare's stirrups, while fixing her gaze into the black horse's simmering, brooding dark eyes.

They locked into each other.

An exchange of some sort passed between them. A rapport stuck, but then faded, evaporated, whisked away as the stallion shook his mane.

Reba prepared for another charge.

Instead, he offered a soft, rattling nicker and rushed toward his herd and led them in the opposite direction of where Hanna Jo created the primitive capture pen. With a flounce of his rump and a swish of his tail, the black horse forged across the farthest swale with his harem. He ran with fluid, swift motion and his black coat glimmered blue as heavy-boned legs pounded, teardrop-shaped ears flared back. He sped away from them like a lash of wind.

Reba thought of an old proverb Grandpa Cole told her—*the wind of heaven blows between a horse's ears.*

They watched until the slowest of them swept out of view.

"I lost control," Hanna said in a kind of daze.

"You're not used to that?" Pearl inquired.

"Not with a horse." Hanna Jo screwed up her face. "Time for Plan B."

Reba stretched her legs and arms, revealing soreness at every patch of her body. "Which is?"

"To be announced. Capturing wild horses in the desert is so much different. For one thing, fewer hideouts." Hanna Jo swiped pine needles off her Wranglers, and marched over to her terrified mare, cowered next to Reba's. "At least our horses stood their ground."

After the three mounted, Reba showed her mother and Pearl the dead cougar.

"Whatever got this guy could be scaring the horses," Pearl stated.

"When I was out here the other day," Hanna Jo said, "I got this eerie impression I wasn't alone. After a while I viewed an enormous, hairy, deep brown animal, at least seven to eight foot tall. He stood on his hind legs and tossed huge rocks at me, like they were pebbles. Then the shaggy creature lumbered away into the trees."

Reba cringed. Was her mother now experiencing hallucinations in daytime? Just when she validated her wild horse story, she blew it by resorting to incredulous fantasy. She studied her grandmother for a reaction.

"Thomas Hawk and his family tell stories of such a being," Pearl related. "I credited it to tribal legends. If we've got wild horses up here, no telling what else ..."

Reba frowned. *Grandma, don't encourage her.*

"Legends and myths often grow out of truth," Hanna Jo remarked. "After it ran some distance, it stopped to beat on the trees and grunt-ed at me. This creature left behind the most horrible scent--skunky, like rotting garbage and burnt rubber. Can't make up a smell like that."

The last remark must have been meant as assurance of evidence. Or a figment of her peyote warped imagination.

"Could have been a black bear," Pearl said.

"A very huge, dangerous, overgrown black bear, who happened to be brown."

"So glad he didn't attack you," Reba finally asserted.

"By the way," Hanna Jo concluded. "Just so you both know, I'm on speaking terms with God again."

Reba sucked in a quick breath.

Pearl dabbed at her eyes.

The three women made their way back to the Cahill barn with alternating visions of phantom beasts and wild horses prancing in their heads.

And Reba haunted by a black stallion, the ghost of Johnny Poe.

Chapter Nine

Pearl thought she heard Hanna Jo slip out of the house very early Sunday morning, probably to search for the wild horses. She tried to go back to sleep, but she heard a faint *tap, tap, tap* against her bedroom door.

She rose up, alert.

A more insistent, urgent *rap, rap, rap!*

"Reba, is that you?" she called out.

A deep, male, raspy whisper, "Pearl." And then a kind of ghostly echo, "Pearl!"

Her neck prickled.

She hefted herself out of bed and yanked open the door into a dark room. She flipped a light switch and saw no one. She wondered why she didn't hear footsteps or a scurrying away.

She sighed. Perhaps she experienced the remnants of a dream.

Plunked down in a chair, weary in body, mind, and spirit, she opened her Bible to Proverbs and read until the second chapter.

Listen for wisdom ... apply your heart to understand ... call out, cry aloud for insight.

Breaking the long, cold, frozen beat of silence, the clock ticked away. She listened some more and tried to release her heart of every unworthy thought that lambasted her. Easing up on her feet, she stole through the house to open a few windows to fresh, high prairie mountain air.

She gulped air as she spied out the front window a shadowy figure slinking away from the Camperdown Elm with a flashlight. The figure soon faded from view behind the bunkhouse. Could be either Wynda or Archie. She exhaled.

Should she try to investigate?

Why hadn't the pair left already? They seemed so eager to be on their way when she left for Spokane.

🐎 🐎 🐎 🐎

"Don't know what happened," Hanna Jo told Reba and Pearl when she returned. "The wild horses are gone." Then she announced, "Someone took a shot at me at the bottom of Coyote Hill."

"You're sure?" Reba remarked.

"Two bullets whizzed right by me."

"Maybe you got close to the tribal hunting grounds," Pearl commented. "And those wild horses might be umpteen miles away by now. Obviously, they're good at hiding. Nobody but you had seen them before."

Hanna Jo's mouth wrenched in that stubborn, surly way of hers.

An hour later, Pearl peered around the barn that also served as Road's End's only semblance of a church, searching for any duty left undone. Ushers Lloyd Younger and Franklin Fraley had moved the horses to the corrals and helped a crew including Younger boys shovel out the stalls.

High voltage lights with naked bulbs snapped on as they set up folding chairs, several metal music stands, and pulled out a stained and varnished rustic podium and portable platform made from old barn boards.

Reba practiced her guitar and sang softly several bars of a hymn in her country twang alto as Seth joined in with his homemade cedar fiddle.

Pearl sprayed a circle of buzzing flies with insecticide. She made sure they dropped before she propped saddlebags that smelled like leather cleaner on the platform for taking the offering.

Pearl marveled at the eclectic, country congregation.

Hefty, brawny Franklin swished off his Fraley Logging Company cap and tossed it on a stable post. He greeted his neighbor, Cicely Bowers, with low, deep voice, his gray coveralls and snoose tobacco can mark in the back pocket.

"Surprised to see you," Cicely said. "Logging slow?"

Franklin nodded. "Available for mechanic work, if you hear of any."

He sharply contrasted with thin Cicely in yellow spike heels, bleached white hair, canary yellow and watermelon pink sheath dress, topped with big pink picture hat covered with yellow roses. She could blend into a Hollywood red carpet event.

Pearl beamed with delight to view Cicely welcome a timid Hanna Jo. Her daughter was in good hands. She'd witnessed that woman charm many a person out of shyness or a snit.

Sergeant Elliot Laws slipped through the open door with a limp and holding his mother Reine's arm. Instead of his Gulf War army uniform, he wore khaki shorts, flowered shirt, and work boots. He aided Lloyd and Franklin in opening the last row of chairs.

Reine headed for the podium and quickly pulled a flute from a case and tuned it to Reba's guitar and Seth's fiddle.

Pearl sauntered to the musicians. "Let's end the service with 'God Be With You Till We Meet Again,' she suggested and pointed at Reine. "You can add the *Godki Píiwewkunyu' Héenek'e* Nez Perce version if you'd like."

"I'll let my father do it. He plans to be here too."

Right on cue, Thomas Hawk entered and strolled to his grandson.

"Too bad Elliot didn't bring his drums," Pearl mentioned.

"Oh." Reine's peaceful face tensed tight. "They are out in the back of my pickup, but ..." She frowned. "He didn't get much sleep last night."

"Hey, I won't mention it." Pearl wondered if Elliot suffered his war scene nightmares again.

She spotted Vincent standing at the door as though waiting for someone. Beatrice Mathwig? He caught her glance and marched right over. A good sign. No matter what, they could be good friends.

Before she could chat with Vincent, Tucker Paddy rushed past them smelling of pine cologne with gelled hair and jumped onto the platform with his acoustic guitar. A full band today for choruses, hymns, and other spiritual songs.

At straight up 11:00 a.m., Archie and Wynda MacKenzie eased into the far back chairs and Pearl started the service with a welcome to all attendees. She went through the motions of leading in worship, the habit of years of church-going, and often in charge.

During the announcements, right before the teaching message, Franklin stood up. "You're all invited to a planning meeting Monday evening to prep for building the new church. We'll start the work on Tuesday morning. We've got the general requirements taken care of. We have the land and materials. We've paid for the building permit and informed the county building inspector. Now, we need as many of you as possible to do the work."

Hands raised all around the room, including from a gray-haired man with wide burgundy tie, who entered late to the service. He sat near the Mathwig sisters.

"I'm in charge of providing picnic fixings all week," Charlotta Mathwig added. "Let me know what any of you plan to bring. Let's make it an old-fashioned barn raising party, without the barn, of course." She aimed a rueful smile at Pearl.

Franklin sat down.

"Whoa, wait a minute," Pearl cautioned. "We're not quite ready to get started. Don't we need an official building committee, with someone in charge with building experience?"

"Got that all figured out," Lloyd Younger insisted. "Champ says he gave you the blueprint. We'll put Franklin in charge and form the committee right now."

Six hands shot up.

"There you go, Pearl. We got it."

Pearl couldn't help add, "But don't we need to wait until after harvest, so the farmers can be involved?"

Franklin rose again. "Meanwhile, the materials sit out there in the open where weather can rot and thieves can steal."

Pearl sensed the press of earnest, eager faces fixed against her. She didn't protest when Franklin said, "We'll have our first meeting at the site tomorrow evening." She'd have a little time to think it all through, to maybe gain a measure of control of the situation.

On the spot she altered the theme of her prepared message from "Standing on the Promises" to "Building on Solid Ground" from the book of Nehemiah.

Afterward, they sang the doxology, "Glory be to the Father, and to the Son, and to the Holy Ghost. As it was in the beginning, is now, and ever shall be, world without end. Amen and Amen." A bit of liturgy from their Presbyterian roots, as the Community Church forged into a new era.

Pearl set out lunch at the ranch house for Vincent, Reba, Jace and Abel, Archie and Wynda—fried chicken, mashed potatoes, shucked peas, and chocolate cake. Hanna Jo grabbed two chicken legs, excused herself, and rode out to the hills again.

"Where did you get your grey windcheater?" Archie asked Vincent.

"Windcheater?"

"Your jacket."

"Oh. We call them windbreakers. Bought mine at Sears & Roebuck."

Pearl and Vincent chatted about church building challenges and then drifted into remembrances of the old days.

"When I taught school," Pearl said, "I walked six miles round trip, managed eight grades, did my own janitorial work, built the fires, disciplined the children, and hoped they learned something along the way. I added the Stroud piece of ranch work after Seth's father died and Seth tried to barber and farm. Not long after, I dropped the teaching."

"How long have you two known each other?" Reba asked.

Vincent wiped his mouth with a paper napkin. "I met up with your grandpa Cole first in southern Idaho back in his bachelor days. We mined for opals and star garnets together. Found enough to put us in business, but Cole sold out his part of the partnership and returned to Road's End to help his ailing father on the family Cahill Ranch."

Pearl grinned. "I was dating Champ at the time."

Reba's eyes widened in horror. "Grandma!"

"As the good book says, forgive me my trespasses. Also, he was much nicer and better looking in those days."

"Even I didn't know that dirty little secret," Vincent teased.

"Well, I broke it off. Champ married Blair within the month. Pure spite, I think."

"How did you and Grandpa meet?" Reba asked.

"Cole told you many times."

"Grandpa embellished it with Scottish fairytales, like the Seal Woman story. Never knew what was fantasy or true."

"As Grandpa liked to say, 'It was as true a story as it could be, for the most part.'"

"I want to hear your version."

"My recollection's much more boring."

"Tell me anyway."

"Well, soon after Champ's wedding, Cole returned to town from his travel adventures, to help his father with the ranch. Saw him at a Grange Hall dance, and when they turned out the lights, Cole immediately asked me to marry him. I said 'no,' because I didn't know him well enough yet and I was on the rebound.

"My friends thought I was crazy. I guess they considered Cole to be a catch. A few months later, when I could see Cole avoided all the other ladies attention, I said to him at another Grange Hall dance,

'You still want to marry me?' 'Yes,' he replied. So we said our vows as soon as we could right there by the Camperdown Elm his father planted. And combined two Road's End parcels of land. The Stroud Ranch was much smaller, but I was so glad to have Cole to share the load."

Pearl gazed at Reba and suspected her thoughts. Now, it was all gone. She tried to brighten the tone. "On our wedding day, he gave me that fancy opal and garnet ring I keep stored in my jewelry box."

"Cole didn't get along too well with his father, did he?" Vincent said.

Pearl stared in the distance as she reminisced. "Finn Cahill was a hot-headed Irishman full of passion about soccer matches, hate of all things English, and prejudice against Chinese. Married a sweet lady, though. Elizabeth was a wonderful mother-in-law, for the most part. However, a scandal surrounded their courtship."

Reba perked up. "Oh? What was that?"

Pearl noticed Archie and Wynda very intent too as they leaned closer. "Never knew the whole gist of it. Very hush-hush in the family. And Cole hated anything that hinted of smelly gossip."

"I sure miss that guy," Vincent said.

Reba nodded and Pearl thought of the kindest, dearest face in her world. She offered Vincent a grateful pat on the arm.

"I dreamed about him not too long ago. He stood right there with me and kept saying, 'Come with me, Pearl.' 'Where are we going?' I asked. 'Anywhere you want,' he said. 'But I can't leave,' I said. 'Got too much to do. Reba and Hanna Jo are coming home. I've got to be here when they arrive.' 'Don't worry,' he insisted. 'We can be gone as long as you want and I'll bring you back. You'll land right here, at this same place and time. No one will know you've been gone, unless you tell them.' It sounded so good. I wanted so bad to go on that trip with him. But I woke up."

"Wish he was here to help with the church building," Vincent concluded. "He'd know all about that project."

"I'm also concerned about bathrooms and Sunday School rooms."

"How about a kitchen?" Reba added.

Vincent picked up a fried chicken leg. "Tell the crew what you need and they'll get 'er done."

After lunch, Pearl changed into old denims and her scruffiest Adidas—flexible, a bit sporty, and so comfortable. Reba and Abel left for the corrals to work with Banner. Hanna Jo still hadn't appeared and Vincent announced he'd nap at his hotel room. Archie and Wynda headed to Lewiston to search for windcheaters and try to find the equivalent of a fish and chip shop.

Pearl searched for the shopping bag she'd tossed in her bedroom. She found it beside the dresser, purchases during her medical procedure trip to Spokane. Inside, a notebook and packet of ballpoint pens and three books: a Mary Higgins Clark mystery; *How To Get Along With Almost Anyone* by H. Norman Wright; and *Dream Big: The Henrietta Mears Story,* about a woman who'd been described on the jacket as a "gutsy lady who influenced a generation of ministry leaders."

Including evangelist Billy Graham.

A fashionable, full of faith woman, she wore big, bright-colored hats, like Cicely Bowers.

She carried the books to her recliner and expected to fall asleep with them in her lap, but a knock at the door intervened.

"Mrs. Cahill?" said the tan seersucker suited man with red tie dotted with tiny golf clubs, carrying a briefcase. "I'm from Camas Realty. A friend of yours suggested I drop by. May I come in for a few minutes?"

"Well, I ..."

The man pushed through and began a barrage of questions. Sable brown hair and deep-set eyes emanated crackling salesman's energy. "I hear you might want to sell your house." His attention darted around the living and dining rooms as he did a quick walk through.

"Excuse me!" Pearl blurted out.

The man stopped to peer up the narrow side stairs. His voice calmed. "I'm sorry for being so abrupt. I just didn't want to take up much of your time. Do you mind my asking, how many bedrooms do you have?"

Pearl did mind, but she replied, "Three on the main floor and one in the attic room."

He hiked up a couple steps. "That's good, very good. You've got a nice charmer here. I'll check the upstairs." He climbed a few more steps. "Can an adult stand up there?"

"In the middle. The sides slope."

He opened the door at the top and peered in. "Why do you have a Laird's Lug?"

"A what?"

"In this attic room, in the wall's top corner. I've only seen one like that in a Scottish castle. They were used by the lord of the castle to eavesdrop on guests when they gathered in the hall below." He leaned forward as though for a closer look.

"Please, don't go in there," Pearl said, ready to grab her revolver from the bedroom dresser drawer and usher this rude man out.

He tramped back down. "Hey, I can see this isn't a good time for you. How about I try again tomorrow? Or any time this week?"

"No need to. I'm not selling my house." At least, not now. And not to this pushy man.

"I'm sure I can find you a generous buyer. I've got contacts as far as California."

She opened the door. "I'm really not interested."

He pulled a card from his jacket pocket and tucked it in her hand as he exited. "Let me know as soon as you change your mind."

Pearl nodded. "Good-bye, Mr. ..." She looked at the card. "Mr. Greysen."

"Call me Harry." He grinned, waved, and drove down the driveway in a late model black Ford Mustang.

Who would give this realtor the notion she wanted to sell her house?

After she settled down, she picked up the Henrietta Mears biography first, read a few lines, and got hooked. She leaned back in the recliner and read for hours, fully awake and more alert than she'd been in a long time. Since before she lost Cole.

"God will lead you and give you the desire in your heart for the one place He wants you to fill," wrote author Mears, from the experience of her long, fruitful life.

Pearl presumed her place to be in Road's End, yet what would she do now that the ranch sold?

Inspired and energized for ministry, she sorted through the ranch papers in her roll top desk and found a blueprint of sorts to give to the men on the building committee, hand-scrawled by Champ on folded drawing paper. Fortunately, Champ used pencil so she could erase and easily change dimensions here and there.

One moment she imagined they could paint the Sunday School rooms in light, fresh colors. Colorful curtains at the windows. Decorate with flowers. The next moment she feverishly began a search in her Bible, writing copious notes, with renewed strength, inspiration, bursting with enthusiasm.

One thing zoomed in clear.

She would delegate all the parts of the church building project and do none of the overseeing or decision making, as per Henrietta's example. Her main role was to teach, to train up leaders, using whomever available in their small, rural church family. She'd garner every resource she could find.

And with that, a vision formed in her mind, a kind of inspired understanding. She couldn't totally blame Champ for his usurping authority by intruding and instigating the building of this local church. He'd been filling their leadership void.

She put on her best walking boots, slipped on a sweater, and grabbed a flashlight. God promised Joshua, "Every place that the sole of your foot shall tread upon, that have I given unto you."

So, she zipped out in her jeep to the construction site to stomp over every square yard of the new church property to claim it for God. Then she rode up and down every street, alley, and side road of the village to do the same.

She returned home from her pilgrimage exhausted, but flooded with contentment. On the porch she watched lightning flash nearby. The Blue Heelers, Paunch and Aussie, and Scat the cat hid under the slatted deck.

The summer storm spidered the night sky in jagged streaks. The air sizzled in the split second before the boom. Intense thunder cracked in powerful rumbles over the house. Hail slapped the ground in small white chunks bouncing on the grass, showing from porch lights.

Pearl hunched her shoulder and lifted her windbreaker high for protection against the pounding, deafening hail as it side-thumped her and the metal porch roof. Wind buffeted her back as she reached for the door. The electric power snapped off as she slipped inside. She searched for a lantern, candles and matches, a lighter, anything to break the blackness.

"Please, no fires," Pearl prayed. *Except Your fire in many hearts!*

She collapsed on the high oak bed made by Polly Eng's Chinese ancestors before the turn of the century and realized God only wanted her to do all she could.

Nothing more.

Nothing less.

One day at a time.

Beneath a Camperdown Elm

Chapter Ten

Reba searched for Jace Monday morning, to go with her to the construction site. She found him at the Outfitters Store. For privacy, she led him outside in the back and handed him the manila envelope with the copies of the ranch sale papers. He slipped the package under his arm, avoided her glance, and pinched the skin of his throat, eyebrows drawn together.

"What's wrong, Jace?"

"I heard from Dad. It seems that ... well, it's Abel's mom, Yvonne ... she's dead. He suspects too much vodka and valium."

"Oh, no!"

"Dad found her at the bottom of the basement stairs."

Reba recalled a scene of Jace bleeding not so long ago at the bottom of those same stairs. She cradled his cheek. "Must be so hard for your dad, finding her like that. Shouldn't we go tell Abel?"

"I ... don't know. He can't do anything but worry about it."

"But shouldn't he know what's going on with his mom?"

"Of course." Jace pushed palms against his forehead. "I'm so sorry, but I must leave for California. Dad needs me. Even though he and Yvonne slept on two different ends of the house, this has hit him hard. Can you ...? Would you mind if I left Abel with you?"

Reba figured she could take care of Abel. They'd hung out together often over the past few months. And he got along good with Grandma Pearl and Hanna Jo. But she couldn't bear the thought of separation from Jace. "Well, I don't have much else to do these days."

"Abel's gone through so much. I don't think he could handle much more right now. Or maybe I'm making excuses, to soothe my guilt."

"When's the funeral going to be?"

"Dad says she's going to be cremated. No public service. When the time's right, we'll do a memorial observance for her with Abel."

"But you've got to tell him now. Be honest with him. It's terrible to learn things long after the fact." As she knew so well.

The shudders started as Reba considered, *what if Yvonne took her own life?*

The ultimate abandonment for the boy.

She wanted to coddle him, wrap him in cotton to protect him from the world. Apparently, abandoners could come in every social strata.

"Okay, but I really can't take him with me. Dad's got lots of stuff for me to handle. He's in financial trouble again." Jace grimaced. "The oil slick buster fiasco didn't help." Jace shoved both hands in his pockets. "I've got another big favor to ask. Could you come with me to talk to Abel?" His face plastered an I-know-I'm-asking-a-lot mask.

"Yes, I will."

Help, Lord.

She silently prayed for wisdom, the right words.

"I'd ask Norden, but the deal is, he's got a gal friend. I can't depend on him these days."

"Oh? Anyone I know?"

"Not sure. He's very secretive about it."

Reba's curiosity piqued, but the more pressing matter of Yvonne overshadowed everything else for now. Yet she couldn't help blurt

out, "I'm going to miss you terribly! We're just getting to really know each other. And I need you ..." to help her figure out the whole ranch thing, what's next for them, what future they might have together.

He pulsed his hand across her shivering shoulder. "I know. I'll miss you like crazy too. I'll take my cellular phone, call you every day and leave a message whenever I can. I'll return as soon as I can." He pulled her close, caressed her, kissed her neck, cheek, and lips, gentle as a down feather.

She longed to cuddle like this forever.

Instead, they returned to the store and took Abel to the apartment.

Jace gently tried to explain that his mother was gone.

"I hope she's in heaven," Abel said, after a few moments. Then he scowled. "Do mean people go to heaven?"

Reba tried not to gasp. She peered at Jace who shrugged. "They've got to make things right with God. Who were you thinking of?" she gently prodded.

"Oh, nobody ... exactly." His eyes grew pensive. He grimaced as he seemed to search for the right response. "Asking you took away some of the scariness."

"Asking me what? About heaven? Or about mean people?"

"I don't know. About everything." He grabbed a gray moth off the wall, opened the door, and tossed it outside.

Reba studied the boy. She couldn't figure out if he exhibited sadness or anger or something else. Maybe he needed more time to process the news about his mother.

He turned to Jace. "You promised me a horse of my own, like I had in California."

"Yes, I did, by your birthday and that's weeks away. We'll start looking when I return."

Abel crawled to the corner of the room, grabbed a toy pistol, and pointed it at them.

"I've told you not to point guns at people." Jace stepped toward him.

"Unless you intend to shoot," Abel repeated. He leaned against the wall, and slid against it to the floor. "I'm practicing for Quigley."

"Quigley's locked up. He can't hurt you."

Reba tried to mentally prepare to care for the boy. "You can talk to me anytime you want, about anything you'd like."

The boy sat still, his attention glued straight ahead.

She turned to Jace. "I forget. What day is his birthday?"

"On Saturday, August 31st," the boy replied.

Tuesday morning, Jace drove to the Lewiston airport in the Chevy, Reba beside him, with Abel behind.

Jace reached over to hold her left hand. "We didn't get a chance to pick out a ring."

"When you get back."

"First thing."

"No, second thing," Abel refuted. "Remember the horse."

"You got it, Buddy." Jace raised his thumb.

"Do you have the ranch papers?" Reba asked.

"In my briefcase." He squeezed her hand. "We'll figure out something."

Reba rubbed her forehead and crunched her nose in doubt.

"I've got reserve funds," Jace said. "If we have to, we'll offer a buy-back price Champ can't refuse. After all, every man has his price and Cahill Ranch belongs to the Cahills."

"Um, I'm not sure ..." Reba began. "Owning Cahill Ranch has consumed Champ for a very long time."

"We'll talk later." Jace pulled into the airport parking lot.

They got out of the car and Reba squeezed him tight before she let him go, too choked up to put words to her good-bye. He strolled away, rolling his suitcase.

"Hurry back," Reba whispered.

On the way home, Reba slipped on sunglasses, so glad to have them to shield her eyes from piercing sunlight and fat, biting tears. No need for Abel to notice.

The boy seemed in his own world.

Pouty face.

Sullen responses.

After he squirmed around for long, cranky minutes adjusting the seat belt and eating a burrito, he finally dozed in the car while Reba pondered how to entertain a ten-year-old and how to help him process his mother's death. Would they regret not allowing him to go to California right away and find closure with a funeral?

Then her mind wandered to why neither Grandma Pearl nor her mother seemed willing to fight for the Cahill Ranch. In fact, just the opposite. Were they really content to let it go forever? Maybe she should too. However, without the ranch, where did she belong? Doing what?

Up until now, the ranch defined her and her destiny, with Jace a critical part of the cast. Perhaps she should muster a measure of humility, cowgirl hat in hand, and beg Champ and Don for a job. Any kind of dirty work would keep her in ranch work. Perhaps a viable opportunity would eventually open.

Really?

On the other hand, wouldn't being with Jace wherever he'd go be a step above? Could she manage another role besides small town cowgirl?

She imagined herself in California, living in a place like Santa Dominga or Casa Tierra. Her friend Ginny George could find her employment with her grandfather's chain of Marketplace George delis and restaurants. Or Jace's father could hire her at one of his businesses.

She thought of living like one of Hugh McKane's wives, Agatha Finley McKane Hempthorn, Jace's mother, or Yvonne McKane, his late stepmother. Padded shoulders dress. Drama hat. Stiletto heels. Maybe gloves. Or power suits by day, sequins at night. Dripping in jewelry and teased big hair.

Reba peered at her plain blue, cotton pullover, denim Wrangler's, and scuffed but comfy boots.

She'd require an extreme makeover.

She'd try hard to find a way to be herself and not embarrass Jace, find a job to earn at least part-time wages, while she waited for her life to make sense.

Aiming down the long driveway to her grandmother's house, she fumbled to park the Chevy, and help Abel with his assorted belongings up to the attic room. She presumed she needed to clean and rearrange before the boy could take up residence there.

Even so, she didn't expect the room to look ransacked.

Stuffed with a store of opened and scattered boxes on the bed, piles of blankets topped antique furniture, drawers open. Old clothing scattered everywhere, along with numerous, tall stacks of yellowed newspapers with busted twine. An oak rocking horse with gold mane had been tossed on its side and a rusty bookcase upended.

She cranked open a tight window in the stuffy room and heard wailing wind, a squawking bird, dog barks, and a coyote howl. A horse neighed below, probably Banner. All was noisy on the western frontier. After a few moments of fresh air swirled in, she tugged the window down.

Pearl considered this room controlled chaos. She knew what was up here and where, whenever she wanted to fetch an item. Now Reba wondered at fresh pine needles scrunched on the floor, signs of someone here recently. She peered closer. Box, drawer, and trunk contents scattered around as if from a frantic search.

Abel pulled off a pile of clothes hangers from the bed and plopped down Rambo and Knight Rider action hero toys.

Reba scurried downstairs and found Pearl in her bedroom, resting in a slatted, mottled woodgrain chair, listening to a Doris Day record on her phonograph. "Grandma, did you start cleaning up in the attic room?"

"No. Why do you ask?"

"Somebody's been piling through things. I didn't want to disturb the stuff, if it was you."

"Been so long since I traipsed up those stairs ... you do whatever you want up there. Tell Abel I'll see him later. Hanna Jo's stalking her wild horses." She pulled up an embroidered, silky lap blanket with a *swoosh.*

The next few days, Abel tagged along with Reba everywhere. He kept a safe distance as she roped and un-roped Banner's neck with careful, cautious repetition, attempting to gain Banner's attention and trust. The mare acted angel one day, demon the next—pinning her ears, swishing her tail, and kicking at her neighbors.

"Raging hormones could contribute to her moods," Hanna Jo observed when she stopped by. "She needs a buddy. I can relate to that."

At first, Banner nickered only when Reba appeared at the corral or sauntered through the weathered barn to drop hay into the feeder. But gradually, to Reba's consternation, the cranky animal turned her favor toward her mother.

Whenever Hanna Jo passed by where Reba held Banner, the buckskin raised her head and followed her mother's movements. Hanna Jo talked to the horse but didn't stop, usually on her way to the hills.

"Why do you keep going out there?" Reba called.

"To be by myself. To think. To spy out the wild horses. And to maybe see that big creature again."

Pearl stayed close to home, provided their meals, and kept checking on the church construction progress. She chatted with Vincent during his breaks.

One day he got bold enough to broach a very personal topic. "Am

I too old for you?" Vincent's mouth twisted as though to brace for a rebuff.

"I think you've got a few miles left," Pearl replied. "And so do I." She pinched his arm. "But what about Beatrice?"

"What about her?"

Pearl took the frank approach. "Are you attracted to Beatrice, in that kind of way?"

"She married a man who invested in Idaho opal mines. That's our main connection. And she reminds me of you. She can be fearless. She believes if a fight's worth fighting, it doesn't matter who wins, because something good will come of it. She's also generous to a fault."

Pearl studied his face. "You didn't answer my question. Do I sense a 'but?'"

Vincent's slow grin warmed her. "But ... she's a bit cantankerous. Too testy and touchy for my taste."

Now Pearl felt a need to defend her. "But she's not bothered when someone doesn't agree with her. That's rare."

"That's 'cause she knows she's right." He reached out to touch an opal ring and matching necklace around Pearl's neck ... fire opals. "I remember when Cole bought those for you."

Time for more frank talk. "Cole was the love of my life and I thought when I lost him, 'never again.' I'd never love another like I loved him. However ..." Pearl wondered how far to take this. With all her talk of being old and tired, she was, after all, sixty-nine, not ninety-six. Still a flutter or two in the aging heart. Especially when a man like Vincent looked at her ... that way.

After a pause that slid into awkwardness, Vincent said, "Pearl, I won't push now or ever, but if I thought for one minute I had a chance ..."

Pearl replied with a hug, partly to hide an unexpected tear. The stark reality of his physical closeness filled her with longing for a man's touch again, the cozy cocoon of a loving embrace.

"I wanted to know if you were okay with ... us being a couple."

Pearl mused for a moment.

They'd been friends for decades. Yet a jump happened she hadn't expected into something more personal. Exactly when, she couldn't tell. Friendship with Vincent displayed signs of turning to love. The heightened awareness of his presence. Missing him when he was gone. A heart skid when they met again. Fascination with his quirks and expressions. Plain ole attraction.

She took the plunge. "I think ... I'm finally willing to see where this leads."

Chapter Eleven

Jace changed into bermuda shorts and cruised from the Burbank airport in a sporty, forest-green, rental Buick Reatta, while a jet screamed overhead. He sped down the highway into the Spanish country town of Casa Tierra past rows of red tile roofs and adobe homes as church bells rang nearby. Perhaps a wedding. Or funeral of a well-known citizen. If so, a person likely known by his father.

Bright yellow, pink, and orange begonias hung in wicker baskets the length of the street, where peacocks roamed free.

He turned on Squash Blossom Road, in front of a horse statue decked with an inverted crescent silver headstall. He stopped at the McKane gated property and found his old key in a zippered pocket of his travel bag.

The first thing he noticed out of place: assorted trash and wads of paper everywhere on the grounds. Had there been a recent wind storm? Not unusual in this coastal town, but where was the groundskeeper? Had he been let go? The second—a new, off-white Maserati in the driveway.

Jace didn't recognize his father at first. Slumped on a couch in the great room, bloodshot eyes, tousled hair, hand tremors, and slurred speech when he attempted a greeting. He sat up and forced his arms into a plaid sports coat to go with a paisley tie and wingtip shoes, not his usual dark suit attire, but still a contrast to Jace's shorts and tank top.

At least here neatness still reined, with grand piano, mahogany mantel, and bust of Abraham Lincoln all dust-free. Jace noted the large painting missing above the brick fireplace of half-sister, Kaylor, pirouetting on her toes in laced ballet shoes. Kaylor, the teen coaxed away from Casa Tierra and killed in an abandoned San Francisco apartment building by Quigley Dalton.

When Jace reached out his hand to nudge his father, he jumped as though petrified. He slapped his proffered hand with a clammy one. "What are you doing here? You're supposed to be in Iowa."

"You mean, Idaho."

"Whatever."

"You called me. Remember?"

The senior McKane sat up straight, slowly emerged from his stupor, narrowed eyes widening to a semblance of alert. He reached for a jeweled box. "I found this. Empty. She kept a canary-colored diamond ring, a single diamond gold chain necklace, and diamond earrings in here--her favorites. It could have been robbery."

"You mean, someone could have ...?"

His father's attempt at tamping down his hair didn't help much. He shot a glance at Jace. "The police hinted I tried to kill her, to avoid another exorbitant divorce." He truly looked tortured, perhaps pained by the accusation or the loss of Yvonne. "The medical examiner believes, the way she landed, she may have been shoved."

That would implicate his father or one of the staff.

"They found her surrounded by Imitrex, for her migraines. She cut out tomatoes and chocolate. No caffeine. Nothing helped. Nothing, nothing, *nothing!*"

"Who else was in the house?"

"Only me, I thought." Hugh stole a look at Jace. "But I did make a call to the Roto Rooter man. I was waiting for him and he was late. Our bathroom drains were plugged and as you know, I don't do things like that." He pressed against his forehead so hard, Jace thought he could see the thrum of his pulse.

"Are you okay?"

"Yes, I'm fine. Apparently, she took a double dose of the migraine meds. She'd done it before. I heard a loud racket that sounded like it was coming from the basement."

"What kind of racket?"

"All kinds of banging, clanging noises. I opened the door and it got louder, so I started down. The stairs were slippery. Then, I saw her. I called for an ambulance immediately. She was pronounced dead at the hospital. The officer in charge thought I was either very clumsy or tipsy. I admit I'd been drinking. The police visited me later and asked a lot of questions. They're doing an autopsy."

Jace plopped down in an easy chair, bare legs rubbing leather. He loosened his Nike laces.

"What? No cowboy boots?" his father prodded.

"Wouldn't matter what I wore. You've never forgiven me my wardrobe *faux pas* since I appeared in black leather jacket and open collar to one of your black tie events."

Hugh opened a cherry wood box with initials *HMK* and offered his son a cigar with teasing smile. When Jace shook his head, he pulled out one of the Double Coronas and stoked it with a lighter.

Jace couldn't recall the last time he saw his dad light a cigar, which usually hung from his mouth, unlit. He also noticed the big plastic box with screen at one end of the dining table. "Are you using computers now?"

"No, that's for you. I try to avoid machines that talk back. But be careful. That thing could turn on you." His father straightened his tie and picked up a gold and diamond Rolex from a stack of unopened mail. "I think I'm being swindled."

"By who?"

"Not sure yet, but I have my hunches. And I lost a yacht. It was stolen by drunk, inexperienced sailors and their girlfriends and sunk."

"Anybody drown?"

"Don't know. Don't care. Just trying to cut my losses."

Jace reeled at the news Hugh hadn't bothered to investigate casualties. But he didn't pry while he assessed what was really going on with McKane Enterprises.

"Where's Dewey?" Jace peered out the rear window beyond the covered porch, looking for Abel's dog supposed to be under Yvonne's care.

"Tied up in the gazebo."

A heavy Hispanic woman appeared with a bottle of champagne on ice, two glasses, Hugh's favorite beluga caviar and crackers, and a blood pressure kit.

"Hi, Sofia," Jace greeted. "How are your kids?"

"Good. Camile got a scholarship to UCSB and Lucien's staying out of trouble." She wrapped the Velcro blood pressure cuff around Hugh's arm.

Jace dabbed a cracker with caviar. "Is this a celebration?"

"Of you coming home so quick," Hugh replied. "You may save my life."

Too bad he couldn't save Yvonne's. "Do you know why she ...?"

Hugh blinked fast. "Yvonne desperately wanted something she couldn't have—her daughter returned."

"She told me," Sofia gazed at her boss for a sign of approval.

"Go ahead," Hugh nudged.

"Relax first and let me take your blood pressure. Breathe deep and close your eyes." She wrapped his arm and the seconds ticked by before she removed the wrap.

"What did Yvonne say?" Jace urged.

"She said, 'I could completely go *poof* in thin air and nobody would know I ever existed.'" Sofia twirled and left the room.

Hugh scoffed. "I'd know she existed by the credit cards she maxed out and left behind."

Jace reeled at the comment. Yvonne drank too much, especially since the tragic loss of her daughter. But she tried to do his dad's bidding, in most things. And she certainly didn't deserve to die like she did.

"Okay, that was unfair," Hugh had the tact to add. "Neither of us can claim superiority in finances." He dragged on his cigar, either contemplating Yvonne or his business troubles. Maybe both. "Jace, truth is, I need your help ... a loan ... it's just temporary ... to cover my worst losses."

"Dad, you've been a millionaire many times over. You need to figure out why you keep losing it."

"I haven't lost it, exactly. I only need a bit of tiding over ... to pay off some debts."

"Who do you owe it to?"

"Oh, some guys."

"Dad, tell me who."

"Okay. But this is very privileged information. Their names are Giovanni and Dink. Most folks call him Rink-a-Dink. They know Bony George and his brother too."

"What are their last names?"

"Don't know. Honest."

"Sheesh, Dad, how could you be so ...?" He hesitated to sort through a rash of pithy word choices.

"Stupid?" Hugh forced cigar smoke from his lungs with a cough. *Insanely stupid! And maybe corrupt too?*

"Okay, how much do you owe?"

"To those guys, $50,000 by tomorrow night."

"That soon? And you don't have that much?"

"I'm deal rich and cash poor right now." He tamped out the cigar and straddled it on a crystal ashtray.

"How about the overseas investments?"

"A fiasco."

"The oil wells in Texas?"

"Going dry."

"What about the Hewlett-Packard stocks I set you up with?"

"Gone. Good news, I sold them for 1/2 a mil profit. Bad news, it cost me nearly a mil to get on several influential boards. And I never forget my friends." Hugh fixed his you-know-how-generous-I-am gaze on his son.

"So, why don't you ask them to reciprocate?"

"People used to think I had more money than God. Well, my

friends' list seems to have changed lately."

"You may need to file for bankruptcy. Again." If he was the father and the roles reversed, he'd show tough love. But what's a son to do? "The thing is, I can't keep bailing you out. I'm engaged to be married. And there have been complications ... with the ranch we hoped to operate."

"But all that's peanuts in comparison. Reba will understand. Besides, McKane Enterprises will all be yours someday."

But he'd have little to offer Reba Mae now. Lesser resources for their own future.

Hugh pulled a mass of jiggling keys from his pants pocket. "Let's go to the funeral home. Haven't made arrangements yet. We can talk more on the way. And there's another thing ..."

A wary Jace ventured, "What is it?"

"I'm having issues with the state department. My lawyer advises ... that is, I want you as a corporate officer."

"I can't. I'm going to live in Road's End now."

"No problem. Meet with the board several times a year. With your signing the papers ... well, basically, I can keep my holdings." He punched Jace's shoulder. "Oh, and I got a great deal on a golf course. It's a small one, only nine holes but a beaut. Let's play a round while you're here."

Jace scrunched his sore neck and tried to relax his clenched fists that had almost begun to spasm into cramps.

Hugh's mood lightened to cheerful. "Steak tartare for a late lunch?"

Jace gagged at the mention. "Only if we get it at Marketplace George. They make it right." *And safe,* Jace wanted to add.

Chapter Twelve

Reba heard from Pearl, controversy brewed already at the construction site.

After they learned there would be a few days delay in delivery of crucial materials, the crew stood around and fussed about how best to begin the project.

She took Abel to play there with the Younger kids while she snooped around. She could hear voices in vigorous discussion as soon as she got out of the pickup.

A gray-haired man Reba didn't know, scar over his left eyebrow bobbing up and down, argued the loudest. "I worked for a contractor to put myself through college," he was saying, wiping grimy hands on his burgundy shirt.

She could see the blueprint tacked to a fence post—handwritten by Champ on a sheet of notepaper. He happened to be viewing the lack of activity from his wheelchair, cheeks flushed, an unsmiling Blair by his side. She caught bits and pieces of the bantering.

"Atch," Vincent addressed him. "Either will work, as long as we begin with a good, firm foundation."

Atch's eyes narrowed. "You should have hired an architect."

"We've got one chance to get this done right out the gate." Franklin seemed to study the stacks of boards and cement blocks.

The crew faced an impasse already.

Adrienne Mathwig interrupted. "We want the rustic look, the wood exposed inside and stone facade outside. We also want the carpet up several feet on the wall, to keep sound from bouncing so much."

"Who does?" Franklin asked.

"Me and my sisters."

"Good. You three are on the Design Committee."

"What kind of roof are you using?" Atch asked.

"Steep-pitched, metal for discouraging fire and sliding off snow," Franklin replied.

"Not worth considering." Champ wheeled over and stirred the proverbial pot.

"And the walls?" Atch and Champ sized each other up.

Franklin recited, "Basic post and beam barn design. Vaulted ceiling. "Let's vote right now on it. Walls first or roof?"

Reba couldn't hear the final results. She asked Beatrice, who was closer.

"The committee sided with Franklin," she said.

"Of course. That Atch Murdock guy is an outsider."

"But Franklin is right and he's in charge."

"That too." They heard cheering. "They're making a race of it. Several are taking bets on how fast they can complete the roof."

"Real bets? Grandma will not be pleased."

Beatrice chuckled. "Definitely not."

Abel bounced over to Reba, waving his arms. "Can I have a puppy? The Youngers are selling Golden Retrievers really cheap. Can we go see them? Can we?"

"Don't you already have a dog?"

"Yeah, Dewey. But not here. Besides, Grandma Pearl has two dogs. So, why can't I?"

That was the first time she'd heard him call Pearl by 'grandma.'

She promised to go with him to the Youngers to check out puppies.

They stayed for lunch when Polly Eng and daughter Kam brought fresh vegetables from their garden in a steaming wok with stir fry Teriyaki Rainbow Trout and a fortune cookie cake. Quite an outdoor feast for the workers and guests.

Reba followed the Youngers to the big house on Road's End's highest knoll after Ursula confirmed they had Golden Retriever puppies for sale. Their ranch sprawled above and behind Seth's place, with one pasture filled with hundreds of Targhee sheep, wooly ewes and lambs guarded by three dogs hard to distinguish from the flock.

In the yard, Abel chased after twelve-year-old Corky who showed off a toy model Navy F-14 Tomcat with missiles and swing wings that changed form in mid-flight. When it crashed, Abel spouted, "Where are the puppies?"

Inside, the boys crouched behind the upright piano to peer at a box in the corner.

Ursula served Reba hot tea made from home-grown mint and dandelions.

"How is it going with the sheep?" Reba asked.

"After two years trial, we're getting the hang of it."

"We've got 350 mammas and 450 babies, many of them twins," inserted eighteen-year-old LaDonna, who bounced baby Aaric on her knee.

"It's basically LaDonna and I doing the work," Ursula explained. "They're our project. I'm helping Lloyd with the farming income and LaDonna's earning money for college."

"Not to mention the great training she's receiving." Reba pulled her fingers through the long-haired fur of a white angora cat sprawled on a teal green settee beside her and felt a gentle purr.

She sank into a sofa splashed with blooms in shades of blue and green. She knew troupes of kids flew through this fabric fashion garden most every day, so she didn't feel uncomfortable in her Wranglers and denim jacket. But she felt damp after scooting through a summer sprinkle, so she sat light as she could.

Soon, the cat shook itself and padded over to Ursula. She pulled him onto her lap and stroked its white head. Reba's forehead beaded with sweat until Ursula got up and adjusted the swamp cooler.

"Did you see that suspicious stranger in town today?" Ursula asked.

"What was suspicious about him?"

"Besides an unkempt beard, he had an eerie and wild-eyed look about him."

"Like a lot of guys who tramp through our town." And live here. "Anything more specific?"

"He avoided eye contact when he asked to use our phone. So, I reported him to the county sheriff's office. Years ago I belonged to a Neighborhood Watch group and I learned to be alert for potential trouble."

Abel rushed over to her. "I found the one I want." He pulled her up and over to the puppy box. He petted the darkest one, with round brown circle markings above each front leg. "I'll call him Patches," he said.

"Can you set this one aside?" Reba asked Ursula. "I need to clear this first with Jace."

"When do you expect him?"

"Not sure." Not sure at all.

On the way home, Abel pointed to a scroungy character riding a sorrel mustang. Weather-lined face and hands, dusty jeans and boots, a tied flowered bandanna around his neck. Long gray hair twisted in a ponytail. Stringy, untrimmed beard and mustache streaked with fiery orange. Slight hump back. "That's the out-of-work cowboy looking for a job. He gave me and Corky a can of sardines out of his saddlebag."

"When was that?"

"At the church building place."

At least he didn't appear to be wild-eyed and eerie. Then again,

maybe that would be in the eye of the beholder.

That evening Reba heard Abel whoop and yell under the over-hanging branches of the Camperdown Elm. She peeked in. Toy soldier figures and horses scattered the grass in a semblance of a battle. They replaced the '55 Chevy and Tomcat miniatures, his usual toys.

"Who are the fighters?" Reba asked him.

"One big army against the big bad giant with the gold rings and gold shield." He picked up a massive sized player all in black.

"Who's winning?"

Abel bent his neck forward. "The giant. He has special powers, you know. So does his horse." Also black. "Is Banner a war horse?" he asked Reba. "Hanna Jo said she's messed up because she was in a war."

"Yes, you could say that."

"I read a book about a war horse named Joey. He got messed up too because he was in lots of bad stuff. War is ..." He stopped as though searching for the right description.

"Horrifying. Very sad. People get hurt and killed."

He nodded. "I hope I don't ever have to be in a war."

"But you like playing with your soldiers."

"That's different."

Smart kid.

As Abel ramped up his battle plan against the gold-ringed giant, Reba studied the Camperdown Elm, the strange Scottish tree spread umbrella style with sticky, velvet green leaves. It seemed so much bigger to her as a kid. She strolled around Abel's toys and gazed at the underside of knotted branches. The contorted crown a mass of convoluted branches with intricate patterns arched high, curved low.

A living sculpture.

Grandpa Cole once related to her the original discovery by a gardener at an estate in Scotland. "All sprawled out on the ground, like a bush, with gnarled branches, as though the roots sprouted upward and out. For it to grow like a tree, upright, it's grafted on an elm along the bark." He pointed to a necklace-like wound in the wood.

"An upside down tree," Grandpa called it.

She reached out and touched a woody branch. "Does the tree have a spell cast on it?" she had asked.

His eyes glazed over. His straight, silvered hair bristled like Scat the cat when she threatened to claw someone.

She asked him again with her best smile and a squeeze on his arm. He nodded in a jerky kind of way, his eyes wet. She thought it very curious he got sad over a tree.

Now, she climbed it, for old time's sake.

Abel scrambled up with her.

A black bird perched overhead and dripped a splatter of droppings. She swatted at it and elicited an indignant squawk. When she couldn't *shoo* it away, they moved to another branch. The bird followed. Reba searched all around the jagged tree for signs of a mother brooding over hatching eggs. No nest propped anywhere.

Irritated by the messy intrusion on this special moment, Reba scooted into the house with Abel and grabbed a long-handled broom. She felt they had squatter's rights to the tree. Out on the porch, she raised the makeshift weapon and black wings fluttered away, as though conscious of an imminent sweep of danger.

She leaned the broom against the trunk and noticed objects sprawled on the ground behind the tree. A dirt-caked hoe, rake, and shovel. How long had those been there?

As she carried the tools to the shed, Abel tossed one of his balsa wood planes, which floated into the root cellar. Apparently, someone left both sloped doors open. He descended the stairs and stumbled onto the floor, wrenching an ankle.

He hollered until rescued by Reba, forced to enter the dark chamber of putrid stink. Rotting boards. The crunch of dried bugs.

The terrified boy screamed, "Spiders! I hate spiders!" Wispy webs smeared his hands.

Back at the house, she iced and bandaged his ankle as he clutched his plane. "I think I'll throw the giant down that hole," the sullen boy proclaimed. "Let the spiders eat him."

That night Abel banged on Reba's door and crawled into bed with her. "There's a ghost up there." Abel pointed to the stairs that led to the attic room. "I heard him moving around."

After the boy fell asleep beside her, she crept out of bed and tiptoed up the stairs to check out Abel's supposed ghost. She stood at the top and slowly pried the door ajar. She waited and listened. A clock ticked. And a shuffling sound reverberated through the far wall.

Reba scooted inside and waited again. *Shuffle, scuff, snore. Shuffle, scuff, snore.* She flipped on a lamp. The noise emanated from the tic-tac-toe grate over a square opening in the wall. Was it coming from inside the walls? A critter skittering around? However, the snore sounded very human.

Something … something downstairs …

Holding the lamp high, she stole down the stairs. She reached her bedroom in time to notice Hanna Jo in gown and slippers heading down the hall to the bathroom with a plate of cookies in her hand.

"Mom," she whispered.

Hanna Jo kept trekking. *Shuffle, scuff, snore.*

Reba crept behind her and tapped her on the shoulder. She snored louder.

She's asleep. And she came from the kitchen.

She nudged harder and startled her mother awake. The plate of cookies crashed to the floor. "Mom, you're sleepwalking. Have you ever done that before?"

"I don't know."

She seemed so disoriented, Reba steered her to her room and helped her in bed.

Back in her own bed, Reba marveled how clear and loud Hanna Jo's movements echoed through the grate in the attic room. No wonder it scared Abel.

Chapter Thirteen

*J*ace pulled on blue jeans, khaki shirt, and black, high top tennies. He wanted to be comfortable while he searched through his father's business documents.

The whole thing bugged him. His father hired sleazy financial advisors and foisted analyzing it all onto his eldest son. More than likely, he'd find out Hugh McKane was being cheated and conned.

Then what?

He scuffed across the floor of his dad's dark office and nearly tipped over a chair. He bumped against the table and knocked over a lamp before he flipped on a light and saw a small fridge. Inside crammed assorted food and snacks, most certainly prepared by Sofia. Ham sandwiches with cream cheese and jelly on sourdough. Grey Poupon Dijon mustard with twisted pretzels. Assorted pickles. Coca Cola and Pepsi. Plus, Haagen Daz Dulce de Leche and Ben & Jerry's Chocolate Fudge Brownie ice cream. All his favorites.

He flounced on the couch with a full plate and gulped on a soda, and forced himself to concentrate. He would need focus and determination to get through this mess. Food devoured, he took a deep breath and dug into piles of paperwork.

Hours later, after a thorough assessment, he realized to rescue his father would take every asset he owned, perhaps including the Road's End store so important to Norden. To bail out his dad, he'd have to stay here in California, protect his investment for both of their survivals, and guarantee his dad didn't make any more poor decisions.

He'd have nothing to offer Reba.

No way to help her regain her ranch.

But then, that might not be doable anyway. No matter, he had to try.

Caught between his father and future bride, Jace faltered in opposing loyalties. He'd always stood by Hugh McKane, no matter what, during countless situations.

A wrecked yacht.

A crashed corporate jet.

Not to mention one recent money sinkhole, oil buster escapade.

Jace kept the peace with at least four ex-wives and girlfriends and their offspring, while keeping the whole mess organized, such as separating out stepkids of former husbands.

More likely than not, Hugh's kids needed a photo to keep him straight. "Remember him?" Jace would say. "He's the one who keeps you in shoes and private schools."

The man he called his father had no business being one, none whatsoever.

Still, he had to admit he'd enjoyed benefits. Jace traveled over the years to far flung, fascinating places like Dublin, Barcelona, Canberra, and Cape Town. He'd been his father's Guy Friday and hadn't minded much. After all, he got to hike gorgeous hills and ride elephants.

He'd accepted his lot in life.

Until now.

He wavered, sensing his entire future in the balance. At the least, his love life.

How could he explain to his father, or to anyone else, that he might rather give all he had and wind up poor in a bunkhouse with a feisty, redheaded cowgirl the rest of his life, than gamble his riches to bolster the shaky, worldwide web of McKane Enterprises?

Where did he best belong?

Would Reba even want him without his financial backing? Or the ranch?

He fashioned an image of her living with him in California as he battled day after day to save the sinkable McKane ship. She could wait for him at their luxury apartment, dinner ready, candles lit. Or she could find a job with the George family in their deli franchises, alongside girlfriend Ginny, and be here when Ginny's baby arrived.

Yeah, sure. That could work.

Something else troubled him. After hours canvassing his father's financials and holdings, Jace detected expenditures from which he could surmise only one explanation. His father also owned a love shack, a playhouse for several women on the side, during his marriage to Yvonne.

He had money and mistresses.

Did that lead also to murder?

The coup d'état happened for Jace when he stumbled upon a Dictaphone in his father's office desk drawer, where he apparently began to transcribe, "A Man and His Mountain/The Hugh McKane Memoir."

Just then, Hugh McKane strode into the room. "I spent time in the vault, thinking." He reeked of cigar smoke.

"About what?"

"I'm captain of a once yaw ship that's going down. I've been stripped down to the essentials. Everything a hardworking man like me has strived for his whole life is meaningless, unless ..."

"Unless what?"

"He's got a fine son like you to get things up and going again. You're the key to my legacy." Hugh's face evolved into a pinched, pained stare. His shoulders humped over, bending his spine. Then sulkiness coated his voice, along with the familiar, arrogant irritation. "As long as no one believes I murdered my wife."

After his father retired to his bedroom for the night, Jace slipped down to the basement, the scene of Yvonne's last moments as well as the long hours of intimacy he and Reba shared when trapped there by Quigley.

He flipped on a light and noticed right away the wobbly step had been repaired. He gaped at the bathroom on the left and peeked into the small, unfinished, empty room on the right with a single window at the top of the door. Although wounded and miserable, here he first realized he loved Reba Mae Cahill.

He blinked around at the sound-proof, half-finished home theatre and wondered how long his dad would stay in this house, now that Yvonne no longer lived here.

On a round table with metal chairs in the long, narrow room in the middle, a cardboard box full of empty cola cans and bottled waters, Cheetos chip bags, and assorted candy wrappers. Quigley's preferred diet.

Strange that hadn't been carted off yet.

Mattresses piled high against one wall between closet doors. And on top, a box of Big Hunk candy bars and a San Francisco Giants baseball hat. Jace reached for them. Why had a paid housekeeper left these here too?

Maybe because they hadn't been here very long.

Perhaps only a few days.

He ascended the stairs and discovered his father in the kitchen.

"The police called," Hugh said. "The autopsy revealed a fatal gunshot wound."

"How did they not know that before?"

"Position behind her ear. The obscuring by the other injuries. They missed it somehow."

Chapter Fourteen

Grandma Pearl left early with a picnic basket for a trip with Vincent, Seth and Hester in the purple Model T. "Don't wait up for us," she told Reba. "We're headed south toward Boise. Vincent wants to check out some issues with his opal mine. We may have to stay overnight somewhere."

Hanna Jo came and went as she pleased, as usual, with sketchy hints as to her activities. Reba had given up trying to pin her down. No sign of her this morning.

So, Reba drove with Abel to Main Street and parked in front of Whitlow's Grocery next to the Outfitters. She hoped to find out when Norden could take a turn with Abel's care. She'd need a break now and then.

More people than usual milled around town this time of day. A crowd formed down the street.

"*Uh oh*, look!" Abel noticed flashing lights on the police car in front of the apartments.

A young deputy Reba didn't know tried to wave people back

from an imaginary line around the apartments as he interviewed several occupants.

Finally, Reba scooted Abel to the Outfitters door and set off the bell. A teen lurked behind LaDonna Younger. Jesse Whitlow, Sue Anne Runcie's younger brother, stared in deep earnest at tins and jars of saddle soap on a shelf, cheeks flushed. LaDonna stopped sweeping floors to greet Reba.

"I didn't know you worked here."

"I started a week ago. How may I help you?"

"Is Norden here?"

"No. He took the afternoon off. Told me he was headed for Skull Cross Meadow on his Harley to get his head on straight. He definitely deserved a break."

"Oh?"

"An intruder broke in last night. Had quite a mess in the back to clean up. And the day before, someone tried to destroy his bike. He said it looked scraped hard with a real sharp object and the rear-view mirror had been broken. Norden heard the noise and tried to grab the guy, but the guy tried to stab him with a knife and then hit him on the head."

"Oh no! Is Norden okay?"

"Yeah, he seems to be, but he's a bit shaken up, understandably."

"Jace will be concerned. Be sure to let me know how he's doing."

"LaDonna, you need help?" a female called from one of the offices.

"No, we're fine, Mrs. Runcie," the girl replied.

Sue Anne appeared from the hall. "Oh, it's you," she said. "Be sure to show Reba the sale on saddle soap." She briskly turned away.

Reba blushed at the dismissal and wondered what her former high school girlfriend was doing here instead of at her father's grocery store next door.

LaDonna explained. "Sue Anne's been filling in. Norden says she's a lifesaver. Caught him up on mounds of paperwork."

Reba felt a tug on her shirt and looked down to see Abel, his knees and elbows bloody, eyes teary. "What's the matter, Desert Eagle?"

"I had a motorcycle accident."

"Oh?"

Abel shushed her and motioned her to bend down. "I ran around to the back of the store chasing a dog and crashed into a parked motorcycle. Please don't tell Norden. I looked it over—it's okay."

"But you aren't." Reba peered at LaDonna. "I thought Norden was gone?"

The girl lifted both hands. "I only know what he told me. He said he needed a long ride to let the wind shake some cobwebs from his mind. Maybe it has to do with all that commotion down the street."

Sue Anne reappeared. "Norden's helping the county sheriff transport a criminal to jail. A guy was caught in the act of breaking into the apartments. I wonder if it was the same guy who ..." She broke out in tears. "It's all too much. Now I'm afraid to go home."

An alarmed Reba started asking questions, but Sue Anne rushed in the office and slammed the door.

"The whole town's buzzing about the robber, of course," LaDonna said. "But I don't know much. I'm stuck in here."

Reba took Abel to the restroom to get cleaned up and bandaged, passing a display of Transformers and talking robots. After she tended to Abel, he began to plead for a talking robot. She rationalized he needed extra activities. She couldn't entertain him every moment. She plopped down money she couldn't afford to LaDonna and then checked out Norden's bike herself, to verify it wasn't harmed.

She took the boy with his robot package to Delbert's Diner, passing the young policeman on guard in front of the apartments where Tim and Sue Anne Runcie lived.

Delbert's Diner advertised a prime rib special and cinnamon rolls, but Reba and Abel wanted burgers and fries. They sat under the huge display of area barbed wire samples with historical stories attached.

Reba recognized every person sitting around the ten tables and six booths. She and these folks could relate all kinds of stories about each other. They heard the rumors over the years, stretched the best of them, or witnessed the events themselves. A certain fondness of identity lingered in such a community. Some may be scoundrels, but he or she was *their* scoundrel.

In the booth next to them, Reba overheard Delbert talking with Deputy Brock Lomax and heard him say he was now "*Chief* Deputy Lomax." He'd returned from a complaint of four large Saint Bernard mix dogs menacing a pet ostrich that got loose from its pen at the Whitlow house.

"I found the bird attacking the dogs and getting the better end of the deal," Lomax commented. "Gave the dog owners a first warning."

The Paddy boys, Amos and Pico, slid into a booth with their mother, Ida. They invited Abel to join their Whitlow Grocery summer league baseball team, playing at Road's End Elementary, 3/4 mile from the ranch house.

"Can I, Reba?"

"Your knees and elbows need to heal."

"Oh, that's nothing." He flexed and hopped around with only the slightest grimace.

She knew she'd have to drive him there. Or maybe he could ride Reba's old bike several late afternoons a week for practice. And then he'd be playing games against the neighboring towns.

There she sat, cowgirl Reba, transforming before everyone's eyes into a full-time babysitter. Or soccer mom.

꘎ ꘏ ꘎ ꘏

When Reba returned home, she and Abel heard a commotion and moseyed to the corrals. She dared to hope Banner wasn't in one of her demon moods. They discovered the mare retreated in a corner with a perplexed kind of look in her eyes.

They slinked on top the fence to listen to Archie MacKenzie sitting on the far side spouting poetry like a bard, complete with wide, sweeping hand motions.

"A harse! A harse! My kingdom for a harse! O for a harse with wings! When I bestride him I soar, I am a hawk. He trots the air, the earth turns dark. The earth sings when he touches it. What a harse should have, ye do not lack, save a proud rider on your proud back.

You charge the earth and go into battle. Your strong legs and flowing mane make the enemy rattle."

Archie bowed before Banner and his audience of two clapped.

"You sound downright Shakespearean," Reba said.

"With a little Book of Job thrown in. Hope you don't mind, I'm practicing for the Worst Poet in Dundee contest. In honor of Dundee's William McGonagall, the *world's* worst poet."

Reba didn't know what to make of that outburst of information. "I'm glad to see you've quieted my horse down."

"Maybe I need to use a horse for the contest. I'll have to check the rules."

They walked with Archie toward the house and the Scotsman headed to the bunkhouse. Reba noticed the rural mail delivery car leaving their box.

"Want to walk with me to the end of the driveway?"

"Please, Reba, let me play with Robbie."

"Who is Robbie?"

He pulled out the talking robot from the bag.

She waved him back to the house and sauntered to the mailbox.

Maybe Jace sent her a letter?

A note from Ginny George?

She picked up her pace in anticipation.

At the bottom of a stack of bills and circulars, she found a typed message on a sheet of paper. No envelope or stamp. No address or name. Must have been hand delivered.

She began to read, a chill pulsing down her neck.

Attention!

This is how your life is going to end if you don't comply.

I am contacting you to see if your life is important to you and your family. I know everything about you. Do you want to LIVE OR DIE?

If you want to live, you will pay $5,000 as soon as possible.

WARNING: do not think of contacting the police or even telling anyone because I will know. A lookout is watching you at this moment.

Good luck as I await your reply with the money in this mailbox.

Her throat strained dry, parched, as she peered around at the cottonwood trees along the road, especially behind her, back at the bunkhouse, toward the ranch house. Her leg muscles tightened as she froze in place. She stayed still for as long as she could.

No other movement.

Nothing suspicious.

What should she do? Knock at the bunkhouse and tell Archie? Call the sheriff, in spite of the threat?

Finally, walking stiff, knees nearly locking, she forced herself to hike down the long driveway, sensing sinister eyes boring into her back the whole way.

Was it Archie? Was he the prankster?

She entered the house, heaved a sigh of relief, and locked the door. She kept quiet long enough to hear the bones of the house creak and moan, and then upstairs from Abel's room a round of clicks, clatters, and machine noises.

She jerked when the phone rang.

With great hesitation, she slowly picked up the receiver and squeaked, "Hello."

A growly, distorted voice mumbled a string of indistinct words, and then said clearly, "Leave the money in the mailbox. No point in tracing that letter. It will lead nowhere."

She cradled the phone with a *thwack*.

Another ring, only once. Then another time. After that, peals of jingles droned on and on. She finally picked up.

"Hello? Hello!" No one answered and she hung up.

Abel ran into the room, glanced at her face, and frowned. "What's wrong?"

"Nothing." She attempted to gain quick control for his sake. "I'm tired. I need a nap." She managed a brittle, forced smile and encouraged him to head to his room to play.

This wasn't funny. Some cruel prank? Or a motive more vicious? It was the sort of thing Quigley would do. Could he manage that from the prison?

With Abel out of sight, she weighed the pros and cons of involving law enforcement, but eventually called the sheriff's office to give a full report. No way was she going to handle this alone, no matter the risk. She read the contents of the letter and explained the crank calls.

"Could be kids with time on their hands playing tricks," Chief Deputy Lomax said. "We'll check it out right away."

On edge, she toured the house, shutting windows and locking doors.

The phone rang again.

With great trepidation, Reba picked up the receiver and offered a hushed, "Cahill residence."

"Hey, I saw a newspaper feature about your town, Road's End," a young female said. "You must live in a regular Peyton Place."

She exhaled a half-relief. What newspaper feature? "Who is this?"

"Jodeen. I work at McKane Riding Company, next to the George compound in Santa Dominga. Remember? I met you there."

Bouncy, tanned girl in her twenties. Long, thick blonde hair. Dark eyes. Bright pink riding boots. Student from UCSB who hung all over Jace. Reba remembered. *"Uh huh."* She clutched the phone tighter.

"I'm sorry to say, I have bad news for you. About Jace."

Alarm buzzed through her. This was too much. An overwhelm of heavy weight. She was in no shape to handle whatever was about to come. She couldn't make herself speak.

"Are you there? I thought you ought to know. If *I* was his girl-friend, I'd appreciate someone telling *me*. So, I figured, I'd do you a favor."

After another pause, Reba rasped out, "Okay." She could hardly breathe.

"You see, Jace has this secret life. Ask him about house payments in San Diego ... and who lives there."

Click!

"Jodeen?"

Buzz tone.

Reba stood in a trance as her hand clamped the phone. What did the girl mean? Was Jace acting out like his father? The proverbial apple didn't fall far?

She fought the rising rage over perceived betrayal. Why had he really gone to California? What was he up to? And why hear about it today, this moment?

🐕 🐕 🐕 🐕

Later, Chief Deputy Lomax stopped by, and she showed him the note and relayed the phone calls that followed.

"Do you believe this is a real threat, Reba?" Lomax asked.

"I'm not sure, but with what I've been through, I believe it may be."

"Okay. Do you want me to have a deputy stay with you?"

Reba hesitated only a moment. "No, that's not necessary, but thanks for the offer. There are enough people around here. I feel safe for now."

That wasn't one-hundred percent true, but Reba craved to be alone, not talk to anyone.

"I'll have someone drive by periodically to keep an eye out. If anything else happens, let me know immediately."

"I will." She watched as Chief Deputy Lomax left.

Reba longed to curl up in her bed and try to forget all the turmoil that swirled in her brain. But she was in charge of a sensitive, young boy who recently lost his mother. She peeked in on him and he was engrossed with the talking robot.

She scampered as quiet as possible to her own bedroom, to calm herself, to think, to plan.

On the way, she passed the hall mirror.

Bad hair day.

Bad life day.

🐕 🐕 🐕 🐕

Later that night, with Abel in the attic room and fast asleep, she hid outside in the dark under the elm with Grandpa Cole's shotgun.

She regretted she'd gotten out of the habit of jogging and practicing the self-defense maneuvers Cecily Bowers taught in her classes. She needed toning, with weights.

She fingered pickup keys in her pocket, coiling them around her fingers, ready to turn them into sharp weapons. And faced ugly suspicions beginning to grow like poison ivy.

Had Quigley escaped? Was he close by?

And the other sneaking conjecture. What about Jace?

She knew one thing. If what Jodeen hinted was true, she'd never love again.

Not ever.

Sick remorse over the possibility wriggled around her innards.

In the midst of all the inner strife, she tried to shut everything down, when suddenly, a comment Archie made earlier reverberated back at her, popping out of the morass of mixed details.

Dundee?

Did he say he wanted to enter a poetry contest in Dundee, Scotland? Did they come from there? Wasn't that the hometown of Grandpa Cahill's parents?

She peered over to the bunkhouse, a dim light and shadows behind the shades.

Who were these people?

The next morning, Hanna Jo grabbed one of Pearl's mares and quickly got the horse whipped into a gallop when the saddle slipped. She grasped at mane hair and nearly fell off. She stopped the mare to take a look.

The cinch strap which fastened the saddle to the horse's back had cracked and torn. Or been cut. She couldn't quite tell if the strap failed due to purposeful action or worn leather.

She tried to shake the paranoid thought, returned to the barn, and got another saddle after checking it closely. She scrambled to the top of Coyote Hill, dismounted, and collapsed beside a boulder, in no mood to canvas the ranch, search for wild horses, or anything else.

She realized she'd been falling apart for a long time.

If only Papa Cole was here ... he once held her together.

He figured out where she was through the years and visited her. He wanted her to come home, but she refused and made him promise not to tell anyone her location, until she was good and ready.

Finally, the time to journey home arrived, and it turned into a more fateful day than she could imagine. She found Papa Cole collapsed beneath the Camperdown Elm.

She blamed herself. Her appearance must have shocked his heart that bad. She saw it in her father's eyes – shock, disappointment, and fading life.

Chapter Fifteen

*J*ace dreaded making the call to police detective Ackroyd, but knew he must. He feared hearing the facts that might force again the specter of Quigley into their lives. Or if not, have to bear any further accusations about his father. He wanted the assurance Quigley remained safely incarcerated, awaiting trial for two separate murders.

"I've been out of the county, finishing up a special state case," Ackroyd reported. "I'll check about Quigley. I do know there was a local TV station feature a while back on inmates who receive fan letters from females. Quigley was included. Of course, his pen pals believed in his innocence. Plus, they commented on his 'hot mug shot.' One of them quoted, 'I think of him as a misunderstood, battered soul.'"

"That's crazy."

"I'll call you back."

A half hour later, Jace's cellular phone rang.

Ackroyd wasted no time. "I'm sorry. Bad news. Quigley escaped after stabbing two guards with plastic knives he made himself."

"When?"

"Three days ago. If I wasn't on that other case, I would have known. In fact, I would have been called immediately to do follow-up detail, as the original supervising detective. Now I'm officially re-instated. You didn't see anything in the newspaper?"

"I've had my nose to the grindstone, checking out Dad's financials. Did you know about his wife, Yvonne? Found shot dead here at the house."

"Ahh. Suicide?"

"Don't think so. Maybe an accident. Or murder."

"What does your father think?"

"He vehemently denies any part in it, though he believes he was the only other person in the house at the time."

"And what do you think?"

Jace could hear the detective tapping on a glass, like the ticking of a clock. "Saw definite signs in our basement here of a possible Quigley intrusion."

"She was shot, did you say?"

"I know what you're thinking. Not his M.O. Unless he upgraded."

"Another thing, a cellmate of Quigley's escaped too, hours later. He was left alone in an interrogation room, somehow worked his way out of the handcuffs and climbed up out of a vent. There's a video of it. Incredible! Not a proud day for the team."

"Could be related?"

"Hard to say. Maybe coincidence. I'll check my sources for more info. Want to do a ride-along with me? You know Quigley as well as anyone. Help me sort out his thoughts, motives, and possible movements."

"Give me an hour."

"I'll give you two. I can catch up on my paperwork."

Jace made two more phone calls. He reached his father at McKane Riding Company in Santa Dominga, the only really viable business he owned, and the other to Reba.

"Abel's coming in the house," she warned.

Jace broke into her hesitation. "What's the matter?"

"I'm wondering when you'll come back ..." He sensed she started to say *home*. "... to Road's End. And I think Abel wants to talk to you."

Abel grabbed the phone.

"I didn't do it," he said first thing through the speaker.

"Do what?"

"Start the fire."

"What fire?"

"The fire in the hay. I was minding my own business when a bat flew at me."

"Did it bite you? Some of them have rabies, you know."

"No."

"So, what does the bat have to do with the fire?"

Abel hesitated. "It scared me, and I dropped the match."

"I see. Why did you have a match?"

"I was practicing."

Jace tried to restrain the frustration edging his voice. "Practicing what?"

"Lighting a lantern."

"Next time, make sure there's nothing around that can catch on fire. What burned?"

"Just some hay. I promise. Well, and my leg a little when we stomped it out."

"Are you all right now?"

"Yes. Reba gave me toast with lots of butter and jam," the boy said with a sniff.

"I'm sure that made you feel lots better."

"Yeah. She's okay. I've got a talking robot she gave me. Can I have a puppy? The Youngers are saving one for me."

"What about Dewey? You still have him."

"Can't I have two dogs?"

"Let me think about it."

Abel handed the phone back to Reba.

"I'll try to watch Abel much closer," she said, "so he doesn't get into trouble."

"Hey, I understand. Par for the course in caring for an active almost eleven-year-old." He quickly made the decision not to mention

Quigley's escape yet, especially with Abel close by. "I'm going to be here a little bit longer."

"Are you okay?"

"Yes. Have more business to tend to."

"For your Dad?"

"And loose ends about Yvonne." There, that was honest, without adding stress on her end. He could explain it all later, after he and Ackroyd got things resolved. "Love you, Reba Mae."

After a pause, he heard a faint, "Miss you, Computer Guy."

"Miss you more, Ranch Boss." He hoped the former walkie-talkie moniker didn't sting her too much.

Reba made her own long-distance call when Jace hung up. The threatening letter disturbed her enough to wonder, who might be her enemy? She suspected only one, for sure. *Quigley.* Waves of angst bumped against her, leaving her disturbed, puzzled, and floundering for truth and safety.

She slowly dialed the number of her good friend Ginny George Nicoli of Santa Dominga, California. They chatted about Ginny's pregnancy, her large extended family, and thriving business venture with the Marketplace George franchise.

Then, Reba asked, "How are you and Paris doing?"

"Relationships can be so ..."

"So hard?"

"Impossible! Messy!"

Amen, sister.

After a pause, Ginny said, "But Paris seems reconciled to helping with the George Deli franchise while moonlighting on the side with writing his true crime mysteries. And I can't wait to be a mother."

Reba tried to nonchalantly change to another subject. "Have you heard anything about Quigley lately?" she said as low as she could.

"Only that he escaped. What else have you heard?"

A stunned Reba quickly quashed any further discussion with a "Nothing" and diverted as soon as possible to more baby talk. She tried to stay attentive, but a well of panic rose higher and higher.

Escaped? How? When?

Jace hadn't mentioned it. Should she let him know?

No. Why give him another worry?

Beneath a Camperdown Elm

Chapter Sixteen

The next morning, two early phone calls broke the silence and they both made Reba jump.

Deputy Lomax called to confirm a deputy was making a loop that included her home, and that there'd been at least two more threatening letters reported, similar to hers. To a random camper in the park. And to grocery store owner, Buckhead Whitlow.

Grandma Pearl called to say she would be home by early afternoon. Reba decided not to worry her with the threatening note or news about Quigley, but she did decide to attend Grandma Pearl's first Wednesday night Shepherd's Class that evening, for several reasons.

First, it was held in their living room.

Second, Norden offered for Abel to spend the night with him.

Third, with Quigley on the loose and Jace in another state, she bided her time with a growing apprehension, and Grandpa's shotgun always in arm's reach. Events she couldn't change nibbled at her nerves. She waited for what, she didn't know, but a snap of anxiety like a raving beast dominated everything.

Plus, with the ranch gone, she had nothing much else to do.

Even Banner, her second biggest responsibility, completely ignored her. She couldn't get the mare to barely slit her eyes open for their bonding session. Training digressed to minus zero progress after a promising start.

But that wasn't the main incentive.

She dreaded the thought this whole new venture of Grandma Pearl's amounted to a huge waste of time. She understood her grandmother's desire to find a constructive, profitable use of the rest of her life. So, to a point, she admired Pearl's courageous step into action.

She could hear all her grandma's sayings over the years. "Depend on God and your anxiety will down-size. He's bigger than any worry. Trust Him, even when He seems to work slow."

However, so far only two members heeded her call for leadership training for this little country church on the edge of town. As much as she loved Seth Stroud, he was a 91-year-old man, and Tucker Paddy, a recently reformed town drunk. What could God accomplish with such meager pickings?

When Grandma Pearl returned that afternoon, Reba greeted her with a little too much emotion.

"What's wrong?" Pearl asked, suspicion in her eyes.

Reba let out a huge sigh, and tears welled in her eyes. "Nothing. I'm all right," she began to say, but Pearls knowing eyes stopped her. Nothing else to do but to come clean with all of the events of the past couple days.

As Reba finished, Pearl, with a set jaw and determined look, fixed her gaze on Reba. "I'll keep my shotgun close."

That evening, Hester ambled in from the kitchen with steaming coffee to join Reba at the overflow, spectator dining table. Tucker's mug rattled as he took his, sloshing liquid in the pottery plate underneath. Reba studied the two shepherds-in-training. Backs straight, they both wore dark ties and white shirts though they rarely did even on Sunday mornings for church. Nervous, uncomfortable, they seemed to stare at the hand on the antique grandfather's clock as it slowly advanced.

Reba opened the screen and wooden doors when she thought she heard a tap. She tried hard to conceal a gasp of surprise. She hadn't expected any of this crew standing there.

Polly Eng quickly explained, "I'm here to observe only, as part of the Chinese Year of the Sheep. Seemed like this theme might fit in."

Next to her, Vincent pulled off a Seattle Mariners baseball cap in greeting. Perhaps he was merely curious or wanted to support Pearl. He'd never done much more than help set up chairs at the barn church before. She did another double-take when Archie and Wynda MacKenzie entered, along with Ursula Younger. Why were they here?

After Polly sat at the dining table with Hester and Reba, the others settled on the deep couches and club chairs and the clock advanced to seven bongs. Pearl stood in front of the fireplace and bookshelves which cast a cozy view. She smiled and nodded to each one, then tugged off her glasses and spoke softly. "Thank you all for coming. I know what you're thinking: 'Why am I here? What will she ask of me? Will I be forced to go to China? Or Mongolia? I'm not ready for this. I'm out of here first chance I get.'"

Seth and Tucker uncrossed their arms and legs and chuckled with knowing looks between them. Vincent grinned with a wink at her.

Pearl pulled out a folder from the roll top desk to her right. "Here's the plan. We'll try a six week experiment. During that six weeks, observe all you can of what God's doing in Road's End and in our country and world. Then, at the end of the six weeks, evaluate what you're learning and where God's leading you. I won't tell you what to do, though I may make a few suggestions, which you can try or not. Discover your own course of action. My aim is to build Road's End Community Church by training one leader at a time, the ones who can say with Queen Esther that they have 'come to the kingdom for such a time as this.'"

Pearl called Archie and Wynda forward. "I asked the MacKenzies and Ursula to come because they know a lot about sheep and this is a Shepherd's Class. A shepherd takes care of sheep. Tell us what you know." She nodded at Archie.

"Ursula has Targhees," Archie began.

"White faces," Ursula added.

"Aye. Our Scottish sheep are black faces. They're very independent and tend to scatter."

"While white faces group together well. I think they're easier to care for."

"Otherwise, they tend to act the same." Archie nodded at Ursula. "You're welcome to continue to butt in whenever you like."

"I'll do that," Ursula affirmed.

"Bringing in the sheep is one of the shepherd's main jobs," Archie continued. "Sheep need protection, guidance, and correction by the rod. The staff lifts and restores them. Working with sheep humbles you real fast. They will bolt in sheer panic at a rabbit jumping through a fence."

When he paused, Ursula jumped in. "As you know, we're all compared to sheep in the Bible. 'My sheep know my voice,' Jesus said. *Yahweh-Rohi* begins Psalm 23, the Lord is our Shepherd."

Reba's attention drifted. Outside through the double-paned windows, shades up, she spied a man with a hoodie on this warm August evening hurrying past the Camperdown Elm and tossing a smoldering cigarette.

She excused herself, snatched up a shotgun, and raced after the guy, shouting at him. He jumped on a motorcycle at the end of the driveway and roared east on the Cahill Crossing road. When the others gathered on the porch to investigate the commotion, she explained what happened. At least, she knew it wasn't Quigley.

"Harassment from the enemy already," Tucker insisted. "The devil's out to get us 'cause we're going to turn the town upside down."

Pearl coaxed them back in to finish the class.

Afterward, Pearl encouraged those who felt ready to go two by two and witness to someone with the lesson fresh in their minds. "You can't expect to lead others in what you haven't done yourself."

Seth left with Hester. "I'm going to practice on my wife and then sit at the whittling bench tomorrow and find a person to talk to."

Tucker asked Reba to come with him.

"Okay," she said, "but you do the talking. I'm the bystander." She wondered who Vincent would choose as a partner. Pearl? Or would he go back to the hotel to get Beatrice? As she left the house, she noticed him conversing with Archie.

She followed Tucker's '75 orange Toyota wagon downtown in her pickup and parked behind him at the Picaroon Saloon, across the street from Jace and Norden's Outfitters store. He straightened his tie and sauntered inside.

Reba stayed in the shadows by the door and inhaled as shallow as possible to keep from gagging. The place reeked of beer and tobacco. As soon as she focused enough to see clear, she saw Tucker, face blazed as hot as any peat fire. She heard snatches of "You will sink lower than the grave" and "You will burn with fire and brimstone."

Chagrined at his lack of tact, she prepared to drag him out of there when he punched the man nearest him in the belly.

"Tucker!" Reba shouted. She debated whether to barge in or not and decided to remain in place. Not smart. Too much testosterone, liquor fumes, and hair trigger reactions.

The man he first hit kept moaning until he blurted out, "Tucker, why did you do that?"

"You showed no reverence for the Almighty of the universe. I couldn't let that pass." Tucker yanked the man up straight. "And why spite the One who loves you most?"

"You better beat it before the law arrives. I'm reporting you to the police."

"Okay." Tucker belted him again, this time in the chest.

The man grabbed both Tucker's arms. "I'd be much obliged if

you'd stop slugging me."

"And I'd be obliged if you'd take this book and read it." Tucker shoved a small Bible in his pocket. "It's got good advice. It says, 'Be watchful. Be alert. Get sober.'"

"How about two out of three? Will that get me into heaven?"

"Only Jesus can do that for you. Call out to him."

The man saluted Tucker, grabbed the Bible, and his half-full bottle. "Here's mud in your eye." He staggered out the door past Reba and fell down in the street.

A relieved Reba followed as Tucker exited too.

"Whelp, I've done my witnessing today." Tucker hooked his thumbs in his dress pant pockets and whistled as he tramped toward his Toyota.

"That's not how Grandma taught you in her class."

"She did say to change things up to fit each special case, didn't she?"

"Well, something like that."

He swung around and high on adrenaline, he marched toward Sal's Saloon next door. The usual rough and rowdy characters lifted their drinks to him. His eyes slit like sharpening blades intent on cutting steel didn't assure Reba he heeded her caution one bit. She grabbed at his arm, but he shook her off.

This time, Tucker sat a while, as though assessing the tone of the place, while the disco music reverberated louder and louder.

Shabop. Ba-Boom. Shabop. Ba-Boom. Shabop. Boom, boom, boom.

Finally, Tucker switched off the video and jukebox and began preaching. In less than a half hour, with tie ripped off, along with the buttons of his white shirt, and sleeve torn, he and seven others got hauled off to the county jail by Chief Deputy Lomax in the MacKenzie's borrowed van, on a charge of brawling, destruction of property, and disturbing the peace.

Reba followed them to Oroston in her pickup and got permission to talk to Tucker in his cell. Rounds of raucous squalls filtered from the direction of several cells.

"We're singing hymns and spiritual songs like Paul and Silas. We started with 'Onward Christian Soldiers," Tucker told her. "Except we ended with '99 Bottles of Beer on the Wall.' Guess that don't count. But be assured, I didn't drink a drop. And you're my witness. First time in my life I did my fightin' and came out of a bar sober as can be. That's a victory all its own."

Reba tried to reply with wise and gentle counsel for this church leader in training. "But, Tucker, you can't manhandle people into the kingdom." She also wondered how wife Ida and the boys would respond.

"Why not? Pearl said, 'whatever your hand finds to do, do it with all your might.' That's what I did." He raised a fist.

Of all the verses in the Bible, he messed up that one. She managed a croak in response when Tucker concluded, "Now, the trick is to find out if my buddies are still saved after they dry out."

She walked to the door and motioned for the jailer to let her out.

"Reba," Tucker called. "These guys are my Gang of Eight—real cowboys looking for job openings. We've got to find them ranch work."

"Check with the Runcies," she replied.

Reba drove home in a stupor to give Pearl her first Shepherd's Class report. She'd try to put a positive spin on it. Maybe if they stayed in jail long enough, Tucker could do his follow-up session with a captive audience. A new slant on jailhouse conversions.

As she turned into the driveway close to midnight, she thought she detected lights flashing on and off around the Camperdown Elm. As she got closer, two streams of light flashed across the field to the road. She spun the pickup around to give chase when the lights switched off. After a while she could see no movement and gave up. She was too exhausted to deal with whatever mischief these prowlers were up to.

Chapter Seventeen

*O*ne moment it was 1920 again. The next, 1991 mixed in. Seth told stories of mule-driven wagons and gold mining while he whittled. Several children played tag. Unleashed dogs and stray cats scampered around them. Youth skateboarded up and down the walk.

"I sorta knew the famous lawman, Stuart Brannon," Seth drawled. "I met him once, when I was five years old. He came for a visit to Goldfield, Nevada, where my family lived. My father was a barber and gave him a haircut. I remember Brannon because he let me sit on his knee and he told me tales. He claimed they were true, not the made-up ones like in the dime novels."

Seth bent down on the bench outside the barbershop, intent on his carving. He shaved a long curl of wood as Hester, beside him, knitted a pair of navy blue socks. His recent bride wore flannel shirt, jeans, and red bandanna. Killer, her black Border Terrier, leaned against her legs.

The old man winked at Abel and showed him the half a whale with eyes, ears, teeth, and blowholes already formed. Entranced, Abel scooted toward the old man and picked up a long, twisted shaving.

A crowd soon gathered, including the whittling bench regulars—Thomas Hawk, long braid encircled with pipe smoke; Joe Bosch from Runcie Ranch; barber Alfred James swiping a razor on a white apron. Even Chief Deputy Lomax stopped by. Archie MacKenzie sidled up behind him, but kept his distance. A few folks from the hotel joined in.

A family with two young girls walked across the street from the apartment complex.

"Are you living here in town?" Reba asked them.

"No, we're at the state park camping," the mom said. "But we've got friends at the apartments. We're going to help them move to Boise. Too much crime here, they said."

Crime? What crime?

Seth held up the half a whale to the girls. "My friend Abel has dibs on this, but if you come back later, I'll have wooden bracelets for you. Would you like that?"

The shy girls both nodded.

"Have you seen any cougars?" one of the girls asked.

"The Idaho Department of Fish and Game says there are recent sightings of cougars near Road's End and around the lake," their mom replied. "Apparently one snatched up a four-year-old girl near the park and left scratches on her stomach and bite marks on her arms."

"How is she?" Reba asked.

"Recovering, according to the ranger. She will have stories to tell. She is getting rabies shots and injections in her puncture wounds. She should be okay."

A startled Reba jumped when hairdresser Richard James crept close and said, "Welcome home. Sorry, didn't mean to shake you up. Time for a Curly Cue full touch-up."

"I know. I'll come in when I can. A bit busy right now."

Tucker Paddy's two sons sprinted down the sidewalk toward Abel. "Found any treasure lately, Seth?" Amos asked.

"Besides them garnets you found around Elk River." His brother Pico's eyes flashed a glow. "We're thinkin' gold."

"As a matter of fact, I have." Seth kept whittling.

After a moment of quiet, Alfred urged, "Well, we're waiting."

Pico prodded, "Come on, Seth, give us a hint where it's at."

Seth finished both flippers before saying, "Tell you what, I've got a riddle for you. You answer and I'll tell you what I found."

The boys nodded and everyone crowded closer, including Archie who pulled a small notebook from a pocket and jotted a note.

Seth spoke in his unhurried way. "You are standing before two gates. One leads to heaven, the other leads to Hell, but you don't know what hides behind either entrance. There are two gatekeepers. You are told by St. Peter, one of them always tells the truth. The other always lies, but you don't know who is the honest one and who is the liar." He completed several dorsal ridges in the wood.

"What's the rest of it?" Joe asked.

Pico bounced on his toes as Abel and Amos traded shoulder punches.

Seth cleared his throat. "You can only ask one question to the gatekeepers in order to find the way to heaven. So, what is your question?"

The crowd murmured and several fumbled with pockets or rubbed their chins.

Finally, the girls' father remarked, "Ask both, which is the door to heaven? Should be able to figure it out from there."

They all looked at Seth for confirmation. "Oh? How's that?" he said.

"It doesn't matter if you ask the liar or the honest guy this question, either way they'll point to the door leading to heaven. The liar just wants to mess with you."

"You think so? That's one way to reason. Keep going," Seth nudged. "I'm looking for the very best answer. Can anyone top that?"

The boys whispered in hushed, excited tones.

"We got it," Pico blurted out. "The liar is guarding hell, because that's where all liars go, right? So, I would hold up a hand and ask, 'How many fingers am I holding up?' Since the liar cannot tell the truth, he would say the wrong number. The honest man would tell the right number and lead to the right door to heaven."

Reba patted him on the back. "Very good job."

Seth raised a finger of his own. "Which way am I pointing?"

"Up!" Everyone shouted.

"Is that the way to heaven?"

Several affirmative answers rang out.

Seth took his time finishing the tail and began the flukes. His question curled and fell away like the discarded shavings at his feet.

"Come on, Seth," Abel nudged him.

The old man twitched like he'd been in a dream land. "Well, we know Jesus went up on a cloud when he left earth. He should know where heaven is, don't you think?"

"Yeah, that's where he came from," Abel replied. "Didn't he, Reba?"

Reba nodded. "Uh huh." She said no more. She didn't want to intrude on Seth's practice session.

Seth blew shavings off the whale, sanded the flukes, and handed the toy to Abel. "Now I need a swimming pool," the boy announced.

The crowd disbanded as Seth held onto Hester's arm and trudged toward his purple Model T.

Archie sprinted in front of him. "Hey, no fair. You didn't answer the question about the fortune you found."

"No, I guess I didn't. Maybe tomorrow."

"Why not now?" He jerked his head toward Reba, so she ducked to avoid the appearance of eavesdropping. "You've been in this town a long time. Is there buried treasure here?" He waved his arm around. "Anywhere?"

"Now, son, could be." Seth's eyes twinkled.

"How about underneath the Camperdown Elm?"

"The one in my yard? Or the one at Cahill Ranch? Couldn't guarantee about either."

Archie gave him a quizzical look and rode off on his bicycle.

Seth turned to Reba. "I'm going right home to put up a No Digging sign. You better too. That young man's treasure hungry."

"Hi, Seth." A man with a large camera edged closer, wearing a big, white hat, tight pants, flowered shirt, and high-heeled, python belly boots.

"I know you." Seth shook his hand.

"We met in Reno. I interviewed you ... Halburt Halstead, reporter for KRNV TV."

Seth grinned. "You made me famous."

"That's right. I was headed to Spokane and saw the Road's End sign on the highway, so thought I'd drop by. Do you know where I can find Pearl Cahill?"

Seth stole a glance at Reba. "What for?"

"I believe I told you I do features on small town, western ranch life. I grew up in Montana myself." He peered closer at Reba. "You were the red-haired cowgirl with this man on his caravan, weren't you?"

Reba nodded. "You asked about doing a feature on me and my grandma."

"That's right. And especially now since Pearl Cahill's been nominated for the National Cowgirl Hall of Fame."

What? News to Reba. "Well, sir, I'm afraid you've appeared at the worst possible moment for her to be interviewed." Or to receive such a nomination.

He chuckled. "You let me be the judge of that."

Hester's black Border Terrier, Killer, yapped at the man's heels. She ordered him away and he crouched behind her, trying to squeeze through her legs, snarling. "The perception of the press around here," she commented, "is they try to get close to you for anything newsworthy, without caring who they hurt."

"I'm not here to hurt anyone. All I want is to find a good story."

"Well, we're not available." Reba tugged at Abel and headed to her pickup.

"Are there really cougars around?" Abel asked as soon as they got in the cab.

"Could be. If you ever see one, don't run. Stay calm and keep eye contact. Slowly try to back away in an upright position. Appear large by raising and waving your arms or opening your jacket. Yell in a loud, firm voice. Don't turn away."

Abel's eyes got large. "That's an awful lot to remember."

"Well, you probably won't. Make a lot of noise and carry a big stick or rock when you're in the countryside away from the house."

"I don't want to see an old cougar."

"To be safe, don't go anywhere by yourself and you'll be okay."

Reba made a mental note to stick pepper spray in her purse.

🐎 🐎 🐎 🐎

Vincent heeded Pearl's admonition to start sharing his faith where he was. He asked Pearl to meet him at the hotel for supper.

She parked down the street from the two-story building before stomping on the wooden sidewalk under a lodgepole pine overhang. A breeze whipped the hummingbird and hollyhock windsocks. A metal monkey swung from the tin roof. Tripled, multi-colored, mini-lights circled the building.

Beatrice joined them at a table in the dining area, her fading brunette hair streaked with highlights, like it was dipped in honey. Her pale eyes shined. She'd returned from a five-mile hike in bright pink tennies and gray sweats.

Vincent tried to stir up conversations by handing out flyers he copied with Beatrice's help about church service times and the new building plans. The visitor at church who volunteered for the construction crew, walked over with a limp in navy sport coat, burgundy tie, burgundy socks, and khakis to take him on.

"Greetings, Atch Murdock." Vincent shook his hand. "You know all about this project already."

"Did you know Atch was a librarian from Lewiston?" Beatrice commented. "And we've discovered he's as handy with a towel and dishes as he is moderating meetings for the regional district public library or speaking at book conventions."

"I'm here at Road's End for R&R, mainly fishing at the lake. I've become friends with this gal ... and her sisters." Atch winked at Beatrice.

Reba did a quick study of Beatrice. No blush. And no eye contact either. Instead, she seemed to try to dismiss him as her gaze wandered around the room. "He's a guest of the hotel," she said.

"And I'm writing a book," Atch proclaimed.

"Oh? What about?" Pearl asked.

"It's an incipient literary project. As a budding writer, I'm very protective of sharing anything about it. But I will tell you, my historical novel is set in Europe ... from the 1600s or maybe 1700s—haven't decided yet. Depends on what strikes my fancy." He pursed his mouth as though to end this vague description. He squinted at Vincent and ignored Pearl with a smooth brush-off. "Who's your preacher?"

"We're working on that," Vincent said. "Meantime, Pearl here is pretty much in charge. She can answer any questions." Pearl scowled at Vincent and he amended himself fast. "Or I can give it a try," he added.

"What do you do for a living?" Murdock asked.

"I was in Idaho opals. Still own a mine, actually."

Murdock seemed impressed enough. "How much do you think you're worth?" he pried.

Vincent studied the man. Pearl knew the type. He didn't really want information. He had a snappy comeback prepared. "You tell me," Vincent said.

"Not more than thirty pieces of silver. The greatest man who ever lived was sold for only thirty shillings."

"*Touché*," Vincent replied.

Atch went on, "I wouldn't worry about you getting a preacher. Put total confidence in any human and you'll be disappointed, every time."

"But that's what God chooses to work with," Pearl countered. "Imperfect people."

"Amen," Victor said and passed out flyers to a group of six entering the hotel dining room and soon got into a spirited debate with one of them about the existence of and location of heaven.

The exchange ended with a firm shake of hands.

Pearl smiled. He'd been preaching to the choir.

Later at home, Pearl heard a knock at the front door and Reba left to answer it. "Grandma, the Reno reporter is here. He wants action pictures of you."

"Like scooping manure?"

"No, like galloping on a horse."

"Won't that produce a blur?"

"Not if I'm patient." Halbert Halstead pushed forward. "And use long exposure and slow shutter speed and a little unconventional processing."

Pearl rose up to the full height of her 5'4". "Do you believe I have a twenty-four-year-old granddaughter?"

"Why, yes, I do," he replied as sassy as can be.

Pearl chuckled. "It says in Proverbs the grace of growing older is to be able to laugh at tomorrow."

"Well, you're doing one better, if you can laugh at today."

"I like you, Halbert Halstead."

"Good. Give me a story. What's up with this National Cowgirl Hall of Fame thing?"

"Oh, that. How did you hear about it?"

"I have my sources. Who nominated you?"

"Ursula Younger and Cicely Bowers, two friends here in town. They think I'm like Annie Oakley. They sent photographs of me and Reba, newspaper clippings of awards and such, biographies and letters of recommendation from a county commissioner, County Sheriff Ed Goode, and a state legislator. A long time ago. I knew nothing about it until I got a call from a gal in Hereford, Texas."

"But now, you have no ranch," Reba said.

They both gave Halbert Halstead a side-long glance, who registered no expression while he fiddled with his camera.

"Yeah," Pearl replied. "I'm obsolete. I certainly didn't expect to be accepted for such an honor. Not everyone nominated is, you know."

"But the reporter knew about it."

"Let me repeat--I was accepted as Nominee. That's the first step toward induction. There are hundreds of others at that stage too. I think as many as 500. That includes a variety of cowgirls—artists and educators, as well as trick riders, ropers, and bull riders. All I did was feed cows and raise mares. Only four or five are chosen."

"It's still an honor," Reba insisted. "Ursula and Cicely and those guys who sent recommendations must have thought you were someone special."

Pearl stared at her mug as her cheeks brightened. "Well, it makes no difference now. I'd have to turn it down or be a hypocrite."

Halstead pointed his camera at the two women. Zoomed in. *Click. Click. Click.*

Chapter Eighteen

Reba slowly rubbed Banner over and under, trying to engage her deep in the eyes once more. She wondered if the horse contacted the chemicals rumored to be used in the Gulf War. Her Nez Perce soldier friend, Elliot Laws, mentioned the possibility of sarin nerve gas. Or perhaps the horrors of oil fires and rockets blasting, the bloody trauma of killing fields, still haunted her.

She talked to the buckskin as she massaged and when she decided she'd done enough for now, she turned to find someone staring at her. "Tim! What are you doing here?"

"You're doing good with that horse," he said. "You've always had a knack ..." He stopped, a grim spin to his mouth, and looked down.

"What's wrong?"

"I've got bad news. Real bad news." His face tensed as he caught her attention. "My wife ... Sue Anne's gone."

"Gone?"

"I can't find her anywhere. And Ginny George said she isn't coming back."

"Ginny? My best friend in California? How did she know that?"

"I called her. She and Sue Anne have been corresponding. I checked the phone bill and found several long calls made there."

"Does Ginny know where Sue Anne is?"

"No. At least, she wouldn't tell me. But she did mention to check with Norden McKane."

"Why?"

"I haven't done that yet. I thought ... well, I kinda hoped ... maybe you would. Could you talk to Norden for me?"

Of all the nerve! So many reasons why she couldn't and wouldn't. She offered one. "This isn't any of my business."

"I'm begging you, Reba Mae, please help me. I can't go barging in on Norden, not knowing what's going on ... between him and my wife."

"Do you have any reason to believe ...?"

"Only what Ginny hinted. Sue Anne must have said something to her. Otherwise, why would his name even be mentioned? I'm afraid I wouldn't act very calm. Not a good idea for me right now to contact him."

Pretty, friendly Sue Anne with Jace's younger half-brother? Didn't seem plausible.

"I think she's mad at me because I wouldn't buy her more ostriches."

"What?"

"She's concerned her dad's going to give over the store to her younger brother, so she's been on a hunt for an income-producing project of her own. She read somewhere about ostriches, how the meat can be prepared tender and tasty, and how many products can be produced from the feathers and skin.

"I did order one for her. It's huge, seven or eight feet tall. Did you know they can kick lions and kill them? I didn't want them around the kids. Besides, I'm sure it's too cold for them to survive the winter here."

Reba presumed there had to be more to it than that. "How long has she been gone?"

"Three days."

"What's missing? What did she take with her?"

He squeezed a tear. "Purse. Suitcase. Toothbrush."

"The car too?"

"No. She left the kids at Grandpa and Grandma's and didn't come back to get them. Now, that's serious."

Reba struggled for a way to best turn down this request and gave up. "Okay, I'll check with Norden," she said, with great misgiving.

"Hey, if you don't want to ...?" He jammed his hands in his Wrangler pockets, his jaw pinched in defeat.

His jibe irritated her. In the old high school days, any attention from him could send goose bumps down her ribs. And begging for more. Now, it made her mad.

Quickly Tim's face softened into remorse and then desperation. "Reba Mae, I don't know where else to turn or what to do."

No way did she want to ask Norden about Sue Anne. But she truly loved those kids, Kaitlyn and William. She could force herself to do it for them. "I said I would."

He thanked her profusely, his trembling hands reaching out to her as she pulled back. "I know how awkward all of this is," he said more than once.

He didn't realize half the gall of it. To Reba, the high school days of best friend and boyfriend betraying her and running off to get married didn't seem so long ago.

"Did you know you're prettier than ever?" He offered a twist of a smile.

Images ignited her mind of her primped for the high school prom in her one and only dress and then getting stood up, while he and Sue Anne stayed out all night. She glared him down.

His eyes softened in chagrin, as though he caught the vision too. "Surely you know how sorry I am. I've changed ... a lot."

Before she could respond, he waved, and drove his pickup toward the Runcie Ranch, past the Camperdown Elm.

She felt thirteen again and remembered the day she crouched under the elm tree, shucking corn when Tim Runcie rode by on his bike on the road. She waved at him and kept on tugging on the cobs. He must have slowed and turned around because the next thing she knew, he plopped down beside her. "Where are your grandparents?" he asked.

"Grandpa's in the fields and Grandma's washing clothes in the barn," she said.

"Good," he said and began to stroke her hair. "You are growin' up, Reba Mae." He quit stroking and she was glad because it was bothering her.

She'd never been that close to him before, his caramel-colored hair all thick and straight like a beaver's, his eyes nearly black as agates. She usually walked behind him after school to the bus stop and sometimes sat next to him.

After that, she saw him cuddled close to a girl named Emilene in their class. "Are you going steady with Emilene?" she asked him outright.

He hopped on his bike and rode away without an answer.

She and Tim grew in friendship over the years and, perhaps, took one another for granted. Maybe that's why he dumped her for Sue Anne. However, from what she knew now about her blood relationships, the matter worked out for the good. She'd been protected. So had Tim. Still, the rejection hurt.

Unreasonable, she privately confessed.

However, she assented to do him a huge favor.

As she and Abel hiked from the corral to the house, Reba almost bumped square into Wynda. "Sorry," she muttered.

"You looked deep in thought," the Scottish girl said.

"I am. Much on my mind."

Wynda reached for her shoulders. "I do massages. Learned a bit at one of my part-time jobs going to university." She pushed and pulled a few times.

"Ah, you convinced me. You can do that anytime."

"How about now?" She followed Reba into the ranch house.

Abel wandered to the video games and Reba stretched out on the couch on her stomach. "How about here?"

"A bit too low for me. How about your bed?"

Reba sauntered to her room and stretched over a bedspread quilted with horses and mountain scenes. After a fifteen-minute rub down of back and neck, Reba rose and thanked her.

Wynda studied the sea painting in Reba's bedroom. Greenish waters, sea gulls, and waves burst against a cliffside. On the horizon, a ship sailed between amber sunset infused billowing of clouds and wind tugging wisps of whitecaps. "Reminds me of a coastal place in Scotland."

"I bought it recently because it reminded me of my Grandpa Cole. He often talked about the ocean. And I spent a lot of time on a California beach during my college days."

As they turned to walk out, Wynda picked up the female wooden warrior Seth Stroud whittled for Reba from the dresser—helmet over stream of hair, raised arm and fist wielding a sword. "Her name doesn't happen to be Lenore?"

"What? Why do you say that?"

"'It shall clasp a sainted maiden whom the angels name Lenore— Clasp a rare and radiant maiden, whom the angels name Lenore— Quoth the raven, `Nevermore.' Edgar Allan Poe."

"Ha! I know a story about a cousin of that poet. His name was Johnny Poe."

"Is that right?"

Reba noticed Wynda didn't follow her into the living room and checked the bedroom again. She still gazed at the sea painting. "I'll watch Abel for you anytime," Wynda offered.

Reba quickly assessed the wisdom of accepting. "You've had experience with kids?"

"I've cared for lots of *bairns*."

Abel entered the room and Wynda hugged his shoulders. "Abel and I get along just fine, don't we, lad?"

Abel nodded.

"Well, how about right now? I've got errands to run."

"Sure. What can we do for you while you're gone?"

"Can you clean saddles?"

"Well ..." Her brows drew closer. Her face tightened.

"I know all about it." Abel's head tilted back, hands plunked on his hips. "Jodeen and Jace taught me. Get me saddle soap, a big bucket of warm water, a rag or sheepskin, a nylon bristle brush, and oil or wax." His eyes gleamed with confidence.

"Well, then, okay. You had pro teachers."

"Oh, yeah. Jodeen and Jace spent a lot of time teaching me the right way to do it."

I'll bet.

Still troubled, despite the relaxing massage, Reba tried to reach Ginny by phone, to talk with her about Sue Anne. Her husband, Paris, answered on the third try.

"Ginny's up north a few days with her mom, picking out baby supplies for people to buy for her baby shower. At least, that's the way I understand it. I'll tell her you called."

Reba finally gave up and drove down Main Street, wondering how she'd handle this awkward situation Tim pressure-sprayed her into.

How dare he?

Why did she agree?

She slipped past the front of the mouse-gray apartments where Tim and Sue Anne lived while they waited to afford building their own house on the Runcie Ranch. The only apartment building in town would never compete in the Road's End Beautiful Property Improvement Contest, if they had one. Wall to sidewalk brittle grass and dry leaves formed the front yard. Quilts or sheets covered most of the windows, except one. Bright yellow cotton Priscillas marked the Runcie place.

She swung her pickup to the side of the road as she decided to check out a few things before she approached Norden. In part, to stall for time. She peered at Whitlow's Grocery next to the apartments. Tim mentioned Grandma Whitlow had the kids, so she presumed they might be there.

She knocked at the apartment door, alert to any sign of activity. Finding no one stirring, she hiked up the hill behind the apartments to check with the manager, Polly Eng, at the gray stone and brick house with the only outdoor clothesline left in town. She resisted the temptation to swing close enough to feel the cool, wet sheets swirling in the breeze and smell the fresh, clean sweetness.

"Sue Anne's gone all right." Polly thumbed a gold necklace with a whimsical goat preening on an octagon shaped locket. "The funny thing is, I helped her do a garage sale last week. Everyone in the apartments contributed, like we did last year. Campers from the park bought lots of stuff. We all made a tidy sum. I couldn't help ask questions when she had Norden carry out furniture and all her clothes into a U-Haul when it was over. She clammed up. Wouldn't say a word." She twisted the necklace chain round in quick, sharp jerks. "My daughter Kam was taking care of the kids. Sue Anne said Tim would pick them up and off she went."

"Was Norden with her?"

"No, I'm pretty sure he returned to his store and she drove away like she was headed out of town."

Reba's stomach lurched as she tossed her purse across her shoulder and tromped down the incline toward the Outfitter's store at the end of Main Street. Polly's account made it sound starkly real.

Reba tromped down the sidewalk to the Outfitters.

Might as well get this over with.

She entered the Outfitters Shop and the welcoming bells rang. But the interior dimmed darker than usual, with indoor lights off. She walked up and down several empty aisles past tack, horse grooming, and saddle supplies. No customers. No employees greeted her.

Hearing the clatter of a manual typewriter in the back, she tiptoed down the creaky hall, attempting to be quiet as possible. She peeked in the doorway of Norden's small office. He wore his usual camo shirt and pants, fishing gear by his side. Through a window she noted the red Harley chained to a post.

Norden turned from the Smith Corona to punch buttons on the adding machine as papers piled on top a file cabinet slid to the floor. When he leaned over to pick them up, he saw her. "Reba?"

"We're looking for Sue Anne. Do you know where she is?"

He got out of the chair and scrunched like the football player he used to be, grabbing the papers. Reba reached down to help.

"I'd like to know myself. It's a mess around here."

"What can you tell me? When did you see her last?"

His eyes flicked away a moment. "She left a few days ago after telling me she was going to karate lessons in Oroston and would return in two hours." He gritted his teeth.

"Return to the store?"

"Yesss ..." He slurred the word, as though holding something back.

Reba crossed her arms and braced for an attack. "Norden, was your relationship with Sue Anne purely business?"

"Biggest mistake of my life."

"What was?"

"Hiring her."

Before Reba could respond, her tummy hitched and her arms flailed as she fought to keep balance. The floor beneath her heaved and trembled, like it had been given a big shake. She reached for the wall to regain her balance. She could hear crashes close by, like dishes or canned goods off shelves.

Norden grabbed for her. "Earthquake!" he said.

In Idaho? A very rare occurrence.

"That must be why the local schools stepped up emergency drills for the late summer session," Norden said. "They must have been warned of possible seismic activity.

When the roller coaster sensation completely stopped, she and Norden ran through the store, assessing damages.

"Could be a lot worse," opined the California native owner.

Moments later, the town's fire alarm blared and a scurry of people rushed the streets, peering around in excitement.

"Anybody need assistance?" Polly Eng yelled, as she held up her EMT bag, used to treat more bee stings, heart attacks, and pregnancy runs than natural disaster trauma wounds.

Reba helped her contact everyone up and down Main Street. Several buildings suffered cracks and broken merchandise and possessions, but only a few minor injuries.

As she reached her pickup, Norden ran over. "If I hear from Sue Anne, I'll let you know."

"Thanks. Tim will really appreciate it."

He gave her an odd look.

After she returned home, Pearl greeted her with, "That earth rumble we had caused Tim Runcie a near fatal tractor accident. His machine tumbled off a hill. Nearly landed on top of him."

Reba collapsed in a chair. "Is he okay?"

"He's one fortunate, but very bruised and banged-up guy. Cracked ribs. Broken nose. Deep gash in forehead. He'll need a few days in the hospital to recover. Then take it very easy."

"I wish I knew where Sue Anne is. She should know."

Chapter Nineteen

*H*anna Jo opened the door early the next morning for Sergeant Elliot Laws. She stared at a large gold key engraved *Road's End 1991* on a chain around his neck. "Mayor Champ Runcie gave it to me. Key to the city." He put his arm around a boy a little older than Abel at his side. "This is my nephew, Malik."

"I brought you all a dream catcher." Malik held up ornaments he pulled out of a leather pack made of bark, wooden beads, and feathers. "Uncle Elliot and I made them. Good dreams come through the big hole and bad dreams are blocked by the netting."

They thanked the boy and each lifted a dream catcher over their heads and around their necks.

"Tell them, Malik, what you told me," Elliot prompted.

"I know where the wild horses are," the boy announced. "Down in a small canyon, hiding. I wanted them for myself, but they belong to you."

"They do? What makes you say that?" Hanna Jo asked.

"Because the big, black stallion told me."

"Can you show us where they are?"

"Sure." He looked at his uncle. "Right now, if you're ready."

Malik hopped onto an unruly pony bareback without bridle, but with added light tack. Elliot mounted a brown and white appaloosa with his long bow tied in front, made from a mountain sheep horn.

"Don't worry," he told his uncle. "My horse is swifter than eagles or cougars and Bigfoot."

A train roared in the distance on one of the trestles. A warning whistle got caught by the wind and carried away.

Pearl yanked her hat off the rack. "Come on, we've got a ride to take."

"But what about Abel?" Reba asked, mindful she'd promised Jace to keep closer tabs on his safety.

"Let him ride behind one of you," Elliot suggested, "since Malik's coming along too."

After hesitation and encouragement by the others, Reba helped a very delighted Abel into the back of her saddle. "Hold on tight," she said. "And obey what I tell you."

"I've done this before with Jace," he said.

"Corralled wild horses?"

"No, not exactly."

They followed Malik north for several miles and then he veered down an old Indian trail, so overgrown they slowed the horses. They forged ahead over undulating, forested hills, and alongside a rocky cliff plastered with vetch, lupine purple wildflowers, and drifts of stirred up bumblebees. Reba never traveled this section of tribal land before. She'd considered their main hunting grounds off limits.

They passed a holding pen, a narrow, long burlap and rebar walled corridor that led to temporary wood stack corrals, more substantial than the one Hanna Jo fashioned on the former Cahill land.

Several miles later, the Nez Perce boy signaled for quiet.

They hunched behind boulders on a cliff overlooking a small canyon, with Hanna Jo and Elliot closest to Malik. They could all see the small herd of horses, their backsides to the humans, and toward the wind.

The black stallion stood still on his high piece of terrain, in full

command. He kept tabs of movements and scents carried by the wind. In an instant, the stallion gave a whistle, a sharp, loud, blowing through the nostrils sound, an alarm to alert the herd that carried over the canyon and through the trees. He reacted to a disturbance and the eight mares below bunched with the four foals into a tight group.

Had he smelled the humans?

Or a cougar lying in wait along a rock ledge or up on a tree limb along the horse trail?

After frantic snorting, the stallion turned and his hooves like flint thundered, trampling brush underfoot. He spun in a circle with puffed chest and thrashing head. He stopped at a rocky wall with a wreath of smoky air out of his nose, but didn't jump toward the herd. And the herd stayed in place.

"Let's listen to them awhile," Elliot whispered, "to gauge their mood."

Time crawled by. They waited for at least an hour as the stallion and his mares finally calmed down.

"How do you suggest we circle the stallion?" Hanna Jo asked.

"Don't need to," Elliot replied. "This herd's led by the old mare down there. Did you notice all the squealing and nipping in that crisis, but she kept her eyes the whole time on the stallion. She kept him and the herd in line. Get to her and we've got them all."

"Unless the stallion abandons the mares," Hanna Jo said. "I've seen it happen."

Elliot squinted. "It's always possible. But I suspect this stallion's going to stay." He looked over at Reba.

"Only way to know for sure is to give it a try," Pearl said. "What's the plan?"

"This isn't my kind of terrain." Hanna Jo eyed Elliot.

The two of them consulted and Elliot gave instructions for position. Malik with Reba and Abel. Hanna Jo and Pearl together. Elliot on point. The goal: penning the head mare and rest of the herd in the trap and hope the stallion followed.

Elliot issued a caution. "Don't let the foals separate from the mares during the chase. The mothers won't return for them."

As they moved forward into the open, the stallion leaped out from behind a boulder above them.

"Keep going. Ignore him," Elliot calmly advised. "We're staying with the mare."

The stallion made moves as though prelude to a battle. Reba knew well enough about agile, stone hard hooves that could kick horse or rider with whiplash speed. Or vicious teeth that can rip and tear flesh. However, Elliot proved right. The feints and strutting turned out to be bluff and bluster.

After much finesse by Elliot and Hanna Jo and following orders by the rest, the mare led her companions and the colts and fillies into the corral.

Then they watched, amazed, as the stallion marched in after them.

The next day, with help from Lloyd Younger and his older boys, they added the captured wild horses to Cahill holding stalls.

Reba fed carrots and apples to traumatized Banner, determined to renew her goal not to give up on her. She'd pay full attention to the horse and forget her agenda. She must get this horse under control before they included her in a pasture with others.

She studied the horse's body language until she realized, unpredictable explosions started with a look, a posture, a twitch. Like a warning. She waited long enough for Banner to tell her she was ready to do what Reba wanted.

The mare stopped and shook her head. She pranced and stomped her foot. Was Banner trying to get her to follow? For one thing, a herd animal required a herd. She should find Banner a partner. Maybe the black stallion, if Hanna Jo would agree.

Since Banner arrived on the ranch, she attempted to establish ranking as leader over Reba. As she grew secure in her new home, she expressed her power as potential boss. She let Reba know she would be led to the barn or pasture only when she wished. She simply planted her feet and refused to move. Reba kept insisting and tried to ease her fears with smooth talk. Still, Banner refused to follow.

Banner responded even weirder whenever Hanna Jo showed up, wearing a different colorful cowgirl hat every day. The mare postured like she wanted to fight Reba, as though she preferred Hanna Jo.

Was it the hats?

Today when Hanna Jo entered with no hat at all and stood in the middle of the corral with hands behind her, Banner sauntered over in a friendly manner and nudged closer, as though telling her to move. Hanna Jo placed her left hand on the mare's chest and backed her up. She repeated that a couple of times, and then turned and walked away.

Hanna Jo pulled a halter off a hook and slipped it over Banner's shoulder while the horse stood in the corner, snorting, eyes brimmed with fright. Then she slid the headstall over her ears, and tied her to the snubbing post, a four-foot-tall log firmly planted in the ground.

"Thanks," Reba said, though conflicted about what to make of the victory.

An hour later, with great ceremony, Hanna Jo appeared with a camera around her neck and leading the black stallion.

"What are you doing?" Reba asked.

"It's obvious. These horses have chosen their owners. Banner prefers me. You get the black." She presented the stallion to Reba, raised the camera, and clicked several times. As simple as that, they made the transfer.

Reba didn't query her mother about the rightness of the switch. No argument or objection warranted. She and her mother experienced their first solid agreement. Reba gravitated to the black stallion without a backward glance at the buckskin.

Without hesitation, she called him, "Johnny Poe. Your full name is Johnny Poe II." Her former horse would now be known as Johnny Poe I.

She sensed an intimate, supernatural-like connection to this animal. She couldn't shake off a notion of the memory of Johnny Poe I with his dying mother at the barbed wire fence. The more she strained to retrace details of that day, she recollected a periphery glimmer, a flash of shadow, a movement in the distant thickness of pines and tamaracks.

Was this stallion there? Another colt? A brother? Perhaps a twin?

This horse definitely identified with her. He grasped a distinct connection. But her attention focused more that long-ago day on the nearest colt, the one collapsed by the severely wounded mare.

And up close and personal to the stallion, Reba noticed several scars that indicated past fights, as well as a slash on the neck, a sign of a cougar attack. Maybe his surrender at the catch pen signaled a kind of acceptance of retirement to a protected arena for him and his mares.

After the informal ceremony of owner changes, Johnny Poe II quickly reverted to his ill-tempered, wild ways, proving to be a bull at times. After all, he'd never been tamed before.

Meanwhile, Banner still postured her disdain for being led. To protect herself, she'd fight or freeze in place, as though she expected pain. So, Hanna Jo insisted on a separate round pen for the buckskin. "It's safer and makes it easier to catch and halter and provides a boundary without using a rope."

They spent half a day erecting the round pen, with Abel and Pearl's help.

Banner soon followed Hanna Jo's direction by moving forward, backing up, stepping laterally, and standing at a halt. Then she reversed her attitude. When Hanna Jo approached, she turned and walked away. When asked to move, she refused by firmly planting her feet. "Can't win all of them all the time," Hanna Jo conceded. "Each horse is different."

Not long after, Banner with the deep-seated trust issues followed Hanna Jo anywhere, like a huge dog, but only when not being asked to do something. Placing boundaries brought out her instincts to run or fight. Hanna Jo kept persisting in discipline in the round pen until Banner knew she was boss.

Meanwhile, Johnny Poe II eased forward for Reba before he snarled at her like a fire-breathing dragon. Then he pinned his ears, reared and lunged, and swung his hindquarters. The herd leader had spoken.

But so did Reba.

She stood her ground and twirled her rope as she heard Hanna Jo, Abel, and Pearl scream at her from the fence, "Move, Reba!"

The stallion headed toward her several more times, each advance closer, more menacing, to maneuver, intimidate. Reba stayed in position, expecting a kick, hoping he'd miss her head or ribs.

Reba held to one main principle—don't balk at times of resistance. She wanted Johnny Poe II as a true partner, not a pasture pet. When he got high-headed and wide-eyed, she'd gain the trust and respect of an animal not used to humans. At the least, she'd provide a home, pasture, mates, plenty of feed, pedicures, mane and tail styling, and veterinary care.

A fair trade.

Maybe the stallion agreed because the black horse stopped his antics, dropped his head, and stared at Reba. Another brief moment of communication between them, as he exhibited a critical show of submission before he galloped away.

Her mother chose that moment to chide her with the question she tried so hard to ignore. "Do you love Jace enough to marry him even if you neither one will ever work on the Cahill Ranch? Or any ranch?"

"I don't know." *I don't know!*

She must accept the facts.

She cherished the idea of Jace in boots and Wranglers, especially now that this Johnny Poe replacement showed up. Maybe that's what she should do to make a living here—train horses and give riding lessons.

That might work. Maybe partner with her mom.

But where did that leave Jace? Would he be interested in horses as a full-time occupation? What venture best fit her and Jace as a couple?

When the stallion graduated to a grassy, fenced arena surrounded by trees, Reba let him investigate on his own. She walked him around the perimeter and emphasized lunging again. Soon she trotted Johnny Poe II along the fence line and circled in the corners.

Finally, she asked him for a canter and he accepted. Reba nearly shouted, "Hurray!" but restrained herself. She didn't dare disturb his rhythm. Or make a big fuss to unnerve him.

"Atta boy," she said, with as much detachment as she could muster.

🐎 🐎 🐎 🐎

Reba headed to the house to check on Abel and Grandma Pearl. They played a boisterous, hand-slapping game of cards on the dining room table. She marveled that Hanna Jo joined them too.

"Sit with us," Pearl invited.

She declined. "I'm going to try to call Jace again. I'm wondering what's happening with him."

"I heard Tim's coming home from the hospital," Pearl said.

"That's good."

She didn't ask about Sue Anne or their situation. She still hadn't told Tim about her conversation with Norden, since he'd been in the hospital. She wasn't sure what to tell him anyway. Doubts still lingered in her mind about Norden's reaction to her queries.

She picked up the phone and dragged it by the long cord into her bedroom. So much to tell Jace. About Tim and Sue Anne. That scary letter. The robberies. Her new Johnny Poe II.

She dialed first his cellular phone he kept in the car. No answer.

Then she tried the number at his father's home three times. Busy signals. She couldn't even leave a message. She heard commotion at the front door.

Malik Laws rushed up, shouting, "Bigfoot is chasing me!"

They tried to calm him and searched around after Pearl and Reba grabbed rifles. They only found a big pile of mauled food and garbage.

"I brought that for bait," Malik admitted and stuck to his story of a Bigfoot sighting.

Something definitely frightened the horses too. Hanna Jo

carefully eased Banner up and put a saddle and bridal on her. She talked to her as she tried to mount. Reba reeled in horror as Banner exploded into the air with Hanna Jo in the saddle.

Rodeo time!

Banner bucked and twisted as her mother brought a rein up and to the side before she lost her balance and crashed to the ground.

Reba helped her mother up from the wet, muddy ground in stunned silence. "You did fight hard to stay on. Amazing job."

Hanna Jo rubbed her hip and shoulder. "Okay, she's not exactly broke for riding yet."

"You all right?" Reba asked.

"Sure. I've been hurt worse than this before." Hanna Jo released a blow of breath. "Well, back in the saddle!" She scrutinized Banner. Flicking ears, wide eyes, dropped shoulder. "Maybe not. Perhaps tomorrow."

Chapter Twenty

*P*earl made a quick trip to the construction site to deliver sandwiches and Kool-Aid. She checked out the progress so far with admiration. She was so grateful for not getting sucked into the black hole of day-to-day building oversight. Capable people took charge here.

Franklin greeted her with startling news. "We uncovered a human skeleton at the construction site last night. A small one. Could be a child. Chief Deputy Lomax and Sheriff Goode are checking missing children reports in the region."

"Where did you find it?"

"Right about where we plan to put a baseball diamond someday. Now part of the construction site is a crime scene."

Pearl walked with him over to the rectangle of fluttery yellow tape staked to the ground.

"The coroner in Lewiston will work on it. That's not all," Franklin continued. "Thieves are stealing from the site and someone broke a window. We've got an overnight patrol sleeping here, two at a time, to keep a close watch. Other than that, we're good. Except for harping by Champ and Adrienne Mathwig. She always seemed so quiet before, but she's terrible. She has to have the last word. She talks and never shuts up, even when no one is around."

"How can you possibly know that?"

"Because I see her mouth moving when I drive up and she's the only one here."

"Give her a part of the project to organize," Pearl suggested.

"Like what?"

She noticed a variety of hardware items scattered on the ground and across a picnic table. "How about making her in charge of equipment and tool inventory?"

His eyebrows squinted in doubt. "Well, I don't know ..."

"Give it a try. And let her join in with a hammer and saw now and then. See how it works. As for Champ ... because of him, we have the land ready and construction materials, including plenty of pressure treated wood, so we didn't need a stewardship campaign or fundraisers. And we've got mostly volunteer labor. Surely, we can put up with some of his mouth."

Pearl putzed around the property and returned to Franklin. "This is working out great. We've got a full five acres to work with ... space for the building and parking and later, playground and recreation area for sports or whatever."

A small crowd of church-goers gathered around them as ideas flowed on how to use the new facility and grounds to reach out to the community. Halloween carnival with a faith theme. Baseball diamond. Basketball court. Game nights. Mini-concerts by local and regional talent.

Cicely Bowers suggested, "Outdoor screen with wooden benches or slots for cars to watch 'inspirational movies.'"

Franklin stopped the brainstorm flow with a comment. "The project's taking longer than we thought. So, we called in the militia, so to speak." He pointed to the MacKenzie white van approaching the site. "Tucker's Gang of Eight." Driver Archie stopped the rig and out poured Tucker Paddy and his former cellmates from the county jail.

"This should go pretty fast, now," Pearl commented.

Adrienne in her denim cap replaced the broken window and while she had the tall ladder out, checked the roof gutters for pine needles or other debris, and made sure they were attached properly.

"I hear you're a dentist. I've got a toothache." Atch opened his mouth and pressed a molar.

"Used to be," she corrected. "Now I bake pies." She reached for a piece each of peach and huckleberry. "Here. This will cure what ails you."

"You're a funny kind of dentist."

"And you're a funny kind of guy. Don't you think I recognize dentures when I see them?"

"How about we go to Lewiston for a little drive?"

Her eyelashes fluttered. "Atch Murdock, are you asking me out on a date?"

"What if I was?"

The city fire alarm blared in the distance and they detected smoke billowing up the lane.

"Big city crime in Road's End," Charlotta warned. "Lock your doors and tuck a weapon under your pillow." She rushed to the hotel to protect her new Viking sewing machine.

Pearl guessed what else Charlotta would be guarding: red, plush side-saddles used to ride in parades, the Mathwig sisters' proudest possessions.

News soon arrived this mishap had been a car fire on the windiest road leading into town from the valley. Another vehicle that couldn't manage that steep mountain grade.

When the county building inspector stopped by, a porridge-faced man with a croaky-voice, Franklin changed his earlier negative tune. "We're close to done," he announced. "Only the doors, windows, and siding left on the exterior. One advantage of doing a pole building."

A remorseless enforcer who aimed to maintain order but drunk out of a smudged water bottle, the inspector handed Franklin a spreadsheet with columns for rooms, item descriptions, quantities, item costs, and total costs. "Fill this out," he demanded.

Later at home, Pearl checked Cole's revolver and shotgun and the

.223 rifles she and Reba carried during calving season to take care of coyotes. She spied Archie in front of the bunkhouse, holding a long pole with small rectangle box attachment on one end and round one on the other. "Anything worth stealing in that van? We're having a crime wave in Road's End."

"The loud and bold-eyed triplet already warned us."

Pearl chuckled. "Must have been Adrienne. She's come out of her shell."

"And besides our instruments, we've got the bikes, a video camera, VCR, and camcorder." He held up the pole. "And this metal detector. Sort of a hobby of mine."

Was he the one they'd seen snooping around? "Better lock your valuables in the bunkhouse."

🐎 🐎 🐎 🐎

Abel spent the night with Norden and had been asked to help out at the store for the day. So, Reba knocked on Hanna Jo's door, hoping to take care of an important pilgrimage. "How you doing, Mom?"

Hanna Jo rose up from her pillow with a groan. "Sore. Every movement painful. Nagging headache blooming into a migraine. Other than that, I'm okay."

"Sorry to hear that. Grandma and I would like you to go riding with us, when you're up to it."

"Any place in particular?"

"Yes, but it's a surprise, a bitter-sweet one."

"I really don't like surprises of any sort."

"I know. Like I said, when you're up to it."

Her mother yawned. "Let me stretch out first, take a shower, and some pain meds. I've got bruises all over after that spill on Banner." Hanna Jo grabbed a wad of clothes and grimaced her way to the bathroom.

The three women mounted Banner, Johnny Poe II, and Pearl's favorite mare. They passed the Camperdown Elm, restless and swaying in the summer breeze. Reba thought she detected sighing and whispering as it bowed low. She shivered, already somber as they headed to a special, private place on Coyote Hill.

They slow-trotted the horses, in no big hurry, so they could chat.

"We haven't discussed it much," Pearl began. "But, you know, you were a twin, Hanna Jo."

"Maidie tried to tell me, but she sounded so confused. I didn't know what she meant."

"That night you were born was very muddled for her." Pearl paused as several large V-flocks of Canada geese scattered raucous honks overhead.

When it got quiet again, Hanna Jo pressed, "What happened to the twin?"

"The boy baby was stillborn," Pearl said. "And Maidie was in such a state … for your safety Seth brought you to Cole and me. When he returned to the house, the boy baby was gone."

Three miles later they reached high growing, perfumed wild rose bushes. They rode through swarms of flitting butterflies as hummingbirds sliced air with their wing beats nearby, even though Bullfrog Meadow lost most its wild flowers and the water at Bottle Lake shimmered low. Burnt or moss-covered tree stumps skewered the field.

Flies buzzed and sage hens purred as Reba led them toward the tiny, decrepit chapel on the other side of the private bridge with the "Cross At Own Risk!" sign. On the side of the chapel, they stepped over a wire fence that gave up long ago and lay on its side. They wound around headstones through tall weeds, Pearl at the lead, until she stopped and cleared away the foliage obscuring a stone marked with *David Daniel, February 23, 1945*.

They stood for a moment, taking in the melancholy site.

"Brings back that chilly, stormy night Seth stood at my door with a precious baby girl and asked us to take care of her." Pearl hugged Hanna Jo.

"Did you know then about the baby boy?" Reba asked.

"No, not at the time. But Champ never should have taken him away. The whole ordeal upset Maidie and Seth terrible."

Hanna Jo kneeled down and brushed off the stone with her hand. "How would my life have been different with a twin brother?" she said. She wondered if she'd lost some part of herself, though they'd never known each other. Would their two halves have made a whole?

The more she stared, the stone looked like a missing puzzle piece.

"That's one of those impossible *'what ifs.'* That story was not meant to be told." Pearl attempted to straighten her jellied legs and the other two women helped her stand and re-mount her horse.

Pearl pointed to the small chapel in a swale of high weeds and pines and down a long path.

"Uriah Runcie built this for his wife, Roberta," she said. "She'd come here when she needed peace and to play the piano."

"Did they ever have services here?"

"No. In fact, Roberta forbid it. This was her own personal, private sanctuary."

"I regret ..." Hanna Jo fussed with Banner's reins, then slid down.

"You regret what?" Reba nudged.

"Disappointing you."

Not the word Reba would use to describe her state of abandonment by her mother for over two decades.

Inside the chapel, rats scurried. A dusty piano decayed in the corner with rusty lid and yellowed ivory keys.

Reba braved another gaping wound subject. "Why didn't you at least come for Grandpa's funeral?"

Hanna Jo's mouth puckered. "I did," she spit out. "I was there ..." She gulped in air. "... for Dad's funeral, but I hid out of sight. I snuck in late and left early. Seth and Maidie saw me, but I made them promise not to tell. I couldn't bear to face anyone."

"What are you talking about?" Reba shook her head in denial.

"I was there, when it happened, underneath the Camperdown Elm. I saw my father's eyes ..." She took another deep breath and winced at Pearl. "... when he knew I was there and he was dying."

Reba's chest heaved and burned as she tried to grasp this claim.

Pearl choked out, "The doctor said he had been dead for at least two hours when Reba found him."

Could he have been saved?

"Why ... why didn't you tell anyone?" Reba's hands shook as she reached for the reins. "Why did you run away?"

"I had my reasons."

"Force of habit?" Reba jabbed. A familiar prick scratched against a sensitive scab on her mind. She always had her reasons.

"You were a handful, you know." Hanna Jo leaped on Banner with ease.

A handful? What did that mean? "So, it was my fault you left me?" If she'd only been a better daughter, a good little three-year-old, she'd deserve her mother's presence.

"I didn't mean it that way. I meant ..." Banner twisted a full circle before Hanna Jo controlled her and blew out a noisy breath. "I knew Mom and Papa Cole could handle you, raise you right. And I knew I couldn't."

Pearl's horse trotted close. "Was that really why you left?"

"That and other things. My life was such a jumbled maze back then."

In the midst of her mother's muddled existence, Reba grew up plain and gangly, with straight, red hair kept long enough to hide big ears and freckled, spotty complexion. She often preferred solitude.

By the time she turned eleven, she knew how to spend the day in the woods wrapped behind them, alone, hunting deer or fishing for trout and salmon. And one fact also grew. Cahill Ranch would one day belong to her, a spot on earth to own, for always. That brought her great comfort when distressed and missing her mother.

While the women eyed each other, each of them intent on her thoughts, the three horses bundled together, nose to nose.

"They're having a powwow," Pearl said.

Hanna Jo broke Banner away. "Race you to the tree," she hollered.

"Which tree?" Reba peered around at hundreds, maybe thousands that filled the forest.

Reba and Pearl could only follow behind as Banner galloped ahead.

Hanna Jo stopped suddenly by a huge Ponderosa pine. Reba and Pearl caught up with her.

As they rested the horses, Hanna Jo cleared the thickness in her throat. "I wish ..." she began. "I wish ..." She paled, cheeks drained to paste, darting glances at both of them.

"Mom, what is it? What do you wish?" Reba prompted. "Might as well tell us." While she braced for what could be painful transparency.

Hanna Jo stretched her neck, eyes closed. "I really wish you could both forgive me."

Pearl didn't hesitate. "Of course I do. I love you so much!"

Reba's windpipe squeezed shut. She watched them with an attempt to pull in her mixed strangle of emotions. In that moment, she once more wrestled with years of past resentment and wondered if she could finally manage to completely bury the hatchet, after a habit born of a thousand repetitions. She coped by striking out. Could she release the pent-up resentment forever, at a moment's notice?

On the other hand, hadn't this been happening in increments already, a bit at a time, throughout this past summer? Like inner chunks of rock beginning to break and crumble.

Lord, help me!

She marveled as she sensed a lifetime's worth of anger dissipate, receding like a tide on a faraway, barren shore. She forced her feet forward in a stiff saunter until she got close enough to reach out and touch each of their shoulders. They landed in an explosive group bear hug.

When they reluctantly pulled away, Reba asked Pearl, "Be honest. Did you regret taking us in? Did we wreck your plans or spoil the peace between you and Grandpa? Especially knowing what you do now."

Her grandmother's gaze dropped as she delayed answering. Reba wondered if she didn't want to talk about it. Perhaps the question embarrassed her. The pause splintered the air with a prickly edge, perhaps supplying the answer.

At long last, Pearl looked them both in the eye, her voice firm.

"Raising you both kept me from early senility and endless bridge card parties. That's worth something."

Warm laughter like a dart of light flashed through the solid wall of decades of deep sadness, lingering long enough to wash over and through them like a cleanse.

"Another thing," Pearl concluded, "there's a lot of similarity between ranching and doing relationships. Both require risk and constant tending, with no guarantee of success."

Chapter Twenty-One

Reba opened a few windows to release air into the stuffy house after Abel and Pearl retired to their bedrooms. She swiped her sweaty forehead and wondered if she had a fever. After easing her discomfort with a cool, wet dishrag, she lingered at Hanna Jo's doorway.

"Hey," she greeted.

"Hey, yourself."

"Good day, don't you think?"

"Bitter-sweet. But yeah, one of the good ones, too."

Encouraged by the recent truce between them, but overcome by a rise of desperation, her finger twitched as she jabbed it toward her mother. "I've got to somehow, at least try, to get the ranch back."

Her mother scowled. "Okay ... list the options."

"I admit, perhaps reckless measures may be called for."

"Like what? Burn down their fields? Shoot their bulls? Murder Champ?"

"None of that would give us the ranch," Reba reasoned, "and

would most likely land us in jail."

"What if we force a showdown with Champ?"

"Now you're thinking. How about this? We could sue."

"Well, it worked for him. If we need a lawyer, I know a great one: Egan Toms."

The Paiute Reba met in the Nevada desert. "But that could get spendy. Does he do *pro bono?*"

"Don't know, but come to think of it, he's from Phoenix. He may not be up on Idaho laws."

"We sure don't want to hire James Howe, Champ's lawyer. However, I don't know any others around here. We'd have to scout around."

Hanna Jo crossed her arms. "There's at least one thing you haven't considered."

"What's that?"

"The one solution that might work."

Reba gawked at her mother. "Okay. I'm listening."

"The first logical step is to stay here in Road's End. Stand our ground, what's left of it. Meanwhile, train and sell as many horses as we can handle. That's a start." Hanna Jo set her face tight, as though that settled the matter.

Reba recalled an old Grandma Pearl saying: *you could have knocked me over with a feather.* That fit now. "Very practical and doable. Also, what if we forget our pride, ask to lease parcels of land from the Runcies, and start from there?"

"Maybe." Hanna Jo added another stunner. "Champ knows about Maidie's stillborn boy, but we have no proof he knows about me. Seth took me away before he arrived at Maidie's the night I ... we ... were born. What if I demand a paternity test from Champ? What if knowing I'm his daughter would change his whole approach?"

Reba both shuddered and thrilled at the prospect. What would be the potential repercussions or outcomes? She imagined the scene between her mother and Champ. How she'd love to make him squirm, to put him in his place. To force him to squarely face the truth. But what if he turned the whole thing around with ugly accusations, with him the victim? He said, she said.

At one time, she considered knowledge of blood relationship as Champ's leverage over *them*, to gain the ranch. Now, with the tables turned, could they make a plea to any part of ranch rights through that same connection?

However, Grandma Pearl sold the ranch to him outright. They had no recourse. And another point. "Proving that fact would also implicate his relationship with Maidie," she said. "Do we want to risk smearing her memory and reputation? Folks would presume she'd been unfaithful to her fiancé Zeke. Better to leave the innocent dead in peace."

"But it wasn't her fault," Hanna Jo stated. "Champ raped her."

"Allegedly. We can't absolutely prove that, even with Maidie's diary account."

"But *we* know it to be true. He also caused fiancé Zeke's death by oiling that roof."

"Also alleged."

With great reluctance, Reba weighed her intense yearning to wreak revenge on Champ versus a fierce desire to protect Maidie. "Forcing a blood test could make the whole matter more public, with possible unintended consequences."

Hanna Jo's lip curled and she flopped in an easy chair. "Okay, forget the test. Let's think of something else."

Then, in a flash, a legitimate, legal, and moral scheme popped into Reba's mind. She shouted at the pure genius, "How much do you think the squash blossom necklace is worth?"

Hanna Jo made a sucking sound, like a gasp.

Reba warmed to her plan and kept plotting. A full image of the necklace formed. Encased in a velvet lined wooden case, with long string of attached turquoise stones the color of robin's eggs in ten ladybug shapes, five on each side, they trailed to larger stones on a double-rowed circular center. Delicate multi-strands of high-grade gold chain and double rows of gold beads. Six gold encased turquoise rounded triangles on each side with gold tassels. Blossom pendant at the end like long turquoise petals ready to burst open.

Pristine condition—no cracks or broken, missing, or loose stones, and nothing bent.

"It's like a mini-mine with all that high grade gold," Reba blurted out. "We could shop it around, find the best deal. We could sell it to the highest bidder. I'm sure we'd get at least a nice down payment to either buy the Cahill property with interest or lease it. That would be an inroad, a start." She stopped as she noticed her mother's widened eyes, face white as milk. "Of course, it's technically speaking your necklace now, but Maidie wanted us both to have it ... in a sort of way." Reba stumbled as a thought hit her. "You don't want to sell it."

Hanna Jo rubbed her hands in long swipes against her thighs, opened her mouth and out came a squeak.

"Just tell me. We'll go from there. I know it was a crazy idea, but I'm stuck. Be honest. What are you thinking?"

"I ... I already sold it."

Reba slowly turned from mush to stone. She strained to catch her meaning. "Sold it?"

"Yes, to Severs Jewelers last week."

"But your mother ... your birth mother ... she wanted you ... us ... to have it!"

"You right now suggested we sell it. I happened to think of it first." She leaned forward, eyes fluttering, as though gathering strength for her defense.

Reba's tongue felt like granite. She tried to lick her lips. "How much did they give you for it?"

"Enough. I don't want to talk about it. I thought you gave it to me. I could do with it what I wanted."

"And what is that?"

"I ... I'm working on it." Hanna Jo posed her closed-up stance. Her jaw set, her muscles tight, her fists bunched in balls.

Reba had learned over past weeks that nothing she'd say would elicit a further explanation. However, Hanna Jo surprised Reba. She visibly softened before her eyes. Her chin trembled and dropped.

She spoke with a steady, lowered pitch. "I thought the ranch was gone for good. I've been thinking my life through, all the things I've tried, what I'd really like to do. I finally settled on what I might be best suited for." She quivered and inhaled a near sob.

"And what's that?"

"A home for women and horses in distress. Horses getting healed and being healers. A sanctuary to provide therapy for women who've been hit by life's blows, unfairly treated, made terrible choices ..." Her face tinted red. "Perhaps abused by their men. They need a retreat, someone to talk to, to listen, a chance to regroup and consider options."

Reba struggled to absorb the shock of this announcement. At the same time, she recognized the plausibility of it. After she regained a measure of composure, she said, "So, where are you going?"

"Right here in Road's End. Cicely told me she planned to sell her large B&B and buy a much smaller place down the street. She wants to stay here and downsize. I got enough from the necklace for a hefty down payment, and this." She picked up the camera she'd been toting around lately.

Reba did a double-take. "You and Cicely have become friends."

Hanna Jo nodded with a shy grin. "It's her hats. I'm fascinated by them. I think they give me courage to be myself. We're going into business together, as partners, only it will be more like a boarding house."

Reba tried to imagine Cicely and Hanna Jo working together. She had to admit the crazy enterprise made a quirky kind of sense.

"What do you think?" Her mom pleaded, her eyes feverish and over-bright.

Reba reviewed a part of her mother's résumé: drove truck with a boyfriend across the southwest ... lab technician in Thailand ... hospital business manager in the Bahamas ... nurse's aide in Vegas. She worked at a jewelry store in Austin, Nevada where she sold both rough and cut stones and later, lived as a recluse as she captured and tamed wild horses in the Nevada desert.

At least part of those experiences, if not all, provided direct or indirect resources for her proposed enterprise. Maybe her mother would finally settle down and in her own hometown. Wasn't that ideal? A happy ending for the wandering, prodigal runaway.

While Reba pondered this unexpected news, Hanna Jo pulled on her sassy stance again. "Let's face it. Horses and needy women are my passion."

Reba tried to maneuver a last-ditch effort why this wouldn't work. "But you've never done this before. How do you know you can do it?"

"Life experience. I've gone through plenty of good and bad. I have few illusions. I know my life's been messy, but no one's perfect. And I do have at least a bit of savvy. They'd come live with me for a time in my home. My mistakes can be someone else's gain." She reached out and gently touched Reba's hand. "And I could take classes along the way too. Don't you see? I finally found a purpose."

Reba released a partial acceptance and reluctantly nodded. She did see, even though it still hurt that mothering duties didn't count as important enough in the past twenty-two years. And they still got no closer to figuring out how to re-possess their ranch.

Hannah Jo continued, "My time in the institution was not wasted. I've seen every tape, attended every lecture, read every book they have to offer. Lots of soothing sentiments. Sorting through the dysfunction, to what was and wasn't my fault. Now it's time for action that will finally free me and maybe others." She clasped her arms in an X shape, as though warding off demons. "For a long time, I believed my existence was a mistake."

Startled, Reba inwardly conceded agreement. *Mine too.*

"We all make mistakes. We all do things we regret." Hanna Jo proffered an absolution of sorts.

"I still want to get back the ranch," Reba concluded.

"Has Jace given you any ideas at all?"

"In one of our very brief calls, he mentioned he studied the sale papers. He thinks Champ pushed Pearl for less than market value. However, the contract appears solid."

Hanna Jo sighed. "She literally gave away the ranch."

"Yeah."

"Well, believe it or not, I'm going to a Chamber of Commerce meeting at Delbert's Diner. The business owners in town have gotten riled by a few issues, instigated by Champ. Think I'll pop in and join the group. Who knows? Maybe I'll come up with another idea."

Chapter Twenty-Two

Champ hired Charlotta Mathwig and Polly Eng to cater the special outdoor banquet he planned in his backyard for the Runcie family reunion. He wanted everything easy, casual, but perfect, in celebration of several momentous events. At his insistence, all three sons and their wives, plus each of the at-home and adult grandchildren must attend—sixteen total—their first gathering since Richie's wedding, fifteen years before.

No excuses allowed.

That translated to everyone, "Don't be left out of the inheritance."

His genius scheme accomplished another lifelong goal. His sons would carry on the tradition. Best of all, black sheep Richie and Randall, on the outs with Champ these many years, would be overwhelmed with his gracious offer. No way they could refuse.

He never forgave the two sons who dared to leave the ranch and get jobs of their own. He tried to sow discord between the three sons. He played one son against the other, in order to keep them apart, to hold all the power. But that ended, as of now.

As a concession, he granted permission for Road's End postmistress, Lisl Monte, to join them, too, though she wasn't family.

"She's become a close friend," Don stated, "and I'd greatly appreciate her being included."

Though the request irked him, Champ didn't show it, an unfamiliar stance. This 52nd anniversary celebration would include vital, *private* family business. Family members only allowed. However, with Blair's nudging and everything else going his way, he could afford another bit of magnanimous generosity. Besides, he presumed Lisl might one day be family—wife to one of the owners of the largest ranch on the Camas Prairie.

Still pumped with vigorous assurance that all was right in his world, he looked up with astonishment as Blair ushered in Hanna Jo Cahill.

"I'm sorry for the unexpected intrusion," Hanna Jo began.

"I'll get iced tea." Blair dispersed into the kitchen before Hanna Jo or Champ could object. An aroma like warm, baked goods, such as homemade bread, slipped in the room and dissipated.

"What are you doing here?" Champ demanded.

"Please, I come in peace." Hanna Jo added a stiff curtsy for emphasis.

Champ chortled, and then burst out laughing, to fit with his rare, jolly mood. He decided to tease a little. "Is that right? Well, I win!"

Hanna Jo fumbled with her jeans' pockets but presented a blank poker face. "I'm not here about the ranch," she retorted. "I mainly want to check how you're doing."

Champ couldn't hide the smirk. "I'm doing fine, considering the shape I'm in."

"I'm curious. What's that strange, big bird you've got penned up out there?"

"You must mean Sue Anne's ostrich. We're tending it until ..." One of many sore subjects. He leaned back with as much repose as he could muster in the wheelchair. "I'm curious too. You've been gone a lot of years. Why did you reappear in Road's End now?"

"I realized ... family is important to me." She scrunched into a chair.

"Okay, spit it out. What do you want from me?" Was she going to beg? Or get teary? He did hear she'd been unstable, committed to a mental institute.

"Champ," she began, "You've done a lot of good for this city. I see a lot of the improvements since I've returned. And the church building will be such a good thing. Folks around here are grateful."

Ah, this was much better. He nodded, overcome with pride in his achievements. Nice to hear such affirmation from Pearl's daughter. He studied her demeanor closely. She did not appear to be an accuser, an arguer, one who stirred up trouble like Pearl. But why was she here? "And?"

"Well, the permit for Cicely's B&B is running out soon. I'd like to renew it for a kind of boarding house. I'm going to call it Mercy House. It will be pretty much used in a similar way as she did, except instead of mainly overnighters, I'll cater to longer stay residents."

He admired her initiative in finding a means of income, so soon after losing their family ranch and her return to town. "So, you plan to stick around this time?" He stared hard enough to make her squirm. He indulged satisfaction in having all the Cahill women under his thumb.

Her eyes flashed an instant's amount of anger. Then she seemed to rein it in. "Speaking of the boarding house, there's a lot of talk around town about the raise in business taxes."

A rustle and clatter caused him to turn his head. Blair entered with a pot of hot water, mugs, and teabags on a large tray.

"No! Go away!" Champ dismissed her with a waffled hand move.

Her glance darted toward Hanna Jo with a shuttered expression, emotions in check, but he detected eyes large with ... apology? Humiliation? Why couldn't his wife show dignity after all these years?

She shuffled away as she edged toward the kitchen and tugged the door closed behind her.

He turned to Hanna Jo to finish their conversation. He registered a bit of amazement at the sudden change in her meek and mild demeanor. The woman before him pushed her shoulders back with a jerk. The muscles in her face tightened to a contorted grimace. She glared at him with no hint, not a waiver of goodwill. "Champ, I changed my mind. I don't come in peace after all."

Taken aback, with a snort and cough, he mustered to regain control. "But ... what about your permit?"

"You can issue it or not. I don't care. And raise my taxes all you want. I've come to tell you a hard fact and I will only say it once. So, pay attention." She rose to her feet and seemed much taller than before. She loomed before him every inch the defiant soldier rebelling against her superior. "I was born on February 23, 1945, and Maidie Fortress was my mother." She emphasized every syllable as though speaking to a deaf man, battering him with truth.

A buried fragment of splintered memories niggled Champ's mind as his chest heaved in outrage. Maidie exhausted in a disheveled bed of bloody sheets. Maidie whining over and over, "The noisy baby is gone. Please, leave me the quiet one." Maidie hugging a naked baby boy, blue, cold, and stiff as stone. Maidie shrieking as he tugged and yanked the infant out of her arms and finally rushed away.

He drove with the tiny specimen to bury the damning evidence high up on Coyote Hill. But all the way there, he kept gazing at the tiny body, so resembling a Runcie form—son Don's cheeks, nose, and spindly legs. And a name whispered through the pickup cab like it was heaven-sent: *fool*. As close to a spiritual moment as he'd ever experienced in his life.

Now, what was this Cahill woman so crudely telling him?

And what did Maidie yell after him, as he stole that incriminating bundle? "Get the noisy one! Give me back the good baby!"

Two babies? Twins?

For a brief moment, abject terror coursed through his veins. What would this mean? Would Hanna Jo push her claim? Make it public? By the time he formulated a proper, sharp retort, she whirled around and forged toward the door.

"You can't prove it," he shouted.

Hanna Jo slammed out of the house.

He could feel his blood pressure rise. No way would he risk a heart attack or stroke due to such a ridiculous outrage. He quickly calmed himself with a renewed sense of confidence. The Cahill Ranch belonged to him now and forever. Nothing could change that fact. Whatever this impertinent woman believed or spouted, he still ruled his domain.

"Blair," he yelled, "Bring me my brandy."

A cowed Blair served her man while he wondered, what caused the sudden reversal in Hanna Jo's attitude? Such an unstable woman. So like crazy Maidie.

On the 52nd Anniversary party day, after taking prescriptions and pain pills, Champ beamed as he zoomed his wheelchair around the yard. He chatted as though interested in their activities with one attendee after the other. He made a show of getting reacquainted with his closest kin.

He gazed with eager fondness at his people, his very own flock, gathered around the picnic tables. They piled their plates from the buffet of oriental hors d'oeuvres, fried and baked chicken, watermelon, potato salad, with apple pie and fortune cookie cake for dessert.

A grand feast for a great event.

All the sons and grandchildren and their spouses gathered around him, paying him homage. His offspring honored their heritage, their legacy, through the hard work and largesse of Grandpa Uriah.

Now, Champ governed his own private fiefdom.

He'd done everything he could to make Road's End the home of the Runcies, and to further their local history. With intelligent managing and deal making, his sons could eventually take over the whole town. That's what Uriah would have done, if he'd lived long enough. Sure, his father was a bitter old man, full of hate at the end, but no one need remember that.

"No hurry," Champ told them. "Everything in its place and time." He relished every bite and morsel. He drank in the full import of this occasion.

Then, he expounded a toast he'd been practicing for days.

"On this momentous occasion, Blair and I are celebrating the fifty-two years we have spent together. Our hard work and commitment to each other have guided us through many years of rough seas and calving seasons. Through our perseverance and the ability to stand strong, we have produced a most wonderful family. One man by himself is nothing. A wonderful family makes a better world." He tilted his glass. "Cheers!" he said and took a sip of champagne.

Each of the three sons proposed his own toast, with a special word for their mother.

Then Champ clinked his glass again for their attention. "First, I'm retiring as Road's End mayor and want Don to take over my place. I'd appreciate your encouraging him to run."

"Hear, hear," said Randall and all the others applauded, whistled, or slapped Don's back.

Champ noted Don and Lisl exchanged looks before Lisl shut her eyes and clutched Don's arm. She surely wouldn't object to his being mayor. After all, this could be a stepping stone to greater positions. Who knew where it might lead, with a little management and ambition?

"Second, as you all know, I've acquired the Cahill Ranch as an expansion of Runcie property. Long overdue. My father believed it belonged to him since his arrival here. Now, at last, it does." He motioned to Blair. She patted a cool, damp cloth on his forehead.

"And now that the ranch has grown so much, I want to announce ... my will names Don, Randall, and Richie to be equal partners in running this spread." He peered at his three sons and noted their incredulous looks and glazed stares, including Don, who he knew expected to gain the whole ranch as the principle manager. He'd give them time to let the news sink in.

"I know Richie and Randall think they're settled in Spokane, in other businesses, but I'm officially issuing the call that you're needed here on the new, improved Runcie Ranch. Now's the time to return to your roots. With all that extra land, you should find it lucrative to return to Road's End and work it yourself. And Don would appreciate the extra help. Isn't that right?"

Don tugged at his tan cotton shirt collar, as sweat sheened his forehead. Beside him, Lisl Monte pressed a knuckle against her mouth.

Champ went on, full of the importance of this moment. "Upon my eventual demise, the combined properties will be divided equally among you three. Lawyer James Howe has already filed the signed papers."

Don locked eyes with his father. "What about Mom? Have you provided for her?"

Champ gazed at Blair, her face wan and pale, working on a brave smile. A bag of weary bones. "Of course. She'll possess the house for as long as she lives." And as long as she doesn't remarry, he had stipulated.

Everyone at the two picnic tables looked down or shifted on the benches. He'd presumed much more enthusiasm than this. After gnawing moments of uneasy, wooden stillness, Champ wheeled his chair in reverse. "Well, then, I'm headed to the family room for a game of pool. You're welcome to join me. The rest can play horse shoes or hoops or whatever."

He heard fierce whispers behind him. Might as well let them talk it all through. They'd soon recognize this as a brilliant plan.

Three of the grandsons, including Tim, played several rounds of pool with him as Blair cheered them on. He resembled his old self, aiming the stick straight, sinking the balls where he called them from his wheelchair perch. Life was good. He had control again.

The rest of the Runcie gang stayed outside.

Later that evening, after Richie and Randall and their families left to return to Spokane, with Blair in the kitchen, Don approached Champ in the living room. "Why are you doing this, Dad?"

"Doing what?"

"Trying to include Richie and Randall in the operations. They don't know what's going on, never enjoyed the work, and want nothing to do with the ranch. Never have."

"Because the situation's way different now. A good living can be made by all of you, with a little work and planning. Surely they can see that and the need to support me and this family, especially you and Tim."

Don sat down and leaned toward Champ. "You're right, but not in the way you mean."

Champ bristled with annoyance at this son of his who dared sit in his former favorite, high-backed chair. He missed the feel of the leather, broken in for decades. A vague evasiveness seemed to coat Don's words. "What's bothering you? Are you angry about having to share?"

Don's face turned chalky white, despite the farmer tan. "Ugly words were exchanged between us all today. I'm afraid everyone got in a nasty huff about this. The wives especially feel pressured by you to leave their homes and friends." He turned away and averted his eyes from Champ's searching gaze.

"You're lying."

He swirled around. "What?"

"You're concealing something."

Don crossed his arms over his chest, his body rigid. "All right. Here it is. Richie and Randall came to a conclusion. They'll sell their portions in five and ten acre home sites. They'll break up the ranch."

Champ clutched the arms of his wheelchair. The stunning admission knifed through him. Blinking lights flared before his eyes. A spasm crossed his chest like a vice so hard he feared a heart attack. "What did you say?"

"I told them this wouldn't sit well with you." Don's searching gaze looked at him with a tinge of pity, but also peace and calm, which Champ interpreted as apathy. "Never liked doing anything behind anyone's back, especially yours."

Champ ruminated a moment before it hit him. "Why would they tell you this now? Why not wait until I'm cold in the ground and spring it on you?"

Don slumped in his chair, licking his lips. "I ... I don't know exactly."

Champ leaned forward. "Yes, you do. What's up?"

His eldest son seemed stricken. "They know about ... my allergies ... they're getting more severe every season ... and ... Lisl agreed to marry me. I wanted to announce it today, but ..." Don rubbed his chin. "Didn't seem the right timing."

"So?" Champ glared, ready to divert this off-track train rushing him.

"Lisl and I ... eventually, we'll live in Spokane."

"What are you saying?" Champ's eyes and temples throbbed. Lights flashed stronger than ever. "And leave the ranch?"

Don's chin lifted, his posture rigid. "I thought the whole piece of land would be willed to me, since I do most of the work. All these years I've put in, thinking someday ... When you ... well, announcing the will thing ... the whole matter cleared for me. My place isn't here. Besides, Richie and Randall offered to get me a job with much better hours and I won't be so sick all the time."

"How ..." Champ snapped, "... could you dare betray me and the Runcie name like that?"

The room resonated with tremors and fissures building up for years. They glared at each other like opposing gladiators.

In the worst kind of comedy of errors, Tim strolled in. "Grandpa, Dad, I want to say this fast, while I've got the courage. With Uncle Richie and Uncle Randall teaming up with Dad on the ranch, this is the time. I want you both to know I'm going back to school." He rocked on his boot heels and held his breath, not realizing he hammered a nail in his grandfather's coffin. "To study for full-time Christian ministry. Maybe be a missionary or minister. Not sure yet. Going to go one step at a time." He flopped into the nearest chair.

Champ truly believed he'd have a stroke. He tried to get his stiff arms to work as his mouth slacked in a frozen, open position. He kept trying to wave them away, to get them both out of the house and away from his presence.

"Are you okay, Dad?" Don stepped forward in alarm.

"Go!" he yelled and cut Blair short with a few expletives when she entered with hot chocolate and marshmallows.

Don sprinted toward her to catch the tipsy tray.

Champ rolled into the dark bedroom, trembling with fury that ballooned his lungs. Betrayed by the whole disloyal lot. How dare they?

Didn't they care anything for him? Or what he'd done for them? And what he'd suffered? He wanted to give them everything he possessed and worked for and they threw it in his face.

Another fact festered in his craw. Owning the Cahill Ranch solved no problems for him nor gave him the leverage he presumed. He thought he'd maneuvered a clever plot for a crucial succession.

While he stewed about this, the phone beside him rang. He answered after five rings and barked, "Who is it?"

"Dr. Gorsuch from the Spokane Clinic. Champ, I finally got the results of those tests we ran at your last visit." A pause.

"Well, what's the report?"

"I wanted to read the numbers again to make sure. I'm sorry to say, you've got onset blindness to deal with. I suggest you set up an appointment soon, so we can discuss your options."

A guttural roar built up inside him. Paralyzed! And now going blind? His family deserting him? What celestial demon tried to torment him?

He didn't deserve this.

If the doctor stood in front of him right now, he'd throttle him, that is, if he could physically manage such a feat.

"Champ? Any questions?" the professional diagnostician repeated with maddening nonchalance.

"No!" He crashed down the receiver with a clatter, picked up the phone, and attempted a feeble throw toward a mirror. It barely projected, tapped against the dresser, and knocked over a photo of Champ and Blair on their twenty-fifth anniversary. Not even enough strength for a solid fit of rage.

Later, after hours of staring into blackness, resenting every syllable of Blair's snores beside him, an old riddle his father taunted him with whorled over and over in his delirious mind.

I am seen in darkness and in light,
I am calm yet tend to fright.
I can be quiet, I can be loud,
I hide in shame, yet am so proud.
I can be different, but still the same,
I am straightforward, yet playing at games.

No matter what reply Champ offered, "A match!", "The moon!", "A heart!" Uriah sneered and responded with a terse, "Wrong, you stupid boy."

Now, Champ knew the answer, spilling over him like an acid wash.

It's me. I'm the fool. The whole joke's on me!

By dawn, Blair got up and headed for the kitchen to start the coffee pot. His eyes closed, Champ pretended sleep. However, a scheme slowly formed out of the gall of bitterness.

He'd get even with the whole lot of them.

He devised each part of the plot until he spasmed into a fitful sleep.

Pearl headed home to squeeze half a fresh lemon into an eight-ounce glass of water. She grabbed a handful of raw almonds and stirred huckleberries and honey into plain Greek yogurt. She'd be healthy or die trying.

After her mini-meal, she stretched her arms and legs while holding onto a high-backed dining room chair, the second round out of four a day. She kept going until she thought she heard a tap at the door.

Soon, a harder rap.

Most everyone in Road's End, sooner or later, tended to pour out their troubles to Pearl. They must have known she was at home by herself because Tim and Sue Anne Runcie appeared at her door with bowed heads, shoulders curled over their chests.

"We need help," Tim whimpered, limp arms falling to his sides. Around his eyes and over his face and arms purpled bruises from his accident.

"Bad." Sue Anne held in a sob.

Pearl ushered them upstairs to the privacy of the crammed and cramped attic room being used by Abel. She cleared away three chairs piled with dusty shoe boxes. Then they sputtered and poured out their whole story of misunderstanding, betrayal, and estrangement.

So, the rumors around town were true. Sue Anne and Norden.

Norden McKane, half-brother of Jace, early twenties and younger than Sue Anne, part Indian, Santa Ynez tribe, and a hard worker and proud manager of the Outfitters Store. That's about all Pearl knew about him. Obviously, Sue Anne saw more than that.

She offered Tim general counsel and nudged him to report to the county sheriff his admitted vandalizing of Norden's motorcycle.

"Norden doesn't want me to."

"How do you know?"

"He was there. I banged on his bike with a huge hammer, broke the rear-view mirror, and when he came out, I lunged at him. Then I grabbed his arm and twisted it. He hollered obscenities, but didn't fight. I raced down the street and he didn't follow. He could have reported me himself."

"Probably guilt," Pearl said. "That's what prevented him."

Chapter Twenty-Three

The coastal sun passed in and out of clouds, casting long, slanting late afternoon shadows.

Jace studied the man stomping toward him on the Casa Tierra beach.

Heavy shouldered in tan trench coat, a hulking form with height and weight to back it up, especially in the black wingtip boots. His permanently down-turned mouth and furrowed brow made him seem in a state of constant exasperation. His hardened, shrewd eyes hid behind sunglasses above a full moustache, and were wreathed under a horrible haircut, as though he chopped it with pinking shears.

"I know where Quigley is," Detective Ackroyd said. "At least, where he might be headed. He's going north."

"Probably trying to get to his mom in San Francisco."

"If so, we should warn her. He's desperate and irrational."

Jace kicked at the sand. "He's never harmed his mom before. He even gave her the squash blossom necklace he stole from Hanna Jo and Reba."

"Well, maybe he wants to show off the girl who has been on the run with him, the one who wrote him in prison. Meanwhile, beach-combers discovered the body of gang leader, Rodrigo Rodrigues, two days ago, right about here. He was shot with the same bullet make as the one they found in your stepmother."

"No kidding! I know Rodrigo's kids, Jip and DeLisa. Jip is Abel's age and DeLisa's much younger."

"Yeah, I know. They yelled at the man who shot their father and attempted chase. Luckily, he merely threw a bucket of salt water in their faces."

"Where are the kids?"

Ackroyd yanked off his sunglasses and rubbed his forehead. "Don't know. But my source has been on a stake-out and says there's a girl with Quigley. Her name's Patsy Ellen Zink. I talked with her parents. She was bored, wanted adventure, and perhaps some cred and notoriety with her peers."

"With Quigley?" Jace couldn't imagine the appeal.

"Unfortunately, she may be charged with aiding and abetting. She bought a change of clothes and an Afro wig for him. Paid cash herself."

"Zink? Does she have relatives connected to offshore drilling?"

"The same. We think Quigley broke into your father's house in-tent on hiding out in the basement. Maybe he also had vengeance on his mind. Perhaps Yvonne happened to be an easier target."

"Easier than what?"

"Your dad, of course. He still believes Hugh McKane is his father, too. He doesn't handle rejection well. We suspect he also surveilled the last known crack house in Santa Dominga that Rodrigo com-mandeered. When Rodrigo exited, Quigley followed him to the beach." Ackroyd slipped his sunglasses back on and surveyed the shore. "He's more dangerous than ever."

"Okay, approach with caution."

"Another thing," Ackroyd continued. "Quigley inspired a gang following of sorts during his short stay in prison. He gained status by bragging about the two murders. He earned a further reputation by beating up the ring leader of a jail boss who bootlegged contraband. His name is Antjuan Bunt, the other guy who escaped."

"So, he's on a sort of revenge tour?"

"To be determined. He's a bad dude incarcerated two months ago. No known address. No family members listed on his sheet. In for armed robbery. He's a big time jewel thief. He can smell gold and gems like a bloodhound. That's his main gig. He boasts it's the easiest money he ever made."

"We need to find those kids," Jace stated, "and see what they know."

After asking around up and down the beach for a couple hours, they discovered the kids along a worn path, near a crude fire ring with bits of charred wood, squatting in a corner of their former tattered tent home.

"My daddy's killed," the little girl said, her face haunted by horror, almost catatonic with grief.

The boy hung his head. In Jip's case, there may be guilt he couldn't help defend his father. Two dirty ragamuffins in loose, layered clothing and ripped jeans, Jace was struck by their desperate situation.

He and Ackroyd decided not to press them right then for information and turned them over to social services. Several hours later, Jace accompanied the detective to question the kids under the custody of Dr. Marbeth Woodall.

"Daddy told us to run," Jip reported. "The man who shot Dad stole drug stuff and grabbed our dog, Skitch. He tried to hunt us down. We watched him from the top of a tree until he gave up and went away."

"What was his name?"

"Don't know."

"Did you recognize the man?"

"No, but he knew my dad's friend, Quigley, and a girl."

"So, there were three of them?"

Jip nodded. "But Quigley and the girl came first and bought drugs from our dad. Then the other man rushed out of the woods, shouting, and started a fight."

The detective showed Jip a girl's photo. "Did you see her?"

Jip looked close and nodded. "I think so."

The detective frowned. "Patsy Ellen Zink, the teen who wrote to Quigley in prison and visited him several times."

"Who's the other man? Antjuan Bunt?" Jace asked.

"I assume. Think, Jip," Ackroyd coaxed. "Tell us anything about the other man you can recall."

"He rolled his own cigarettes from a plastic bag full of tobacco."

"Good. Anything else?"

"He was dirty and smelled like beer. His jeans were ripped." The boy looked down. "Worse than mine."

"What about his face? What did he look like?"

"He looked mean and carried a bucket, with water in it," Delisa whispered. She clutched a single white flower in a tiny white ceramic vase. A candle flame flickered next to her chair.

The detective looked at Jip for confirmation. "Maybe he was trying to catch things with it, not sure what." He inquired of Jip, "Did you notice tattoos on his arms?"

"Don't know. The man told my dad he knew where to find gold," Jip continued. "He said he'd take him to where it was. But then they had a big fight about a bag." He looked down. "I know it was drugs. Then he shot my dad. Quigley and the girl hid in the trees."

"Why'd he leave the kids behind?" Jace wondered aloud.

"Yeah, they're eye witnesses," the detective mused.

"When they chased after Skitch, we got away," Jip explained.

"I'm so tired of dealing with Quigley," Jace said.

Ackroyd pierced him with a sharp glance. "Time to take him out for good. And Antjuan too."

"Jace, your mother, Agatha, heard I was holding the kids," Marbeth told them. "She volunteered to take them both, at least for now. She's on her way over here to pick them up."

After they left Dr. Woodall's place, the detective received a call on his cellular. Several miles north, another body found on the beach—a fifteen-year-old female runaway named Summer, in the foster home system.

"Whether the two murders are related or not," Ackroyd said, "too early to tell. If so, this could be a serial killing crime spree in action."

"I say you stay on Quigley's trail," Jace suggested.

"I agree. That way I can maybe protect the girl and possibly cross paths with this Antjuan."

"He's got an agenda that includes Quigley."

"Looks that way. I'll send in a report of what we know." He thumped Jace's arm. "You want to stay with me?"

"If I'm allowed. This may involve what happened to Yvonne too."

"My call. You got a concealed carry permit?"

"*Mm hmm.* But only for Idaho."

"Okay, then. Stay alert. Stay close. Duck when the shootin' starts."

At the next Shepherd's Class, Pearl applauded Seth and Vincent and even Tucker. As she shared her delight in their courage, her hand pressed against her chest as the door opened and shut. Her startled stare caused them all to turn around.

There stood a red-faced, sweaty Tim Runcie still displaying purple bruises and stitches. He rubbed the back of his neck as his left eye fluttered and blinked. "Is this the church meetin'?"

"Sit down and make yourself at home, Tim," Pearl said. "Reba, bring us all hot drinks."

While everyone wondered why Tim could possibly be here, Reba served strong black coffee to the men and green tea with honey and cinnamon to the gals.

Pearl talked a while about the four spiritual laws, then how to lead, to inspire, and the importance of encouragement and listening. "Be good listeners," she repeated. "People won't care how much you know until they know how much you care."

"I believe Teddy Roosevelt said that," Seth remarked.

Pearl closed with, "I have never had any aspiration to be a preacher or minister. I tried to convince men like Pastor Kiersey to come here. As you know, he does fill in on occasion. But he has his own church and youth ministry."

"What did you do before the barn church?" asked Tim.

"Before the barn church ..." Pearl paused. "Reba, you tell it."

"Not much to tell. Grandpa did a Bible reading. I led the singing. And Grandma preached. In good weather, we met under Grandpa's Camperdown Elm. In the winter, in our living room." Reba considered whether to say more. "I've seen a small, ancient looking chapel on the side of Coyote Hill, on the way to the meadow. Was that ever used?"

"Oh. Haven't thought about that in a long time. That was Roberta Runcie's personal place," Seth said.

"Ah, yes," Tim remarked. "Grandpa Champ's mother, Uriah's wife, kept her faith very private."

"Uh huh," Pearl said, "There hasn't been a proper church here for quite some time. Finally, one night God rolled me out of bed and told me to bloom where I was planted. And where I was planted is in Road's End. There's not many of us and folks come and go. But leaders can be raised up from among us, right here."

"Do we have to speak the message in the church service?" Tucker asked.

"Only if you believe God has called you to that task."

Tucker displayed a slow smile, let out a huge breath, and flopped in his chair. "He hasn't said a word to me about it."

Pearl smiled and announced, "Now, let's sing, 'Stand Up For Jesus.'"

They greeted this suggestion with great gusto, jumping to their feet when Pearl handed out hymn books.

After completing all four verses and ending with a long, drawn out, final "shalllll ... reign ... e-ter-nal-ly," Pearl called out, "Now, anyone who gives their testimony of coming to faith in Jesus can sit down."

After stunned and embarrassed looks at one another and a long pause, Tucker pulled on his suspenders.

"It's all Seth's fault," Tucker gushed. "That man and his trip in the purple Model T to Goldfield, Nevada a few months ago got me out of myself and my addictions. Those long days on the road without a bottle to nurse, the evenings with my family and all the rest who joined us on the caravan, it's what I needed. Seth got me saved." He pounded the old man on the back.

After that, each of those in the room told their story. But everyone was most intent on the last man standing, Tim, the unexpected new member of their group.

Tim shuffled his feet and began. "As some of you know, Sue Anne and I got two miracles recently: the saving of our marriage and the saving of my life. Surviving a near-death experience and problems with my marriage, I'll never be the same. Coming that close to losing everything, well, God got a hold of me and I'm ready to learn everything I can." He stared at Pearl, on the brittle edge of tears.

She touched his arm and nodded.

Tim plopped down in his chair.

After everyone left, Tim lingered behind the porch shrubs and surprised Pearl by coming out of the shadows. "Pearl, I've decided to go into Christian ministry, to be a pastor."

She tried to hide her gasp of shock. "But you've always wanted to ranch with your dad and grandpa, since you were a small boy. Even after you got married, you poured yourself into that job."

"True ... but I've changed my mind. Long hours in the hospital and on the tractor rearranged my priorities."

"You know that would mess things up for your grandpa and dad."

Tim sighed. "Maybe at first, but they can hire someone in my place."

"Wouldn't be the same. Not at all. What does Sue Anne think about it?"

"She's, uh, working it through, trying to get used to the idea. We've had some good talks from it though." His mouth skewered. "Hey, I thought you'd be excited about my decision."

"Seems like you should stay on the ranch."

"But, Pearl, don't you want me to serve God full-time?"

"It's not up to me. It's between you and God."

"Well, I think He wants me to serve Him."

"You can do that anywhere ... even on the ranch. Leaving is a very serious life changing decision that will affect a lot of people." Pearl studied his face. Did he truly have 'a call' or not?

"I've never been more sure of anything in my life. It's on my mind day and night. Besides, I know how hard it's been for you and the church in this town to find a trained leader. I want to be that for some place that might need me."

Pearl studied his earnest expression, seared with zeal. "All right then, let's figure out your next step."

"Thank you, Pearl, for understanding. I've always suspected that there is more to life."

"Like what?"

"Just ... *more*. It hit me again at my grandparents' anniversary party—now's the time to decide to go and not look back."

"Have you talked with your dad or grandfather?"

"Dad talked to me first. He's moving to Spokane, at the end of harvest, to go into partnership with Uncle Richie and Uncle Randall ... and to be with Lisl Monte. His allergies are getting worse and so is Grandpa. Dad can hardly bear to be around him anymore, especially the way he treats Grandma. He's becoming very skilled at intimidation from the confines of his wheelchair, manipulating us. And I can't stand it when he shames Kaitlyn and William for not riding horses, when he's been told they've got allergies to horse hair."

"Sorry to hear it. He's probably afraid of losing you," Pearl assessed.

"That's not all ... Uncle Randall and Uncle Richard plan to sell their two-thirds of the ranch, subdivide each portion into a development of home sites with acreage for horses. I'm guessing Dad will do the same, eventually, with his third. Of course, all of this will happen after Grandpa's gone."

Pearl fought the rising tide of nausea at the thought of both the Cahill and Runcie ranches split into pieces and decimated. They would fade into distant history forever.

Tim kept on. "Grandpa and Grandma will be cared for. Dad and his brothers plan to hire a live-in nurse, to help them both."

Chapter Twenty-Four

Wynda charged into the house carrying two large grocery bags, Archie trailing behind. "We brought you some groceries. It's a trade. I need to borrow some things. I promised the Mathwigs I'd make some Scottish treats for the Grange Hall dance coming up." Wynda disappeared into the kitchen.

Archie leaned into Abel playing Pong on the TV. "Did you know I almost drowned in sheep dip once?"

Abel faked a gag.

"When do you expect you'll be heading out of town?" Hanna Jo asked.

"Straightaway. Within a week," Archie replied. "And with that repartee, I shall have a wee day out." He strolled outside, hopped on his bike, and punted and pirouetted his way down the driveway.

"When's the Grange dance?" Hanna Jo asked.

Reba tried to peer in the kitchen to check on Wynda. "This weekend, I think. Grandma should know for sure."

Hanna Jo cleared her throat. "I, uh, called Eleanor Dalton,

Quigley's mother. We had a long talk."

"About what?"

"All sorts of things. I invited her to stay with me at the inn when we get it in gear. She may be my first client, if you want to call it that."

A sudden chill hit Reba. "I ... I don't understand."

"She's in a tough place. She blames herself for her son and Dax is being sued for insurance fraud ... after he gets out of rehab. He most likely will do prison time. She's divorcing him, to protect what little she owns."

"She wants to come here?"

"She's a shattered woman. I know what that's like. I can be a friend who listens, feed her healthy, homemade meals, and vitamins. I know a thing or two about homeopathic medicine too." She sneezed and blew her nose. "Including Echinacea against colds, if I'd remember to take it."

Reba remembered the instant empathy her mother showed when they visited Quigley's mom in her San Francisco apartment earlier in the summer.

"I'm not trying to excuse Quigley in the least," Hanna Jo continued. "but his stepfather, Dax, got him started in criminal activity. And his mother claiming Hugh McKane was his real father, and Hugh rejecting him, only brought him more disappointment and bitterness."

Before Reba could thoroughly assimilate all they'd discussed, a custard-colored Mercedes-Benz rolled down the Cahill driveway. When the doors opened, out stepped Jace's mom from California, Agatha McKane Hempthorn. Crimson lips matched her red bouffant hair. The woman inhaled first thing. "This place smells like Christmas!"

Two children climbed out too ... Abel's friends on the beaches of Santa Dominga, California. Jip and DeLisa Rodrigues shied toward her with a tan and white Spaniel at their side. "This is Skitch," DeLisa said.

Skitch portrayed pure innocence. Head tilted down, adorable eyes looking up. Who could resist him? Reba hugged them all, including the dog.

"I'm sorry for dropping in without warning. I don't like flying," Agatha explained, "except on a McKane jet. But the pilot I trust was not available. So, I drove. I would have called ahead ... I should have, except ... I found out that a room with two beds became available at your local hotel."

Agatha turned with a wide grin when Abel yelled, "Aggie!"

Hugh's first wife, mother of Jace, engaged the boy as if she thought him her own.

Later, Reba scrambled to wash down her filthy pickup as the three kids played in the yard and Agatha checked into the hotel and wanted to look over the Outfitters store. "I'm half owner now," she announced.

Tentacles of doubt seared Reba again. She wondered why Agatha really came all this way. To take Abel home to California? Did she bail Jace out of his part of The Outfitters Shop because he wasn't coming back?

The disquieting notion gripped Reba's heart. Had Jace abandoned her? She tried to remember every word they said the last time they talked. What clues did she miss? She felt small, hurt, and lost, like when she was a child left behind by her mother at the Cahill Ranch. Only this time, not even the ranch still existed for her.

She considered a ride to the top of Coyote Hill. However, she needed to stay close by for Abel and the kids. She sauntered to the elm tree, hunkered down next to the trunk, and tried to hide from everyone, even herself. She wished she could bury a lifetime of bitter resentments here and find a fresh future for herself.

Did she cherish Jace as a person, as he was? Or the idea of him, as a potential rancher husband in training? Her view of love seemed to be, "What will this man do for me?" When did she ever ask, "What could she be for him?"

The whole marriage scenario scared her to death until ... she got excited thinking of a partnership, that is, *him* coming alongside *her*. She'd never once considered, *wherever he goes, I will go.*

Losing Grandpa Cole so suddenly meant no good-byes, no last words. But she knew he loved her. She swiped and patted the place on the ground where they found him, longing for one more hour or day with him, another long talk.

Now, she missed Jace terribly.

She saw in Jace a safe space, a familiar face she'd grown to love. She yearned to get to really know him. His wants and needs, his likes and dislikes, his interests and habits. What made him happy or angry?

But without the ranch, what did they have together? Did she want more than anything to be with him, wherever he was? Wasn't that what marriage was all about?

She hurt all over.

Bruised ego.

Aching spirit.

Later, Agatha returned. "What on earth do you do around here for fun?"

"Lots of things," Abel replied. "Stuff together. Hang around."

"Ah." Her face wreathed with smiles.

"Would you like to go riding?" Reba asked.

"A day's road trip would be nice. Shall we go in my Mercedes?"

"I meant on a horse."

"*Awk,*" she sputtered. "The only horses I've ever ridden were hand-carved, bright colors with stripes, gold hooves, and black glass eyes. Why don't we all go to Delbert's Diner for hamburgers. My treat."

Reba begged off to go to her favorite place, with Johnny Poe II.

She trailered her horse to a parking lot and rode the three miles around the 105-acre Road's End Lake.

As they sauntered along, she relished moments of peace with the black horse. Inhaling pine and herbal scents, she viewed the forest scattered with Ponderosas, Douglas firs, and aspens, hiding wildlife, such as white-tailed deer and skunks, raccoons and muskrats. In the distance, a children's playground, fishermen on the banks and in boats, and campsites with tents and RVs.

Families and couples on vacation. Grandpas and grandmas fishing with grandkids for trout planted annually by the Fish and Game Department. The harmony of play—all's right with the world.

Canada geese honked overhead, flying in a V-shape. Bald eagles flew to the tops of trees. Great Blue Heron and Osprey waded the banks while assorted varieties of ducks quacked their broods into single file. On occasion, otters frolicked in view and a painted turtle might be spotted.

She passed the area where yurts could be rented—domed, circular tents with hardwood lattice walls and clear Plexi-glass skylight roofs, fully insulated, that could withstand high winds and heavy snow loads.

Her attention diverted to a sudden movement in the trees. A man prowled and teetered around like he was high on some substance. Bared arms exposed a number of tattoos. His gaze engaged hers and he jumped into a nearby old pickup and tore off. The rear door to the trailer hooked to the vehicle flew open and stuff flew out with a crash.

Thud! Thud! Thud!

In a frenzy, Johnny Poe II began to rear up, his head in the air with mini-hops with his front feet. She attempted a sideways move and tried to bend his head down. Sensing him still frantic, she forced a small, tight, fast circle right, and then quickly spun him left.

"Whoa," she kept saying as calmly as possible until he stood still. "Good boy. Good boy!"

Johnny Poe moved forward in a steady motion. She stopped him and got down to pick up a pair of cracked binoculars and assorted other items that clattered from the trailer.

Reba reached the gift shop and gazebo where a female employee collected fees for day visitors. She reported the suspicious happening.

"Sounds like that combative camper I've asked to leave several times," the employee replied. "Saw him earlier this morning banging his head on the flag pole. I'll report him to the authorities."

Beneath a Camperdown Elm

Chapter Twenty-Five

When the phone rang, being the closest, Hanna Jo got up to lift the receiver. Reba watched as by degrees, Hanna's face switched from nonchalant to a definite register of alert and then pushed to alarm. "I can't talk," she rasped, her eyes wild, as she pushed the slick, sweaty receiver toward a puzzled Reba.

"Hello? This is Reba Cahill."

"Miss Cahill, as I was saying, a commercial fishing vessel is missing at sea, one that Griffin Cahill runs. We're informing next of kin for both Michael Cahill and Griffin. They were listed as onboard."

Reba reached out to touch her mother's stiff shoulder, to offer comfort as well as support. "What else do you know?"

"There were six crewmembers. Debris was found—a life ring and buoys. Later, they also rounded up an empty life raft, emergency radio beacon, and survival suit. We got a report of a roll in very rough seas. We suspect they capsized in 30-knot winds. We did recover one crewman who did not survive."

Dread attacked her. "And his name?"

"I can't give out that information, but it wasn't Michael or Griffin. We're doing everything we can to locate the ship and other crewmen. And there was a name on Michael's emergency contact list: Nina Oscar. I haven't been able to get a hold of her. Would you be able to?"

"I'll try." Michael's most recent known blonde girlfriend, last known taking pre-med classes at University of Idaho in her goal to become a pediatrician.

"And Miss Cahill?"

"Yes?"

"I want you and the family to know that Captain Cahill kept a meticulously maintained ship."

Reba hung up and stalled long enough to pray hard for her mother. How many losses could a sane woman take, much less one with a mind deemed impaired?

⚘ ⚘ ⚘ ⚘

The next morning's newspaper article about Griff and Michael's missing boat in the Lewiston Tribune also listed other Alaska fishing boat tragedies over recent years. Not encouraging and certainly not comforting. Reba didn't realize the dangers involved.

She studied Hanna Jo's twitching face, riddled with anxiety.

Her mom's eyes pleaded. "We all deal differently with stress."

"Mom, I'm here for you, whatever it takes. Let's do this together. But I'm just being honest when I say it's going to take God's help."

She surprised Reba by sitting straight up and reaching out her hand. "I know. You have no idea ..." She gasped air. "... what it means to hear you say that."

Reba clutched her arm and they held each other as Hanna Jo's sobs bounced off the walls. After a while, she eked out, "I tell myself when I think I'm losing it, "Hold on. Hold on!"

"You've been through lots of ups and downs. It's going to be okay," Reba kept saying, as much to convince herself as to assure her mother.

Hanna Jo blurted out, "Biggest mistakes of my life ... almost." She grimaced at Reba. "Using peyote and losing Griff. Griff was ... a slow dance, a heady waltz. We seemed perfect together. But in the end, a sad story."

Reba held her tongue, afraid to say anything to derail her mom from further revelation.

Hanna Jo whispered something. Reba leaned closer to hear. "I want that kind of devotion again. That closeness. I think I was ready to commit again—the constraints and everything. Now this!" Then another sob rattled her chest before she gulped out an actual prayer. "Dear God ... please, please protect Griff and Michael, right now, wherever they are."

The seconds ticked by on the wall clock.

"You know what?" Hanna Jo continued. "You and I ... we might not have liked each other, if we grew up together."

It's nip and tuck now.

Her mother grinned and punched Reba's shoulder before her face pulled into serious again. "I believe I came to know you at just the right time."

Reba pondered her statement with mixed feelings. "Sounds almost theological. Did you learn that at the clinic?"

"According to the docs, my stress and agitation levels signaled deep, chronic depression."

"I'm sorry," Reba began. "Could be side-effects of the peyote."

Hanna Jo gave a slight nod.

"What did you appreciate most about Griff?"

She didn't hesitate. "He sometimes prodded, actually goaded me. He poked around in my life, asking questions. So many questions. But he didn't react at all when I ignored him. He simply left me in peace. He cared, but he gave me space. Even so, I considered marriage to be a sacrifice. I realize now, too late, he was my salvation." Hanna Jo got up, pulled on her boots, and headed for the door.

"Where are you going?"

"To my other salvation ... my horse ... alone!" She squeezed the door shut behind her.

Beneath a Camperdown Elm

Chapter Twenty-Six

Sprays of daffodils and daisies in colored glass decanters spread across the tables, with a larger arrangement on top the piano at the Saturday night Grange Hall dance.

Hanna Jo seemed a little loopy. "Took some cold pills," she told Reba and finally collapsed on a folding chair.

Archie showed up in bottle-green slacks and denim jacket.

"I was expecting a tartan tie and kilt," Pearl said.

"Not this time," he said. "You know, kilts have become like tuxedos. For formal occasions mainly."

Abel rushed over to him, wheezing with excitement. "Malik says they found a monster in the lake."

"Oh? Was it Nessie?" Archie said.

"Who's Nessie?"

"The Loch Ness Monster. Those who claim to have seen it describe it as like a dinosaur or long-necked reptile."

"Cool, but our monster's a giant fish. We think Bigfoot would like to eat it."

Archie grabbed a tray of the Scottish treats to pass around. "Stuffed artichokes? Marzipan cake? Deep-fried Mars bars?"

Reba and Hanna Jo took tentative bites of a mixture of bacon and dates.

"What do you think of the devils on horseback?" Archie asked.

"Interesting. Salty and sweet."

"I like the crunchy texture."

"Crunchy."

"I'm addicted," Archie said. "I won't be offended at all if you don't like them."

LaDonna pushed forward, away from Jesse Whitlow. "What's the difference between American and Scottish girls?" she asked.

"American girls want to know why you do or say things," Archie said.

"We're more curious?" LaDonna responded.

"Or you want to control, be dominant. And you worry more about your grooming. You choose Madonna over Mother Teresa. And you tend to have a sweet tooth. You also add sugar to foods that should be savory."

"And what are Scottish girls like?"

"Less demanding. They don't constantly ask guys to explain themselves. They let you be yourself and get on with things."

"Archie the philosopher."

He seized the girl in one swift, smooth movement, flung her about, then stomped and whirled around her, then handed her off to a flustered Jesse.

Wynda swayed gently to the music of the fiddle and sang, 'Lochaber No More, a heart-rending lament that made Reba feel sad.

After it was over and Wynda saw Reba's face, she said, "At least that song's better than a Gaelic psalm. They're really dirges."

The little home-grown band concluded with *Good-night, Irene.*

After the dance, Reba gathered Hanna Jo and Pearl to take them home. "I can't find Abel anywhere."

With the full moon and flashlights, the three of them scouted around the Grange Hall, engaging the help of the few guests left.

"Do you want me to call the police?" Beatrice asked.

"Not yet." Reba's imagination took nosedives as she continued her search separate from the rest of them. The mournful wails of coyotes sent shivers down her back. Her flashlight flickered as though about to die out. "Abel!" she called out numerous times. A boy could get dangerously lost in an area like this.

Hanna Jo and Pearl rode up to her in the Jeep.

"Malik's gone too," Pearl reported. "Elliot thinks they're after Bigfoot, down at the lake. He's headed there now."

Rather than further alarm, Reba gasped relief. The experienced Indian boy could provide protective company for Abel, especially at night.

She hopped in the jeep with the women and Pearl drove toward the state park. They took the three-mile loop all the way around the lake, alert to any activity. Soon back where they started at a gravel pull-off, Hanna Jo asked, "Do you think they headed down there?" She pointed to a gravel trail looming in the deep, dark woods. Strange things could happen in a place like that.

They peered all around by the jeep's headlights, shushing through ground cover and ferns, near the heavily forested road. Lots of nooks and crannies for boys to get in trouble. Reba studied the light and shadows for signs of them hunched down, trying to avoid rescue.

She took a deep breath, willing her lungs to work, shuddering as she stated the obvious. "We'll have to walk."

They pulled on light raincoats as large splats spread on the windshield in swirls and wisps. Pearl fished around in the back seat for an umbrella too. Moving spotlights approached ahead of them on the trail. They waited as three men appeared.

"There's a huge search team looking for them," Elliot reported. "One of the campers has a bloodhound. They said they'd stay out all night, if needed. There's nothing more for you to do."

Pearl eyed Reba, "I guess we'll go home then."

"I'm ready," Hanna Jo responded. "And I'm sure they'll be okay," she amended.

Reba wondered what Jace would want her to do. Going home and giving him a call made sense. However, she dreaded having to confess Abel vanished while under her care. "I'm staying with Elliot."

Hanna Jo nodded and squeezed Reba's arm. "Elliot, please phone us if you learn anything."

An hour later, Elliot and Reba appeared at the ranch house door with two soaked, young adventurers. They shivered on the porch, waiting for Pearl to bring them large towels.

"We had cans of Pepsi and a flashlight," Malik said, too excited to pretend guilt or offer apology.

"We did see a very large, scary monster," Abel said.

"Bigfoot," Malik insisted. "He wanted that fish."

"Yeah," Abel agreed.

"But first, we saw a huge cat."

"More like a lion," Abel said. "We stayed very still and slowly raised a tree branch as high as I could. We didn't run."

"When he saw us, he tried to hide. We didn't get close or try to scare it away. We stayed like that a long time. Finally, Malik said, 'I think that lion is gone.' That's when we heard his Uncle Elliot yelling for us."

They both jumped when the wind rustled and swished around them, even picking up pieces of roadside gravel.

After Reba let Jace know the boys were found, she followed Abel upstairs to tuck him in bed. "Why didn't you tell me where you were going?" she scolded.

He bunched up the covers and squeezed into them. "Because."

"Because you knew I wouldn't let you do it?"

He nodded.

"Abel, I'm responsible for you. You scared everyone and forced them out at night to look for you. What if you had gotten hurt?" Or worse. She added the final chide. "You shouldn't do things you know Jace would forbid."

Abel yanked down the sheet. "He would have gone with us."

She considered his statement. Perhaps he would. Would she have even thought to suggest such a thing? "But I've got to know where you are," she concluded.

"I know. Next time, I'll tell you."

"Asking first would be more considerate."

The boy yawned and lay down. "I never walked that far before. I tried hard to stay awake while we waited, but I got so tired. I kept falling asleep." He yanked out a blistered foot. "My leg muscles kept hurting too."

Two miles from the Grange Hall to the park. Another mile to the back of the lake where Elliot's crew found them.

Reba started to go get salve, when the boy began to babble, "I learned something. I think heaven is leaking through the holes in the sky ... through the moon and stars. I wonder if Mom was up there, trying to see me."

Reba stayed still as possible, silently urging the boy to let her in and share his private world.

After a bit more rambling, Abel stared deep in her eyes. "I'm not afraid of Quigley anymore."

"Quigley's not here." She wondered if he needed a night light.

"Yes, he is. He's in my dreams."

Chapter Twenty-Seven

Jace and Detective Ackroyd drove to San Francisco and staked out Quigley's mother's apartment. The second day, they spotted Quigley with the wig, thinner than ever, with gold rings on each finger and left ear lobe. He wore black eyeglass frames with no lenses. They inspected him for a possible knife threat as he fixed a glare their way.

"Do you think he recognized us?" Jace asked.

"Could be. Not likely, though, with the baseball caps and sunglasses. Plus, he's not expecting us."

Jace studied his female companion. Dark, lank hair, aquiline nose, flat-chested, drab clothes, and no make-up. "Why in the world did that girl go with him?"

"He offered excitement ..."

"You mean, danger."

"Living on the edge. That's what appeals to gals like her. I understand she did grow up in a nice middle class neighborhood. Decent folks with good jobs. No obvious problems."

Quigley strolled up to the apartment building's entrance, the girl in tow. He pointed up toward his mom's apartment, and the girl ascended the stairs while Quigley headed down the street. Once out of sight, Ackroyd opened the car door, "I'll call SFPD and let them know Quigley's here. You stay put." He shut the door quietly and hurried a block away to a pay phone.

As Ackroyd disappeared around a corner, another man in brisk stride entered the apartment building. Broad-shouldered like a football player, oil creased the man's skin. Dirty hair crammed under a soiled hat.

Jace looked down at the mugshot lying on the floor. Very close resemblance.

"Antjuan Bunt! What's he doing here?"

Jace looked back in the direction of the pay phone, but Ackroyd couldn't be seen. He jumped out of the car and shadowed Antjuan up the stairs and hid in an alcove while Antjuan banged on Quigley's mom's door.

"Who's there?" a female said.

"A friend of Quigley's."

"He just left," she said, leaving the door closed. "If you hurry, you can catch him."

Antjuan stepped back several feet and crashed against the door twice, gun in hand, breaking through. "Give me the gold necklace," Antjuan demanded, "and no one gets hurt."

"What gold necklace?"

"The squash blossom with turquoise. Do it, now!"

"I don't have it," Mrs. Dalton said.

"Did Quigley take it with him?" Antjuan yelled.

"No, I told Quigley that red-haired girl and her mother insisted it belonged to them, so I let them have it."

A slap, a scream, and a thump.

Jace watched as Quigley, three stairs at a time, rushed to the apartment with a knife. Jace figured he must have heard the scream. Quiqley charged into the apartment, knife ready. A gun fired. Quigley staggered into the hall, calling out something incoherent, and collapsed.

Ackroyd also rushed up the stairs, gun drawn, and crouched outside the door. He quickly glanced inside the room, in time to see the girl descending the fire escape, Antjuan already gone.

Ackroyd yelled, "Someone call 911!" as he leapt up and gave chase.

Jace ran over to Quigley, kicked away the knife and felt for a pulse. A weak one. Mrs. Dalton hovered and sobbed over her son.

Jace called 9-1-1 and stayed behind with Mrs. Dalton and Quigley.

An ambulance arrived to take Quigley to a hospital.

Police questioned Jace as Ackroyd returned empty handed. He flashed his badge and told his story to a just arrived detective. They heard the news that a doctor declared Quigley dead on arrival, which sent Quigley's mom into hysterics.

After Ackroyd and Jace repeated their versions of the story one more time to the detective in charge, the detective reported the incident to his Santa Barbara police precinct. Later, news features on TV included Antjuan's mug shot with profile of both sides of his face and photo of tattoos of a muscular hand clutching a lightning strike on both arms.

The emergency line flooded with calls of sightings.

When Reba picked up the phone at the ranch house, she heard, "Finally reached you! I've got something I need to tell you."

"Jace, what is it?" Reba waited, heart beating fast. This could be anything. Was her life about to change again?

"I thought you should know. Quigley's dead."

"What did you say?"

"Quigley Dalton ... he was shot to death in San Francisco, in his mother's apartment." He told her the whole account.

She tried to assimilate the news.

Quigley gone? Forever?

Her mind scattered with what this meant. No more fear. Home free. No longer a threat. "What about the girl you said was with him? What happened to her?"

"Don't know for sure. They're looking for her. Antjuan Bunt shot him, then he and the girl ran off. We think they may be together."

Something nagged her. What if Quigley didn't send the menacing letter? And the muffled phone call? Must have been kids on a dare or a random tramp passing through town. Would she ever know?

"Hey, Reba Mae," Jace signaled through the miles. "Are you ready? I'm coming home."

A crackle of peace loosened her spine. "So good to hear you say that." Real good! *He's coming home!*

Before he hung up, he added, "This Antjuan guy—he's an avid jewel thief. He knows about the one-of-a-kind gold and turquoise squash blossom necklace. Tell the local police to be on guard ... and you too."

"But we don't have it anymore. Mom sold it."

"He doesn't know that."

Later in bed, she pushed and pulled at her pillow as she tried in vain for hours to fall asleep. When she finally did, she dreamt of a mystery man with a gun, a professional jewel thief desperate to grab an expensive gold necklace, worth a lot of money. And she wore it around her neck. She woke with a start and clutched her chest. The images seemed so real and gnawed at her.

Where is this guy, Antjuan?

Chapter Twenty-Eight

The Horizon plane droned overhead, descended for a landing at the Lewiston airport, circled the field, and careened in to line up with the runway.

The rest of the Cahill gang stayed at Road's End and insisted Reba go alone to meet Jace. A metal fixture rattled near her and passengers entered the gate. Then he appeared. A shimmery mirage walked toward her. Tall, familiar span of shoulders with shock of shaggy, dark blond hair, beard stubble, broad smile and wearing a black t-shirt and black jeans. She caught the heady scent of lime shaving lotion.

She reached out to his forearm, felt his muscles flex and pushed aside every doubt and smidgeon of mistrust to plunge into his embrace. She kissed his chest until his lips mashed hers, leaving a tingle in its wake. He pulled her so tight she heard the pound of heartbeats knocking against her ribs. She clung to his arm until they reached the Chevy.

Jace drove them to the walkway along the river. They got out and strolled.

"Have you heard any news about Michael and Griff?" he began.

"No. Nothing. I know Mom's worried sick."

They watched a couple speed boats whizz by. Finally, he scratched his head in furious frustration. "We can't keep going on like this." His lips pinched together for emphasis. "I won't leave again until I know everything about you, Reba Mae."

She let go his hand and grabbed his forearm. "First, tell me something I don't know about you."

"Okay ... I used to stutter as a kid. I learned to fly a plane before I could drive a car. And I moved to Road's End to hide."

She jabbed him with an elbow. "Why? Got a secret life? Are you a wanted criminal? Or a movie star in disguise?"

He shook his head, crinkling his nose in that way Reba adored. "I was ducking the pressure of a dishonest part of the business world and from my father's drama. Didn't work, did it?"

Now that their initial warm greeting cooled a bit, she zeroed in on what simmered between them. She squeezed her arms against her waist and blurted out, "What about that girl ... the one you send money to ... the one in San Diego?"

His eyes enlarged and he leaned back. "You mean, Robin?"

Mention of a name stung. So, it was true. Her heart scuffed, pumping double-time beats of dread, about to shatter in a million pieces. "I guess so."

"Robin Crosby. She's going to college there." His eyes softened, either in defeat at being caught or because of a sweet memory. "I told you about Joanna, the girl who drowned. Robin's her younger sister and she's disabled. I'm doing what I can to help her out, since Joanna's no longer here. That's all the family they had, the two of them."

"Oh," whooshed out. The moment stalled with a catch to her senses. Losing Joanna was also part of why Jace journeyed to Road's End. He meant to spend the rest of his life with her. Now, did she believe him? Could she trust him enough to let the suspicions go?

Air pooled in her throat while his expression stayed taut, tense, waiting. "I think it's time ..." She couldn't get the words out, like she'd bit a chunk of jerky and couldn't chew.

"Time for what?" He managed a semblance of his charming, crooked smile and held her waving hands.

"Don't do that. Now I can't talk."

"No, you can't." He released her. "Be yourself." A benediction of sorts.

She fought for control as tears flowed.

He gently wiped her cheek. "What is it, Reba Mae?"

Her lips compressed and cheeks bellowed as she blew out slowly. "I just … I want you to love me as I am."

"I love the Reba Mae I know, all of you."

They fell into a long embrace until Reba nearly choked with elation.

They sauntered back to the car and ordered burgers and sodas at a drive-through.

Halfway up the mountain on Highway 95 toward Road's End, Jace mentioned, "I'd like to see the original ranch sale papers, rather than only the copy."

"What difference would that make?"

"Looking at it more closely on the flight here, something caught my attention. I want to check it out."

"Sure. No problem."

"Also, I want to check out inclusion of mineral rights, or allowance for hunting on the property. Mineral rights are not automatically transferred when property is sold. Have to go to the county recorder's office and maybe back to the 1800s to figure out who owns those mineral rights to mine on that parcel of land."

"What do you expect?"

"I'm looking at all angles." Jace grinned with a touch of lechery. "I'll strive to always take care of you and work alongside you, for as long as I'm able."

"Sounds like vows to me. Does this mean we're already married?"

"I'm ready, if you are." His leg brushed against hers. He fondled her hand. "Why wait?"

Reba relaxed in the knowledge he meant them to be together, no matter where. But real soon, they must figure a next step, at a specific place and doing a particular job that made sense to them both. And he should know the whole truth about her.

She avoided eye contact as she quietly, carefully prepared the words. "Jace, there's something I need to tell you."

"Okay, let it all out."

"About Champ Runcie ..." She couldn't make herself say it.

"You mean, that he is your real grandfather?"

She released a ton of air. "Who told you?"

"Seth, when we were in Nevada."

"Oh. Okay." One hurdle jumped. "And Don Runcie ... did you realize he is my biological father?"

Jace jerked back on the seat. "Whoa, didn't see that one coming."

"Mom didn't know about Champ and Maidie at the time. However, Don was married. She knew that part was wrong." Her breath caught in hitches. "If you want to call the whole marriage thing off, I totally understand."

He slowed the car and pulled over to a wide spot at the side of the highway. He hugged her as close as he could around the steering wheel. "All I see is a terrible, awful burden you've had to carry because of choices others made." He ruffled her hair in an affectionate caress. "Reba Mae, you're not defined by the sins of your parents. However you got here, you're a special creation and very precious to me."

The dam broke and she balled the fabric of his shirt as she gushed all over it. "I'm sorry, I'm sorry." She dabbed as best she could at his stained sleeve.

He handed her several tissues and she clenched her face muscles to get a grip.

"Come on," he said. "Let's go see what's waiting for us at home."

Later, at the ranch house, original ranch papers in hand, Jace detected white-out with no initials, on the document made out by Lawyer James Howe. "Either sloppy office work on Howe's part or something more sinister," he told Reba, before he left for Norden's apartment.

Reba got up to go to the bathroom and look for a snack in the kitchen. She noticed a light on at the bunkhouse. At 3:00 a.m.? Maybe they were finally going to continue their journey to Canada. If so, she wanted to issue one last farewell to their Scottish visitors.

Outside, dead silence. The dogs didn't bark. Alarm bolted through her when she found Scat the cat unconscious on the porch. What foul person could do such a thing?

Pop! Pop! Pop!

Three sounds like shots fired around the house. A pellet gun?

She held still until she heard tapping and shuffling sounds.

She lurched against a woman crawling on her hands and knees across the lawn, bloody all over. "Wynda?" she called. She got closer and didn't recognize the young woman who collapsed at her feet. "Who are you? What happened?"

She could hardly spit out a name. Gasping, and then unconscious, not breathing. Reba knocked at the bunkhouse to get help and noticed two bolt locks broken. She pried open the door.

Inside, she found mayhem.

Phone ripped from the wall and cord missing. Belongings strewn around, including a gas station receipt with a handwritten telephone number. A smashed pair of glasses with shattered lens and cracked brown horn rim frames that she hadn't noticed either one of them wearing. A lamp broken and across the room. A large orange marmalade jar smashed on the coffee table, spilling out jelly on Scottish magazines. But it wasn't orange scent she smelled.

Kerosene!

That's when she heard pitiful cries, like a kitten or a young child. As she got closer, she stared at a woman prostate on the ground with swollen neck and ragged breathing. She stopped her approach as a figure slipped into the darkness behind the bunkhouse, a murky form barely discernible as human. A flash, a spark revealed a lamp in hand. Another strike of a match to the mantle and pulsing light pushed out a glowing circle. Then the flicker of a lighter tossed against the side of the bunkhouse.

An instant later, the glare and sweep of headlights as an engine revved. A vehicle zoomed past the building and drove across the woman prone on the lawn and then down the long driveway. Reba screamed, "Stop!" The MacKenzies' white van.

She couldn't attempt to give chase. These women needed help. "Wynda, what happened?"

"A vicious man with a pickaxe and gun came at us out of nowhere. I kept throwing things at him. There was a girl with him who tried to stop him. He gun-whipped her and slammed her with the flat of the axe several times."

"Where's Archie?" Reba asked her.

"Down the ... " She gasped and coughed. "... cellar."

"The root cellar?"

"Aye."

When smoke began to choke the room in a charcoal swirl, in a crouch, Reba grabbed Wynda under the arms and shoulders. The air in the room quickly heated with thick smoke, choking visibility. She convulsed with a cough, tried to get her bearings, and scooted Wynda out of the bunkhouse, by grabbing and dragging. She positioned her carefully on the lawn and checked out the other woman. Clothes askew. Blood seeped through her chest. Deep scrapes bruised her face and bare legs. Nose piercings and barbed wire tattooed her arms and neck.

Reba couldn't find a pulse, even after an attempt at CPR.

She sprinted to the ranch house. "Fire!" she shouted, as she wrestled open the door. "At the bunkhouse."

Pearl and Hanna Jo raced out of their rooms.

"I'll grab the extinguisher," Pearl said. "You get the hose extender in the back of the house."

"I'll call the fire department." Hanna Jo sped to the kitchen.

"We need an ambulance, too," Reba told her. "Wynda was attacked. So was another woman I've never seen before." Then she called Jace and the emergency number.

Jace arrived and he and the women did their best to water down the flame-engulfed bunkhouse. Inside, a searing blaze, an angry inferno. Their feeble attempts to water it down produced scalding steam against the fierce flames and grinding heat.

They leaned against each other, away from the toxic fumes, to watch the fire burn.

By the time the fire truck and ambulance arrived, they found a mass of charred remains, and no response from the unknown woman. Tortured face. Contorted red mouth. Smudges of thick, black liner around cold, hard eyes wide in shock. Legs and torso smashed and twisted by the desecration of tire tracks.

They pronounced her dead at the scene and EMT Polly Eng gently shut her lids.

Reba noticed a muddy canvas bag several yards from the ravaged girl. She picked it up and opened it to try to find identification. She pulled out a wrinkled, monogrammed towel caked with dust and dirt with initials PEZ. She showed it to Jace.

"Patsy Ellen Zink. That's the gal who was with Quigley."

"Are you sure?"

"No doubt. Sad end to her adventure. Detective Ackroyd told me her parents filed a missing person's report. Age seventeen and their only child. She was interviewed in the newspaper article Ackroyd showed me. She wrote to Quigley in jail, visited him, and then ran away with him. Not sure what she's doing here ... unless Antjuan Bunt somehow enticed her away."

Hours and days ago this young girl brimmed with potential. A full future ahead of her. How fragile the divide between life and death.

Volunteer Fire Chief Buckhead Whitlow tapped Pearl on the shoulder. "Sorry, we've got to head right back to town. More fires reported."

"Where?"

"On Main Street." Chief Whitlow and his crew left, siren blaring, lights flashing.

The EMTs carried Wynda on a stretcher to the ambulance as she stirred to consciousness. As the doors slammed shut, Reba requested they wait until they looked for Archie.

Jace and the gals, plus Polly Eng, crept in the darkness toward the cellar, guided by flashlights cutting orbs of large circles at their feet. Reba and Pearl opened the broken double door. Rats and cockroaches scurried around in the sudden streak of light. They found not only

Archie, but Abel too. Phone wire tied their feet together and hands behind their backs. Archie's forehead bled from a gash and when they untied him, so did one of his arms.

Polly fashioned a tourniquet to help stop the bleeding.

"I tried to keep the boy calm," Archie said.

"He told me lots of stories," Abel affirmed.

"What are you doing here, little buddy?" Jace ran a knuckle down the boy's cheek. "I thought you were up in the attic room."

"I thought I heard Bigfoot stomping around outside. Then this man grabbed me and forced me down here with Archie."

"The man had bunches of tattoos and a gun," Abel said.

"What kind of tattoos? Did you get a good look?"

Archie provided the description. "A muscular hand clutching lightning on both arms."

"Like on Antjuan," Jace asserted.

"Well, he provided a first for me. I've never been tossed on a hard, dirt floor in a pitch-black root cellar and left to die before." Archie passed out from loss of blood before he could say anymore.

The EMTs carried him to the ambulance and they pulled away after Abel assured them the mean man hadn't hurt him.

The boy rode in the Jeep, which now smelled like a smoky campfire gone bad, with Jace and the women as they followed the ambulance. Forced to take a side route out of town as Main Street blazed, they ogled the incredulous flames. Reba worried for everyone's safety in the intense heat as shifting human silhouettes moved up and down the street.

They slowed down to watch four men load a huge trunk into a pickup.

Pearl rolled down a window. "Need any help?" she asked Lloyd Younger. A hot ember brushed her cheek.

"Not now, though the heavy ash could come alive again."

They could hear glass crunch beneath his heavy boots. Shattered lightbulbs, twisted wood, and bent metal scattered the area. A nasty sharp smell of burnt chemicals, such as cleaning supplies, permeated the air.

"Everyone's pretty much saved what they can," Lloyd continued.

"LaDonna wrestled this thing out of the burning Outfitters store and down the steps. Have no clue how she did it."

"I think we've rescued homes and most of the businesses," Franklin Fraley told her. "Except the Outfitters and Hotel next door are gutted."

"The Outfitters blew up something fierce, right after LaDonna got out. It was full of combustibles," Lloyd added. "She also recovered a set of leather-bound books."

"Where is she now?"

"They took her to the Elkville hospital for observation. Ursula and the kids are headed there now."

The lake itself seemed on fire as they passed by, with watery reflections pulsing and smoldering.

"It's a wonder the fire didn't wipe out the whole town," Pearl said.

Beneath a Camperdown Elm

Chapter Twenty-Nine

Sheriff Goode and Deputy Lomax questioned Archie and Wynda at the Oroston hospital and allowed the three Cahill women to be present, at the twins' request. Seth and Hester stayed with Abel out in the waiting room.

"We were packing the last of our items and getting ready to leave town," Wynda explained, as she sucked on ice chips. "A girl with a nose piercing knocked at the door. 'Our car's having trouble,' she said. 'Can we use your phone?' As soon as she entered, all of a sudden, this man crashed into the bunkhouse with her and demanded we give him a gold and turquoise squash blossom necklace. When we told him we knew nothing about that, he grabbed a metal box on the table we were about to pack and we got into quite a row."

"Had you ever seen him before?"

"Maybe. There's been several suspicious looking guys around the park lately. One of them, when we were making our video, kept getting in the frame."

"So, you have a recording of the guy?"

"Why, yes, we do." Archie stopped. "*Argh.* No, we don't. If the video was still in the bunkhouse, it burned up."

"And if it was in the van, that man took it with him," Wynda said.

"Did he take the metal box with him?" Jace asked.

"Aye," Archie said.

"And what was in it?"

"Personal effects," Archie quickly responded. "Letters, a journal ... and other stuff."

"We've put out an APB on the van and alerted everyone in all the towns up and down Highway 95," the sheriff said. "We hope to catch the guy soon."

When the officers left, Archie asked the women to shut the hospital room door. "May we have a word?"

"We have a confession to make," Wynda said. "We came to Road's End because ... we didn't have anything else on ... and on purpose, too, to find our family heirlooms."

"Our *great-grandfaither's* icons," Archie corrected. "We believed if we could return them to Scotland, we'd gain a reward or heirship from our elderly father."

"All the property goes to our older brother at his death and we get nothing," Wynda explained. "It's the law and tradition. And yet, our brother is not suited. He resents his duties and neglects them. Everything could be lost."

"And what were these icons?"

Wynda looked over at Archie. "Go ahead, tell them," he said. "There's no reason to hide anything now."

"First, we told the officers a half-truth. In the metal box, we uncovered yellowed letters, a framed black and white photo of our great-great grandparents, a lock of hair, a Bank of Scotland fifty-pound note, and a whaling ship log. Most would have value only for our family." She motioned to Archie to continue.

"However, there were four main contents: a ruby encrusted cross, two rare Roman gold coins, a whale bone scrimshaw with whale ship scene, and a black pearl ring with diamond in the center."

Wynda winced. "We don't blame any of you, but these valuables were stolen from our family, by Elizabeth MacKenzie, when she ran away at the age of eighteen to America with Finn Cahill."

"He was lonely. She was grateful to get away, as we heard them tell it," Pearl said. "She told me once she ran with Finn because he made her feel like the smartest, most beautiful woman on earth."

"And they are gone: aye, ages along ago;" Archie opined, "these lovers fled away into the storm."

"Don't know if it was dark and stormy or not," Pearl filled in, "but they eventually reached America, after many months on a whaling ship. Not very romantic, so Cole's mother told it, but quite an experience. They finally traveled west and landed in Goldfield, Nevada, enticed by its being the last gold strike left."

"What was she like, Elizabeth?" Wynda asked.

"Pretty. Full of fire," Pearl said. "But at the end she was wracked by a nasty cough. She was like a little bundle of black rags when I last saw her."

"Any siblings of hers in Scotland?" Reba inquired.

"At least one elder brother was killed in the war. Another inherited family land. Elizabeth couldn't inherit any, even if she'd stayed. Eldest son got it all."

"So, in revenge, she stole the family jewels?" Jace remarked.

Archie waved an arm. "*Amor furor brevis est* ... love like anger is a brief madness."

Reba reeled at the revelation that more scandal infested her history from every lineage, both natural and adopted. "They must be worth a fortune," she said.

"We don't know for sure the monetary value. However, we were told from our childhood that the ruby cross meant more," Wynda explained, "as a bond with our great-great-grandparents ... of their faith, of who they were, and as a symbol of what held our family together during desperate times in the past."

"How did you know where to find them?" Pearl asked.

Wynda glanced down at the bedsheets. "First, we searched your house ... including behind the Laird's Lug in the attic room. We strongly suspected they'd been hidden there. No luck. Our deep and sincere apologies."

The attic room disarray.

"When that proved fruitless," Archie related, "we finally found a strike with the metal detector under the tree."

"The Camperdown Elm?" the women echoed.

Wynda lay back on her pillow, the welt around her neck pulsing. "We should have asked your permission, we know. We've been digging under the tree every night since. We kept covering our hole with the grassy plug and hoped none of you would find us out, until we were long gone."

"Abel almost caught us out," Archie confided, "with playing the war games with his soldiers. That made us very nervous."

"Why didn't you tell us about this from the beginning?" Pearl said.

"We tried to feel things out, in our way. We concluded you didn't know anything about it. Then we didn't think you'd believe that those things belonged to us. Or you would insist on keeping the heirlooms yourself." Archie squinted his eyes shut. "Now, none of us gets them. They're gone."

Pearl mused, "Cole sprawled there under that tree with an axe, because he wanted to free our family from a curse. He thought it came because of the wild-headed tree, so he tried to chop it down. But now we know, any supposed curse derived from a theft long ago, the treasures buried under the tree."

"Did Grandpa know about any of that?" Reba asked.

Pearl rubbed her forehead. "I'm not sure."

Archie seemed to bite back something he started to say. He reached for the water glass instead. "The original tree survives, you know."

"You've seen it?" Hanna Jo prompted.

"*Och aye.* We've got several ourselves at home, made from cuttings, of course, same as yours."

"It's a sad tree, don't you think," Wynda said, "with its drooping shape, like folded, closed up wings?"

"Maybe that's why it gave Grandpa such a gloom and doom feeling."

"His father, Finn, too," Pearl said. "Although Idaho has lots of lakes and rivers, Finn missed the sea. He wanted to be a merchant marine and would take an ocean voyage on any excuse. I heard his stories of his time on a whaling ship out of Dundee."

"You've got to come there sometime," Archie said. "To Dundee. See where it all started."

Pearl rose from her chair. "At the end of his life, Cole's father, Finn, wanted so bad to visit Scotland one more time, but it didn't happen." She turned to the Scottish twins. "Perhaps he meant to make restitution."

Back at the ranch house, they investigated the grounds. Smoke from the town fire had blown the other way, but the air reeked of soot and gassy fumes from the still smoldering bunkhouse blaze.

A disk implement created a fireguard of black dirt in the field around the house. The volunteer rural fire department and neighbors with plows kept crop and property damage to a minimum throughout the area.

Jace took Abel to check out their apartment and move all their belongings to the attic room.

Hanna Jo and Pearl headed to Main Street.

Norden and the Younger family, plus the Mathwig sisters and Atch Murdock knelt at the former business sites and sifted through wet, cold ashes to retrieve anything of value. Both Norden and the Mathwigs insisted, "We'll rebuild as soon as the insurance comes through."

"My place didn't have a chance," moaned Norden. "My stock was so highly combustible." His nostrils flared. "If they ever catch the guy who did this, I'll pulverize him."

"Have you gotten an update from the sheriff yet?" Pearl asked.

"Nope. But the perp was driving a white van."

"Like the same guy who attacked the MacKenzies and burned down our bunkhouse," Pearl stated. "Why would he bother to burn your places too?"

"Perhaps he figured that would occupy us, while he made his getaway."

"Well, it worked," Pearl commented.

Charlotta, ever the supreme hostess and homemaker, opened a card table in front of the Pick-Me-Up saloon, set out iced green tea with lemon, warm-from-the-oven chocolate chip cookies, and a donation jar. That doubled the bystanders in an instant.

"Got to keep busy doing something," she quipped.

🐎 🐎 🐎 🐎

Reba crept to the barn to check on Johnny Poe II and the other horses. Large flies flitted around her and out the door when she swatted them. Folding chairs used for the barn church still lined one wall, along with several metal music stands. The rustic podium and platform made from barn boards crowded one stall, not yet moved to the new church building.

Several pitchforks stuck in a pile of hay bales stacked to the rafters. The loft had been left open. She made a mental note to close it after she tended the animals.

When she backed up to leave the stallion's stall, she froze. She sensed she was being watched. Panic clawed at her chest. She veered around, prying for something wrong, out of place. A shiver of silence ticked away. Was she flinching at a phantom?

She listened to the barn, straining for a telling noise. Out of the usual earthy smells, she detected the stench of stale tobacco.

Then, without warning, a menacing creature stalked out of the shadows swift and intent on a prey, slamming her against the stall. She wheezed at the sharp cobra-like jab from behind. Seized around her neck, a hard yank wrenched her left arm back.

The terse order came from behind her. A bristly voice jeered, "The gold and turquoise necklace ... tell me where it is and you'll live."

Her nose filled with a mixture of pungent herbal, woodsy weeds and rank sweat. And something else clung to the stale air ... a whiff of kerosene fumes. "Can't ... talk," she gagged.

He loosened the neck hold, but kept her arm twisted and restrained. She alerted herself to the possibility of a knock-down-drag-out fight. Leverage to her knees. Balance on her feet. Any clothing to grab. A way to roll, scramble, and flee.

She thought she heard the distant slam of a car or pickup door. Probably at the house. Who returned? Or came to visit?

The sound agitated her accoster. He cursed with a blister of scorn. "The necklace," he hissed. "Tell me quick or I'll shoot up the house and anybody in it."

"Who are you?" She tried to pry loose but the man tightened his grip with his vein-laden, bulging biceps tattooed with lightning strikes.

Could this be Antjuan? She thought he left in the MacKenzie van.

"I'm going to count to three. There will be no four," he growled.

"We don't have it. That's the truth. My mother sold it to a jewelry store."

"Well, then, give me the money or I'll have to kill you. You've seen too much." He clutched her tighter.

Rage overtook panic. She remembered one of the tricks Cicely Bowers taught them. She silently counted a quick *one ... two ... three* and back-kicked with her boot heel as hard as she could, while dropping completely limp, dead weight, to the floor. He yelped and she scooted away. Boots were made for maiming.

She grabbed the first mean tool she could find, a pitchfork. "Stay away!" she warned. "I know how to use this."

He whipped out a gun, cocked and aimed it, and she noticed the busted knuckles. "You shouldn't bring a pitchfork to a gun fight," he snarled, his look fierce, cold, calculating.

Reba tried another tack, a play for time. "Why did you kill that girl, the one with Quigley?"

"So, you know who I am ... allegedly, that is." He cinched his mouth into a sneer. "Alleged ... I love that word. *Innocent* until *proven* guilty." His snarl exuded the raw power of controlling his world by getting rid of anyone who messed with him or got in his way. He reeked of rage.

He didn't know her, yet he loathed her. She suspected he'd gladly cut her heart out. She kept talking as calm as possible, trying to maneuver a break.

"What was that girl's name? Patsy?"

"She's not my problem." His eyes seemed glazed, unfocused.

She smelled liquor. He could be drunk. "We thought you left the area, in the van."

"I did. Then a jerk pulled over next to a ditch, turned the flasher on, and pulled his hood up. I stopped and offered to stay with his car, if he wanted to use the van to go find help. He thought *I* was the stupid one. He didn't know I messed with the brakes. I then hitched up with a chatty fisherman, going to the lake, and hid in the hayloft of this old barn until you showed up. Stupid. Stupid hicks, all of you."

Why did he risk coming back? He possessed all the MacKenzie valuables. Perhaps the oldest motive in the world—greed. He wanted more. The necklace, too. A jewel thief going after the full heist.

Behind him, she watched by peripheral vision in fascination as Johnny Poe II stalked out of the corral. Without hesitation, the stallion rushed the man, butting him in the back. The man yelled, bumped forward, and flailed to regain his balance. After a plummet to the ground, he rolled and raised with a swoop, gun still in hand and aimed at the stallion.

"No!" Reba plunged the pitchfork into his broad back and shoulder with all ten tines.

Bam!

The man shot high and howled in agony before his weapon dropped. The barn echoed with a ricochet sound as Reba furiously raked the gun toward her with the bloody pitchfork. Johnny Poe II reared, lifting his hooves high in the air. Flustered, Antjuan screeched and scrambled through the back door, as it swung wildly.

Reba corralled the black stallion, quieted him down, and sprinted to the house. She noticed the '55 Chevy parked in the driveway. "Jace, are you here?" she shouted through the open door.

He ran down the stairs and she collapsed in his arms, spilling out a semblance of the story in word gasps. She grabbed Pearl's shotgun and tossed a rifle to Jace. "Abel, you call 9-1-1 and tell them to get here fast."

"And stay in the house and keep it locked," Jace ordered. "And push the bolt," he added.

Jace pulled ahead of Reba on the run toward the back of the barn. He scanned the landscape of corrals and pasture. Reba helped him watch for movement.

"He surely had a transportation plan, a getaway option."

Suddenly, an engine revved nearby before a motorcycle roared toward them, appearing from the other side of the barn. Speeding faster and faster, the wheels weaved with a slip and slide over gravel and rock. Jace raised his rifle.

"Move!" Reba yelled.

Jace squeezed the trigger and leaped out of the way, as the cycle careened into a barbed wire fence. Rider and bike flipped over the bent fencing. Jace held up his hand for Reba to stay back. He approached the scene with care, rifle ready. She edged forward for a peek anyway.

Antjuan sprawled on the ground, limbs like dishrags wrenched in awkward angles, blood gashing from his forehead. Bile in her chest threatened to come up.

Metal can and contents scattered across the pasture. While Jace guarded the unconscious man, Reba found the rich and deep-colored, foot long, ruby encrusted cross. She hesitated to touch it or pick it up, but didn't want to leave it on the foul ground. A few small stones seemed missing. She carefully searched around, but couldn't find them in the grassy field.

She restored each of the MacKenzie treasures back to the partially busted metal can. Sirens blared in the distance.

Beneath a Camperdown Elm

Chapter Thirty

 Reba slept late the next morning after a troubled, restless night. She reviewed and replayed over and over the scenes at the bunkhouse and in the barn.

The trauma.

The peril.

The risks.

The *what ifs.*

Finally, she yanked off the bedding and the onslaught of images. After a long, hot shower for the chill in her bones, she pulled on a tan button shirt over brown tank, brown Wrangler's, her most comfy and clean brown leather boots, and pulled from a box her favorite tan cowgirl hat. About as coordinated and dressed up as she ever got.

At 11:00 she settled into Jace's strong and protecting presence, as he drove her across the high mountain prairie. "First stop, Severs Jewelry," Jace announced.

"Before you invest in a ring for me," Reba said, "I think you ought to know I'm only good at cooking three main dishes: basil beef stew, dill beef veggie soup, and tamale pie with Grandma's jalapeno cheesy cornbread recipe on top."

"Okay, good. We'll start with that." He offered her a goofy grin.

She pecked his cheek. "I am partial to guys with contagious smiles."

"However, before you accept my ring ... well, this is awkward and pretty much foreign to me ... but I must confess that at the moment, I'm basically broke. Most of my money and investments have gone to bail out my dad."

Reba felt the very air cleanse between them in this honest exchange. "We can wait on the rings. We can wait on everything. Really."

"Nope. We're not going to wait. I've got enough to get something simple."

"That suits me fine."

She loved this man more than ever. His quiet steadiness, practicality, and common sense settled her down, made her full of confidence.

They gazed at the gold and turquoise squash blossom necklace on display in a locked case at the back of Severs, but in a town this size it attracted more onlookers than serious buyers. Jewels glittered under glass on each side the long aisles—diamond rings, sapphire necklaces, emerald bracelets, ruby brooches. They took a careful study of ring choices and finally settled on a plain, double-set of middle-sized gold bands, not too wide or too narrow.

"Someday, you'll get diamonds," Jace promised.

"All I want is you." Reba meant that with her whole heart.

"Reba Mae, let's get married right away."

"How about Christmas?" When he frowned, she compromised. "I could get things ready by the end of harvest." Maybe Thanksgiving.

"How about September 1st?"

"That's the proposed new church dedication day."

"Yep."

"Whoa, cowboy, hold your horses. It can't happen that fast."

"Why not? We need no more than you and me, a witness or two, and the preacher."

"There are many more details."

"Like what?"

"Like where do you suggest we live?"

"Let's ask your grandma if she minds if we put a double-wide on that flat piece near the Camperdown Elm."

Reba recalled his parents' homes in Casa Tierra, California. "Are you sure? After what you're accustomed to?"

"You mean, sharing an apartment with Norden and Abel?" He winked, and she laughed. It felt really good to be making plans.

Afterward, they watched "Dances With Wolves" at the movie theater and then dinner at the Hong Fa Chinese Restaurant.

"I've decided something. I'm going to sell this Chevy and get a used family car." Jace handed her an ad sample:

'55 Bel Air Chevy convertible with white top, cobalt blue body, red interior; 300 HP Chevy 350 with TH350 transmission; proved solid on 1,200 mile road trip; front disc brake conversion kit.

"Don't you think we should keep it? As aaccn investment?"

"We're starting nearly from scratch, Reba Mae. I'm willing to do what it takes to make us a decent living. We could maybe buy a few acres at least. Lloyd Younger thinks he found a new crop for up here: winter hardy apples. He's speculating a good percentage will survive the below zero temperatures."

So, he envisioned them staying in Road's End, without the Cahill Ranch. "Diversified farming."

"Maybe you could run a candy apple store out of a trailer, and take it to fairs and rodeos. The apples would be ripe in September and October. You could travel around to various regional events. Dip the apples in caramel sauce or melted red cinnamon candies. Or use taffy. Cover them with sprinkles or nuts. We could include a cotton candy making machine and other fun stuff. Plus, sell boxes of apples as well."

Reba glowed with pride. Jace left California but brought his business savvy with him. Hope stirred within.

"Or I'll become a cellular phone entrepreneur."

Reba looked at him skeptically. "Cellular phones? Really?"

"Sure. A car phone can cost several thousand dollars, and lugging portable big, brick phones are not always the most convenient form of communication. But they are electronics, and electronics always shrink in size and cost as the technology advances. Once they are small enough to carry in a pocket and the price is affordable, I think a lot of people will have them. Maybe as much as twenty-five percent of the population."

Reba still wasn't convinced. "And how will you make money on that?"

"Easy. Cellular phone companies will be looking to expand their cover, and they'll need towers to hang their equipment on. If I build the towers, they'll rent space on them. Why go through the hassle of building their own? Real estate isn't just dirt, it's vertical, too."

She decided on the spot she would follow this man anywhere.

Jace, Abel and Jip planned a full day. Haircuts at the barbershop. Shoot baskets at the elementary school. Wash the '55 Chevy to prepare for sale.

Because of the hotel fire, Agatha rented a room from Hanna Jo at the B&B, which wasn't fully operational, but she seemed a good sport. Then she hung out with all the gals.

They helped Hanna Jo move her belongings to Cicely's place and DeLisa took over her bedroom at the ranch house, helping her fix it like she wanted for her temporary stay, "until the wedding."

Kaitlyn Runcie came for a visit and shared a doll with DeLisa. They drew a picture of the two of them with Reba and Johnny Poe

II. Reba taped it on the fridge until she could find a frame for a wall hanging. When DeLisa brought Reba her guitar, she played while they sang "The Farmer in the Dell" and "This Little Light of Mine."

Agatha announced, "I love being here. The kids and I will stay the rest of August."

"Yay!" hollered Jip and DeLisa.

"That's good. You'll be here for our wedding," Reba said and instantly added for Agatha's sake, "It's going to be small and plain, the smallest and plainest you've ever seen."

Agatha hugged her as the children did flips and circled the women with whoops.

When they all headed out to watch Abel play ball, Jip revealed such a longing look, Reba asked the coach if he could play too.

"We're doing a double-header today and several of the boys couldn't make it. I've got an extra uniform." The coach glanced at the brown-skinned boy. "Might be a little snug on him and he'll have to sit on the bench most of the time."

They soon discovered Jip could run fast, hit the ball hard, and never missed a catch. The second game he played first string outfielder and received loud cheers from the crowd. Reba wondered how that affected Abel. He clapped for his friend as much as anyone and seemed content to remain sub for third base.

Later, back at the barn, Reba spied Jip and Delisa hunkered with Abel in one of the mares' stalls. "Jip wants to learn to ride," Abel said.

"Only if it's okay with Agatha."

The older woman made a thumb's up signal.

Jace carried a cement block to help Jip mount one of Pearl's mares.

Reba held a riding crop as she studied his style. "Relax a little," she coached. "Hold on with your knees."

"How's he doing, Ranch Boss?" Jace inquired after the first lesson.

"He's a natural."

Chapter Thirty-One

*P*olice sirens and a clanging fire truck assaulted the country-side, this time forging toward the Runcie Ranch.

Lawyer James Howe found Champ at home and slumped over in his wheelchair, with Seth Stroud trying to rouse him. Howe told Deputy Lomax and Sheriff Goode, "Champ called me and said he had something urgent to show me. I came as soon as I could."

"He did the same for me," Seth asserted. "I knocked several times and heard sounds like gagging inside. I finally tried the door and it was unlocked, so I let myself in."

When Seth found an unresponsive Champ, he called Hester, who contacted the emergency line and Pearl. All three Cahill women arrived after the lawyer and an hour before Blair. By then, Champ had been declared deceased.

Blair's pale blue eyes turned to steel when she heard the news. Pearl led her to a chair and they all sat with her as she started talking nonstop about their history together as a couple, as though she'd been dammed up for years.

At last, she described their last morning together with deadly calm. "We played Rummy, Checkers, and Chess, at Champ's insistence. Then he told me to go to Oroston to pick up a new supply of calcium capsules. He said the bottle on the end table didn't look right. He'd been in good spirits when we played our games, rare for us. I told him to get a nap since he looked tired and then drove to the pharmacy."

"Anything else you can tell us? What was his state of mind recently?"

"Well, the day before yesterday he begged me to drive him to the top of Coyote Hill. I finally took him and he wanted me to position his wheelchair in the most open place, with no trees or boulders to obstruct. He told me he wanted to roll down. So I rolled a couple boulders to find the safest path.

"I tried to talk him out of it and then told him he couldn't go alone. I sat on his lap and unstopped the brake with the belt strapped tight and my arms raised high. I screamed all the way down, like we rode a roller coaster." Her eyes gleamed bright, unblinking. "I felt like a kid again and I think he did too."

Blair's chin trembled. "You don't understand Champ unless you knew his father too. He was totally controlled by his father. 'You will toe the line so hard, it squeaks,' he told him growing up. Champ tried to do the same to his sons, thinking to make strong men, ranchers, out of them." She abruptly transitioned to hostess. "Would you like tea or coffee?"

"No, thank you," Pearl replied. "Is there anything we can do for you?"

Blair seemed not to hear. "Roberta has always ruled this house," she noted.

"Champ's mother?" Pearl gently scooted her chair closer to the sudden, new widow.

Blair nodded. "Nothing ..." her arm swept the room, "can be changed. It must all stay as she left it."

But now, with Champ gone, couldn't Blair do as she chose?

Blair changed the subject again. "Look at all those pills. Champ had to take so many."

Prescription bottles covered the end table, plus a pitcher of water.

"The good thing is," Blair said, "It's over. Took only minutes." She stared in a daze at the table.

Her statement jarred Reba, the implication.

Hanna Jo quietly asked, "Do you think he committed suicide?"

Blair looked down. "Why is Seth here?"

"You don't think he had anything to do with this?" Reba spurted.

"Champ and Seth weren't close. Why would he be here?"

Her question bounced in echoes around the room.

They could see through the front window a pickup pull up the driveway with Don and Tim inside. The Cahill women rose to leave.

"I tried hard to keep our sons close," Blair was saying, "to help them reconcile, and bring everyone together." Her hands fidgeted and twisted in her lap, her face contorted. "I always wanted a daughter."

Did Maidie's sorrows still cast a long shadow?

On their way to the Cahill ranch house in Pearl's Jeep, Reba asked what they all wondered. "Why did Champ call Seth to come to the house?"

Hanna Jo blurted out, "In the wild chance he might get Seth accused of his murder."

"Or to bring resolution to the whole controversy between them."

"We'll probably never know." Pearl sighed. "I'm glad Blair wasn't there when he took those pills. One of the few kind things Champ did for her was to send her away."

As Pearl steered down the Cahill Ranch driveway, she began to muse about the Runcie patriarchy. "At one time, Champ's father, Uriah, practically owned the whole town of Road's End. In fact, he named it. 'Finally,' he said, 'we've found our home, the end of the road.'

Pearl continued, "Uriah infused the town with industry, with his compelling personality, and the formation of the logging mill. When the mill closed down in the 1960s, Uriah encouraged the development of the state park at the lake. Champ wanted that heritage to carry on, making this town a sort of Runcie fiefdom."

Reba sighed. *And you helped him accomplish that.*

Reba admitted in the same instant, she should try harder to accept the things she couldn't change. Champ had been no shirker, no genteel Sunday farmer. He worked hard on the land inherited from his father. But he also lusted after the pasture on the other side of his fence.

"Don't take this wrong," Hanna Jo blurted out. "Blair already seems much more peaceful."

"She'll have tough times of withdrawal, I'm guessing," Pearl said. "All those years together ... too ingrained a habit."

"Road's End will be a ... a sweeter, kinder place now to live in," Reba ventured.

"Also, less interesting." Pearl confided, "I will miss him. Butting up against that man helped sharpen me, including the intensity of my faith."

🐎 🐎 🐎 🐎

Road's Enders showed up in droves for the funeral of Champ Runcie and crammed into the not-quite-finished, new church building. His loss softened the tone of his worst former enemies as comments buzzed around the building.

Pearl opened her Bible at the podium and it fell open to a verse from Ecclesiastes 5: "All his days he eats in darkness, with great frustration, affliction, and anger."

Instead, she read aloud what followed, about the satisfaction of hard work, and how it was good to enjoy God's gifts of wealth and possessions, in the appointed years of life. "This was Champ's lot and how we'll remember him," she concluded.

After the service, Tucker grabbed hold of Franklin and Vincent. "We've got to get this place ready for the wedding. I'm offering my

Gang of Eight to come help."

"You got a gang, huh?" Franklin remarked with a grin.

"Yep. Trained them up in the jail. We're ready to serve. You tell us when and we'll be there."

"Alrighty. See you in the morning, bright and early."

Vincent turned to Pearl. "With their help, we'll surely meet our deadline."

Lawyer James Howe pushed through the crowd of mourners toward Reba, Hanna Jo, and Pearl. With no preamble, he stated, "Champ requested in writing all three of you attend the reading of his will."

Pearl's eyes widened in astonishment. "What on earth for?"

"I know it seems irregular." He dabbed a hand toward his forehead as though warding off a migraine.

One last revenge, a final dagger to the heart, to witness the parceling out of their former property?

"Well, I'm not going," Hanna Jo retorted.

"He especially wanted you there." Howe reached out to her with a fluttery movement, while his glance darted around the crowd, probably trying to see if any of the Runcie family stood in earshot. Then he stepped closer to all three of them. "Please help me honor his last wish. If not for Champ, do it for me."

Pearl studied her daughter and granddaughter, both as flustered as she was. Would there never be an end to Champ and his dominance over them all? Even in death, he must have the last word, humiliate them once more. But the lawyer seemed determined to complete this final mission on behalf of his client. She couldn't help but feel a bit sorry for him.

Pushed into a corner again by that maddening man, she exhaled. "Okay, I'll go."

"No, you won't," Hanna Jo replied. "Not alone. I'm going too." She swirled around toward Reba.

Reba huffed a sigh. She gave in to the inevitable. "Grandma, we'll be there with you."

Chapter Thirty-Two

The room bristled with tense stares as the Cahill women entered, at 10:00 a.m. sharp. Tim and Sue Anne arrived a minute later.

"What are they doing here?" Randall hissed, none too quietly. "We know what's in there. Why include them?"

Reba had an inkling of motive. Champ desired to dig the wound deeper, to tamp down their personal loss. One last poison arrow from the grave as they witnessed the division of their own property.

She'd never felt more out of place in her life.

Get this over with!

Blair looked anything but a picture of health. Her face flushed with fever as she coughed deep from her lungs. Maybe bronchitis or pneumonia.

Reba pinched her mouth in annoyance. Blair shouldn't be here. The sons should have rescheduled for her sake. Reba sure didn't want to be here—anywhere else in the world would be an improvement. Another vivid reminder of her and her mother being shut out by

Grandma Pearl.

Lawyer James Howe opened Champ Runcie's will, slowly unfolded the paper, crinkling the page.

"I don't understand," Randall Runcie burst out. He sat the closest to the lawyer. "That's not the document Dad showed us."

"No, it's not. It's holographic, a handwritten will in black ink that cancels the previous one. Be assured I checked out all the legalities."

"But the other one was dated, signed, witnessed, and notarized," Randall sputtered as the other sons crowded closer.

"Get back, all of you, so I can read this," the lawyer ordered.

"Don't worry about it," Don whispered to Randall. "Maybe he added more for Mom too."

"Then, why are *they* here?" His fierce nod aimed at the Cahill women.

Howe cleared his throat and rambled about how he found the new will. "Neither I nor Blair had anything to do with it."

"Read it already." Richie uttered a surly growl.

Howe's deep frown in his wrinkled face hinted that was the last thing in the world he wanted to do. At first, he stood and shook the paper. Or was that his hand shaking? He slunk down again and pulled off his glasses.

"I, Marion 'Champ' Runcie, of Bitterroot County, Idaho, being of sound mind and under no undue influence, make this my last and final will and testament, revoking all previous wills and codicils."

The lawyer paused to gaze around the room.

"Keep going, James!" Randall shouted.

Howe continued. "I direct that all my just debts and funeral expenses be paid as soon after my death as possible." This time a hesitation before he read again.

"I appoint James Howe as my personal representative, to serve without bond. If he is unable to serve, I appoint Pearl Cahill as my personal representative, also to serve without bond."

A breathy gasp around the table.

"I give my personal and household effects as follows, including the primary house, garage, storage buildings, and vehicles, to my wife, Blair Runcie, to be owned by her as long as she lives. I also bequeath to Blair Runcie all stocks and bonds and CDs that remain after payment of funeral expenses.

"I give to Don Runcie the sum of $1,000. I give to Randall Runcie the sum of $1,000. I give to Richard "Richie" Runcie the sum of $1,000. I give to each of my grandchildren—Tim Runcie, MaryBeth Runcie, MaryAnne Runcie, Peter Runcie, Roxie Runcie, and Harry Runcie—the sum of $1,000 each.

"I give all my ranch and farm property, including barns, outbuildings, machinery, cattle, horses, and other equipment necessary to the operation of the ranching and farming business, to ... " Lawyer James Howe looked up with a twitch in his eyes and a nervous gawk around. "... Hanna Jo Cahill.

"If anyone contests this will, they will receive a total of $1.00.
August 15, 1991
Marion 'Champ' Runcie
Road's End, Idaho"

Randall and Richie stood up so fast, their chairs banged against the floor. Their faces blazed several shades of scarlet.

"Outrageous," Randall hissed and stormed out of the room.

"Well, we're not left out with nothing," Tim noted.

One by one, the Runcie family members departed the room, backs stiff, no acknowledgement to the Cahill women. Don lingered last. He conferred in heated, hushed tones in private with Howe, and then he also left, head down.

Reba studied her mom. She fumbled with her chair, her eyebrows squished together. "What on earth happened here?" she mumbled.

"We got back the fences," Pearl said, her face full-blown wonder. "With the others thrown in. Isn't that right, James?"

The lawyer handed Pearl and Hanna Jo copies of the will. "Looks that way. I'm as surprised as you are."

On the ride home, Reba asked what they all wondered, "Why would Champ do that?"

"Maybe to punish his family by humiliating them, the pursuit of power over them to the bitter end," Pearl surmised.

"Yeah, how dare they choose to make lives for themselves, apart from him?" Hanna Jo commented.

But why name Hanna Jo and not Pearl as sole owner?

Perhaps he finally admitted in death how he was responsible for her life.

🐎 🐎 🐎 🐎

Hanna Jo stomped to the house with brand new, full quill ostrich boots, sea green eyes shining, and strawberry blonde hair coifed in a soft curl bob down to her shoulders. "Well, now we know." She shoved papers at Reba and Jace. "Champ's so cunning. I knew there must be a catch."

Reba shuffled through the documents and dreaded what might come next. She hesitated before she asked the expected, "What's that?"

"You know how weird it feels to me to now own both ranches, unless, of course, the Runcie brothers wriggle a legal way out. However, they may not want to. James Howe told me Champ owed years' worth of back property taxes."

"Ha! Same as Grandma," Reba noted.

"Now we or I have to pay his and hers."

Reba tried to absorb that information. "Why would he do a stupid thing such as not pay property taxes? He was the mayor, for Pete's sake."

"I guess he thought himself untouchable and entitled. Who knows? Also, I'm now liable for the estate taxes."

Reba glanced at Jace, his face grim. "Wow, just wow!"

Her thoughts slid to Tim. No wonder the property didn't go to him instead. He didn't want to burden his grandson.

"Greedy and manipulating to the end," Hanna Jo commented.

"But you got to feel for the guy, in spite of it," Jace finally put in. "He never fathomed for a second that all three of his sons and his grandson would refuse to carry on the legacy of the Runcie Ranch."

"So, are we to gain both ranches and lose them all?" Reba said.

Jace swiped his shirt and jeans. "You know what? I've been in worse fixes than this before. At least you have the land, the property, and all that goes with it to run a proper ranch. No matter what the ultimate bill owed, we can pay it off, sooner or later."

Reba studied this man of hers—shoulders back, chest out, chin high—and believed every word. With a lot of hard work and ingenuity, eventually they'd make a go of it.

"I put you two in charge," Hanna Jo said.

"Of what?"

"Everything. I've got my own business to run."

"Grandma too. We'll figure out a compatible team, with trial and error, I'm sure."

"My first suggestion," Jace injected, "Let's get started right away clearing rocks for seeding winter wheat."

Hanna Jo high-fived him. "Agreed. See? I'm going to make a great boss." She reached out to hug her daughter.

"Mom, we've had a number of very rough years. But we can look out for each other now."

"I've been thinkin' about us. You and I were grafted onto a Scots-Irish trunk by adoption. We got a rocky start, but Pearl and Cole cared enough to include us in their circle of love."

"That's right," Reba affirmed.

"We're wild shoots grafted in with ancient roots, a whole new family in the making." She paused for a quick breath before her conclusion. "A graft does require a wound and healing and cultivation to work."

Reba brimmed with gratitude for the peace between them right now. They were family—strong, together.

"If only ..." Hanna Jo's voice cracked. Her shoulders drooped as she rubbed the heel of her palm against her chest.

Their lives littered with pathetic *if onlys*. "What is it, Mom?"

"Michael ... Griff," she wheezed out.

At the Grange Hall, Reba and crew cleaned up the building and grounds in preparation for the upcoming reception. Reba and Jace decided on the simplest of weddings and to marry on the church's dedication day.

Sheriff Goode and Deputy Lomax busted in on them.

"We found the white van," the sheriff announced. "The driver didn't navigate a tight turn on White Bird Grade very well."

"You got him in the hospital, Sheriff?" Tucker asked.

"No, he's at the morgue. He got thrown badly wounded into a canyon and a big black bear finished him."

Abel and Malik both yelled, "Bigfoot!"

"Antjuan's still in the hospital," the deputy said. He's releasing information like a sieve. He's bragging about his exploits, including his murders. He heard Quigley boast about all the jewelry at the McKane house, so he stole that. And Quigley blabbed about the exquisite squash blossom necklace at his mother's place in San Francisco. His main goal was the jewelry. He killed those who got in the way of that goal."

"How did Antjuan know about the valuables in the metal box?" Jace asked.

"He'd been skulking around the Cahill place," the sheriff explained. "He caught the MacKenzies in the act of digging up the box from under the tree."

Jace nudged Abel. "Hey, guys, did you see those big prints in the dirt by the cemetery?"

The two boys raced outside.

Jace eyed the sheriff. "Do you think Antjuan had anything to do with my stepmother's death?"

"The authorities in California strongly suspect so. They're asking for extradition."

Jace blanched white. Reba stood closer and rubbed his back.

"Since he escaped the California jail," the sheriff continued, "he's been after Quigley, the girl, and any valuables he could find, especially the infamous squash blossom necklace. His jewel thief's mind twisted with obsession at owning that gold and turquoise. Meanwhile, he nearly burned down the town in order to escape."

"And isn't he responsible for the death of that driver on the side of the road?" Reba inquired.

"I believe a case could be made."

Chapter Thirty-Three

The next morning, Hanna Jo made a list of possible things to do. First, she grabbed her new camera to photograph the crime scene and aftermath of the fire at the bunkhouse and downtown. She included footprints around where the van had been parked.

Reba walked out in her bathrobe and slippers. "Mom, what are you doing?"

"The police might need details. Things are easily forgotten and should be recorded."

"They have their own photographers. Besides, the perp is dead. There won't be a trial or anything like that."

"I know. I ..." She tried to focus, to better explain. "I'm so jittery."

"Have you been taking your meds?"

Hanna Jo closed her eyes. "Yes, but I also need to keep busy."

"We've got a ranch to run. There's going to be a Church Dedication and a wedding. You've got your business to start up. There's a bazillion things to do."

"You're right. I can't seem to settle down. It's like I'm ..." Hanna Jo searched for a word.

"Maybe you need to rest, take a day off."

"No. I must keep busy, keep my mind occupied. Or I'll go ..."

Reba stared at her in alarm.

"I think I know what it is. Griff and Michael—I can't stop worrying about them."

Reba hugged her waist. "Come on, Grandma's fixing breakfast. You give her a hand while I take a quick shower."

Reba led her by the arm to the ranch house. Hanna Jo stopped her at the door. "There's something else I've been wanting to discuss with you. Now's as good a time as any." She looked down at her boots and sorted through the words. "Because of Don ... and Champ ... and Maidie in your lineage ..."

"I know, Mom. I don't plan to have any children."

"Okay. Higher chance of birth defects. But that's not all." She scuffed a heel across the wooden plank deck. "You should also have regular medical checkups. You might inherit more than our craziness."

"Like what?"

Hanna Jo would gladly sink in a hole and never come out again. "I don't know exactly, but it gnaws at me something fierce. You're liable to be plagued with major health issues."

"Mom, leave it be. It is what it is." Reba tromped to the bathroom.

Hanna Jo sauntered toward the kitchen where Pearl fussed with a carton of apricots and cobbler crust. She never felt more alone in all her life. No one could understand the deserted island she felt stranded on. No matter how many people tried to draw near, or gathered around her, she couldn't feel completely free of her mistakes.

The guilt began to swell so badly, she thought she'd burst. The notion kept pricking her as a dinette chair she pulled out stuttered across the floor. She flopped down.

"What's wrong, honey?" Pearl said, white flour dusting her clothes and face.

"Everything."

"No, it's not. We're going to work it out."

Hanna Jo suspected she meant paying off the ranch debts. "Some things we can, but others ..." Her nerves thrummed an insistent, sad tune, a habit from her runaway days. As she studied her mother's longsuffering face, she worked hard to resist the gloom. "Love you, Mom." The simple statement lessened her load, waged war against the quicksand of inner desperation.

Pearl's face lit up. "Love you too." When the phone rang, Pearl nodded at her to pick up.

Hanna Jo stood, dragged her boot heels across the linoleum, and grabbed at the receiver, ready to hand it off to her mother as quick as possible. "Hello."

A crackle over the line, then she heard, "Hey, Jo!"

Every muscle stoved up, her nerves electric. She held the instrument harder, closer. Only one person in the whole, wide world addressed her that way. "Griff! Is that you? Where are you?" The last trace of her melancholy melted in a tiny puddle as she nearly cried with joy.

"Hey, girl, been ridin' under a midnight sun. Now, I'm lookin' at gem-colored waters, bald eagles flying, and jagged, snow-covered peaks from my window."

"I don't understand. I thought ..." Her mind blanked. She couldn't take it all in.

"I'm in an Anchorage hospital, until I can make my escape. That is, me and Michael."

"So, you're both okay?" She caught herself. Raw with hope, she half-feared she listened to an imposter playing some kind of game. She listened harder to every nuance.

"We will be, as soon as they finish interrogating us, and we take care of business loose ends." His voice crooned in an unmistakable, familiar tone. She could hear music in the background—"Tulsa Time" by Lee Greenwood, one of Griff's favorite country singers. Hanna Jo's sucked-in breath slowly released. "What happened?"

"All of a sudden, the water got brutal. A real squall. We got in trouble so fast and we didn't realize we had a leaky pipe."

"How many crew members did you lose?"

"One too many."

"I'm so sorry." She paused, not sure what else to say about the sad news. "Now what?"

"The thing is, I ... we ... want to get out of Alaska for a while. We've been talkin'. You see, we'd head your way, you know, to Road's End, if we ... if I had *any* inkling of some sort of welcome reception."

Hanna Jo sat down, kept repeating his words silently. A few of them penetrated. She tried to make sense of them. It sounded an awful lot like Griff was asking her something. "I'll be here," she managed to eke out, her mouth dry, scratchy.

"Okay ..." He hesitated, like he expected more.

Hanna Jo's head spun. She slowly stood up, focused on the far wall and gently moved her head up and down, right to left. "I'd like to see you ... both," she replied, knowing full well she'd fly right then and there to Anchorage to be with him, if he even hinted a request.

She heard a slap or punch against a hard surface. "Good! We're practically on our way."

"When ...?" she began and heard a *click* and dial tone.

Numb and dazed, she could only swallow in response to Pearl's questions. Finally, she managed, "They're all right! They're coming here!" To us. *To me!*

The next few days, Hanna Jo tried on fake eyelashes, fussed with makeup, and highlighted her hair. She wanted to look better than her best if Griffin Cahill dared to show his hide in Road's End.

🐎 🐎 🐎 🐎

Michael and Griffin arrived in town in Michael's 1980 bronze Mustang Cobra with Michael's blonde, med student girlfriend, Nina Oscar, scrunched between them.

Nina stood back near the Mustang while Michael rushed forward to hug and swing the three Cahill women around, one by one. When he let go of his mother, she circled around until she faced her former husband.

Griff and Hanna Jo did a slow, bashful dance toward each other, not quite a two-step or a waltz. More like a country style ballet.

"Jo," Griff began.

The intimate word swallowed her up and stirred her deepest longing. "You've been gone an awful long time," she said. "Forever, in fact."

"I'm back," he replied. "How about you?"

"I'm home, Griff." She looked him fully in the eyes. She wanted him to believe and trust this statement like nothing she'd ever said before to any man. "You're my home."

He gently tugged her toward him. They simply held each other.

Michael and Nina strolled away toward the barn and corrals. Soon, Pearl and Reba left Hanna Jo and Griff to be alone and followed after the other couple.

"You need a big crew for this expanded ranch," half-brother Michael announced.

Reba recalled his left hand with two short stubs, blown off in a fireworks accident.

"I'll help with the horses," he insisted. He headed for the pasture. "You know I've got a knack with rowdy horses."

"Yes, you showed off enough times with Johnny Poe I. The stallion out there is Johnny Poe II."

He took a quick look all around and wasted no time with an assessment, with no apparent finesse. "The wild ones graze together fine. But in the corral, they push, kick, and bite each other, when they aren't grooming one another."

Neither Banner nor Johnny Poe II reacted to his presence, except with calm and acceptance.

"I bet I could get on them from the right side with no fuss," he goaded.

Reba didn't take the bait. No way would she let him ride Johnny Poe II. "Don't you dare try."

"You're right. Not today. The stallion and buckskin told me they want time together. Alone." Michael winked.

Griff and Hanna Jo appeared at the corral gate, beaming, arm in arm.

"I told Griff we could use another hand with the horses," Hanna Jo said.

Griff shook his head. "That's not really me, though I wouldn't mind helping in a pinch. I do hear there's an opening for ranger. The present one resigned to go to a bigger state park."

"How on God's green earth did you know that?" Hanna Jo said.

"I have my sources."

She punched his side. "Won't be as exciting as Alaska."

Griff's eyes twinkled. "We can visit Anchorage anytime we want and I can help out a crew now and then."

"The county sheriff is looking for another deputy too," Reba mentioned.

"Looks like I've got a whole passel of options." Griff squeezed Hanna Jo closer and she didn't pull away, not one inch.

They stayed there like that as the others walked away. As soon as she knew they were totally alone, Hanna Jo said, "It's so incredible to see you, to be with you. But I don't know ... I'm such a wimp."

I'm terrified.

Griff snuggled into her. "The way I hear it, you've been locked in closets and car trunks, beaten up and choked, and you survived."

"But I'm scared of scurrying rats and cockroaches." And risking love again.

"However, you're smart, resourceful, and tenacious."

"My room looks like chaos." Same as my life. "I'm still no housekeeper."

"But you're a fighter. I've seen you war against an incompetent world and a toxic environment."

She touched his cheek and whispered, "I have learned to trust my gut."

"And what's your gut telling you right now?"

She pushed out every ounce of clenched air, forced herself to relax, and breathed in a peck of peace and a touch of trust. She leaned over, and kissed him soft but firm on the lips. "To go for it again, with you."

Early the next morning, Hanna Jo nudged Pearl and Reba out of bed. "We're going to Spokane, to shop," she announced.

Reba tried to crawl back under the covers. "Are you crazy? What are you talking about?"

"For once in our lives, we're going to be gloriously glamorous and romantic, for your wedding. We're going to wear dresses!"

"No, I'm not," Reba snorted. "I told Jace I'm wearing my cleanest, newest Wranglers and he didn't mind one twit."

"Nope, nope, *nope!* That won't do."

"Mother, it's 5:00 a.m. and you sound drunk."

She hiccupped. "Maybe I am still a little tipsy. Griff and I stayed out pretty late. Come on, you two, get ready. Your chariot awaits and I need a designated driver." Hanna Jo turned to leave.

Pearl reached out for her arm. "Girls, before we go, I've got a confession to make."

Reba stopped still and studied the gray-haired woman's face. Grandma Pearl's look was more coy than shy. A fractured smile through a crimson blush.

"I had a special night too." She slid her hand into the pocket of her satin pink nightgown. She pulled out a fist clutched tight and slowly opened it. In the middle she cradled a round, brilliant-cut, diamond solitaire ring.

"Oh!" Hanna Jo gasped.

"Stunning!" Reba gushed. "Does this mean … Vincent?" Reba was too stunned to say more.

Pearl nodded with wet eyes and slipped the ring on her left hand.

"Mom, tell us all about it," Hanna Jo said. "Don't leave anything out."

"There's not a lot to say. He took me to dinner at Rooster's Landing. We ordered salmon and stuffed halibut. He insisted we have dessert and he sat this ring on top my huckleberry pie *à la mode.*"

"Then what?" Reba prodded.

"He mentioned he knew Cole already gave me lots of opals. Would I be willing to wear this too? Then he asked, would I please meet him at the church Sunday night? He'd be the one standing by Jace. I said I would."

"And by Griff, too," Hanna Jo added.

"Really!" Reba squealed.

Hanna Jo stretched her mouth in a lopsided grin. "It was going to be a surprise."

"Can you believe it? We're all three engaged at the same time," Reba said.

The three women began to whoop and holler and hop around.

When they finally calmed down, Hanna Jo again headed for the door.

"Wait, Mom!" Reba stepped to her dresser and rummaged around in her sock drawer. She pulled out the wooden female warrior who clutched an outstretched sword, the one Seth carved and sanded with such care. A woman with wide, deep eyes, helmet and long stream of hair, ready to do battle, peered at her.

Why hadn't she seen it before?

She recognized that face.

"This belongs to you, Mom. You're the warrior among us. I know it took a lot of guts for you to return to Road's End. And you're the one who found the wild horses and my new Johnny Poe and persisted until we brought them all here. And you confronted Champ. He did a turn-around, giving us back our ranch and his too." She handed Hanna Jo the trophy. "You so deserve this."

"I ... I don't know what to say."

Pearl, her eyes glistening, wreathed in a huge, wrinkled smile. "I'm not sure I believed I'd ever witness such a moment as this."

Hanna Jo swiped her nose. "I couldn't have done it, any of it, without the help, perseverance, and support of both of you."

The three of them collapsed into each other's arms.

Hanna Jo finally nudged away and balanced the wooden warrior on top the dresser. "Okay, gals, no more distractions. It's time to shop till we drop."

Chapter Thirty-Four

After breakfast, Reba left the kids with Agatha and Pearl and entered the Main Street barbershop. She passed the Burma-Shave ads, photos of Moses Stroud and son, Seth, and antique sign which revealed, "Liquor used for pulling teeth and taking out bullets."

Conversation buzzed between owner and barber, Alfred James, and several customers, one in the chair and one waiting.

"They've started clean-up on the Outfitters and Hotel. Hope they can get them both up and running again."

"What happened to the crazy guy who started them fires?"

"They found the white van over the side of White Bird Grade. Transmission and brakes plumb went out on a tight turn and over the side it tumbled and got totaled."

"So, he ups and rips off those nice Scottish twins."

"He's liable to get a curse put on him."

"Everyone suspected old Finn Cahill buried something under that dadgum tree."

"I heard it was gold."

"Purtneer was."

"Used to be a small town like ours was free of big city crime."

Alfred sharpened a razor and spit out chew into a wastebasket. "Hi, Reba. Richard will be right back. Go in and make yourself comfortable."

She entered the salon through the cloth hanging at the doorway and plopped into the revolving chair. She grabbed a white cotton wrap and several styling magazines.

Soon Richard James entered the rear door, recognizable in the low light by his curved nose, prominent bridge, and pushing the single-wheeled unicycle he used as his mode of transportation around town.

"Did you ever do an act, like in a circus?" Reba asked.

"No, but I've been exchanging riding and daredevil tips with Archie MacKenzie. They asked me to join them when I can for a presentation, if I could get up the nerve."

Within three hours, Reba's hair bounced once again with Richard's creation, the full Regal Red, Curly Cue treatment.

🐎 🐎 🐎 🐎 🐎

When Reba arrived at the ranch house, Agatha took Reba and Jace aside. "Reba Mae, Jace, I have a sort of wedding gift for you that I need to explain." She watched the kids play in the Cahill yard around and under the elm tree. "Jace mentioned you'd be interested in taking on Jip and DeLisa."

Reba aimed a smile at Jace and clutched his hand. "I may never have kids of my own, so ..." she let the sentence dangle.

"Well, here's a further incentive. I'm going to set up a trust fund for them—for their care now and college fund later."

Reba speared Jace with a look, intent on taking her cue from him. Would he agree to her generosity?

At first, indecision flicked across his face. But soon after, Jace grabbed Agatha by the shoulders and kissed her cheek. "Mom, that's great!"

Then Reba felt free to hug her. "It's incredible. Thank you so much!"

Within an hour, Hugh McKane flew into Road's End's small runway with his private plane, wearing white slacks, collared blue-striped suit, white shoes and navy jacket.

One moment tagged a sad note when Abel commented, "I wish Mom was here too."

Hugh showed enough presence of fatherly empathy to promise to take the boy fishing before leaving Idaho. He soon after agreed to allow Abel to stay with Jace and Reba for the coming school term.

Later, Hugh confided to Jace, "I purchased a company which supplies valves for off-shore wells all over the world. It's a winner. I'm going to stick with this one business and make it work, so I can pay you back, with interest."

Jace rubbed his brow and seemed at a loss for words.

That evening, Abel, friends, and family celebrated his eleventh birthday with a buffalo burger barbecue. He finally, officially received his very own appaloosa pony from Jace and Reba, which he promptly named Little Foot. Other gifts included a teepee from Malik, Reine, and Elliot Laws, and the puppy he wanted from the Younger family. From that night, the Golden Retriever stuck to the boy like Velcro, so that quickly became his name.

In the shades of purple twilight, one happy boy experienced what he dubbed, "My best birthday ever."

Chapter Thirty-Five

SUNDAY, SEPTEMBER 1ST, 1991

The morning of the church dedication service, people gathered at the building site from all over the Road's End village and surrounding area. News about the new church grew for weeks with a buzz of excitement. Members and visitors arrived early and congregated in groups outside and in the sanctuary.

The Mathwig sisters supplied juice, coffee, and homemade donuts on a large, rolling cart in the social hall.

The crowd swelled larger when Tucker Paddy's Gang of Eight arrived in a car caravan, all cleaned and spiffy, with a timid entourage of family members in tow, decked in their Sunday best. Tucker ushered wife Ida and sons, Amos and Pico, to front row seats.

A noisy cacophony of music rose before the service with each instrument tuning up. Elliot Laws on drums. Atch Murdock with trombone. Seth Stroud on fiddle. Reba and Tucker with guitars. Wynda and Reine Laws on flute with Wynda double duty with violin too. Dapper Archie appeared in a velvet dinner suit and green tweed kilt jacket with horn buttons and blew his trumpet, with bagpipes at his side.

LaDonna handed him a small Bible. He tucked it in his breast pocket.

"Will you read it?" she asked.

"Yes ... *ach,* no ... to lie about such a thing ... but I find comfort in having the good book close to my heart."

"But a book is for reading," she scolded. Then she grabbed Jesse Whitlow's arm.

Reba heard Jesse used a chunk of his summer earnings to invest in a gas card, a going away gift for the Scottish twins.

After picking wildflowers on the Camas Prairie for the altar that morning, Wynda wore a flowing green Paisley dress and brown suede boots, complements of Reba and her friend, Ginny George Nicoll of California, who showed up because of the wedding later.

Pastor Kiersey of Oroston arrived with his wife, Iris, and children, crammed in his battered coupe. Behind him, a dually pickup contained four youths. "I'm training them for ministry," he explained. His dark brown hair swung as he introduced them. "This is a field trip for them."

"It's like the church is starting again from scratch," Pearl commented to Reba.

Cicely Bowers made quite an entrance in wide-brimmed, flaming red hat, cocked to the side, black mini-dress and heels, looking like a scarlet tanager in the midst of sparrows.

"*Fantoosh,*" Reba heard Archie say with a kind of whistle.

Cicely called out, "Hey, Franklin, all you guys did a terrific job with the church building project."

"Thanks! Did you know I'm going to Vegas for my birthday?"

"I didn't know you were a gambler," she noted.

"I'd like to see the lights and pass through Seth's infamous Worthy Mountain Mine area, after all the stories I've heard."

"Hey, if you happen to see my niece, Neoma, the one who visited me earlier this summer, tell her to give me a call."

His eyes twinkled clear and steady with not a sign of blush on his tanned face. "You mean, Neoma Buzzwell Hocking?"

"How on earth did you know my niece's maiden name?"

"We've been communicating ever since she left here."

"Well, I'll be hankered, as they say in these parts." Cicely thumped Franklin on the chest near his heart. "So, there's more going on here than I realized."

A tape recording of Maidie Fortress playing the flute using a portable player enveloped the crowd. The din of noisy conversation and musical tune-ups slowly quieted down. At the conclusion, Pearl stepped to the podium.

"It was my husband Cole's idea that we start a church in our home," Pearl began. "We soon needed more room, so we moved to the barn." She relayed the history of the little country church. "This dedication provides a chance to advertise our existence and invite everyone in town and countryside to come."

When she concluded, Wynda and Archie played "Amazing Grace" on violin and bagpipes.

Then came the special dedication of Maidie Fortress's Memorial Bell, presented by her uncle, Seth Stroud.

"Maidie Fortress was born November 15, 1912 in Goldfield, Nevada, and died in Road's End, Idaho, May 1, 1991. She moved to Road's End in 1913. Many of us often heard her playing a flute solo from her cabin balcony. We remember her wearing bright-colored smocks and making up silly rhymes. Her favorite color was purple, which is why I painted my Model T that color. At times, she'd tell me she heard church bells. Now every Sunday and on other special occasions, we'll hear her bell sounds too."

Pearl added, "The bell was purchased through the generosity of the late Champ Runcie. We can use it to summon folks to church with three dings and warn of fires in the area with multiple pulls of the chain."

Reba noted only Tim, Sue Anne, and children, Kaitlyn and William of the Runcie family attended.

Pastor Kiersey preached the inspirational message with a visual he created on a poster board. His theme: "God draws His story with permanent ink straight through our crayon crooked lines."

Reba's mind spiraled as Maidie Fortress's bell rang out at the end of the dedication. Most everyone present took a turn.

Pastor Kiersey announced, "You will also hear three bongs from this bell this afternoon at 4:00 for our extra-special wedding gala."

Chapter Thirty-Six

The three Cahill brides decked out in western style dresses—Pearl in taupe, Hanna Jo in yellow, and Reba in white—with matching boots, and each wearing a hat specially chosen by Cicely. Their steeds crunched up the gravel driveway as each arrived on her own horse—a brown mare, a buckskin, and a black stallion—along with red side-saddles borrowed from the Mathwig sisters.

Abel McKane and Jip Rodrigues served as ring bearers and DeLisa Rodrigues scattered the aisle with yellow, red, and white rose petals.

Seth Stroud walked the three brides down the aisle.

The weddings began with vows spoken and rings exchanged one at a time, the first such observances in the new church building.

Reba and Jace McKane stood with Maid of Honor, pregnant Ginny George of California, and Best Man, Norden McKane.

Best Man, Michael Cahill, and Maid of Honor, Cicely Bowers, accompanied Hanna Jo and Griffin Cahill.

And Pearl and Vincent Quaid crowded the front with Best

Man, Franklin Fraley, and Maids of Honor, Beatrice, Charlotta, and Adrienne Mathwig.

Reba sang in her country alto, "I Can't Help Falling In Love With You," accompanying herself with the cedar guitar Seth crafted for a wedding gift.

Before the couples kissed, the three grooms presented *silver* and turquoise squash blossom necklaces to their brides, with ores taken from the recently re-activated Worthy Mountain Mine in Nevada, through Agatha McKane Hempthorne's arrangements. None of them were replicas, each style fashioned different and unique, like their owners.

Later, Reba and Jace led the long caravan in the '55 Chevy, top down, to the Grange Hall after an eventful, but peaceful Idaho summer day.

Now, under an expansive, starry night sky with a full western moon, Reba watched the arc of a shooting star.

Her heart brimmed with joy.

Whatever lay ahead, this was another God hugged day.

THE END

Beneath a Camperdown Elm

Epilogue

The Monday afternoon after the weddings, two of the new-lywed couples primed for work on the Cahill-Runcie Ranch. Hanna Jo tidied up Mercy House to prepare for both a new horse and human arrival. Griff pulled on a borrowed ranger uniform and reported for duty at the Road's End Lake Park.

Meanwhile, Wynda MacKenzie planted sweet and thorny, white Scottish roses, purchased from a Lewiston nursery, in Maidie's garden and in front of the Cahill Ranch house. And she set slips from the white roses at Elizabeth MacKenzie Cahill's grave.

By the end of the week, the MacKenzies rented another van and loaded their belongings, including the metal box with ruby encrusted cross, gold Roman coins, whale bone scrimshaw, photo, and pearl ring. They left the letters and journal with the Idaho Cahills and drove northwest into the sunrise, toward the Canadian border.

The following Spring 1992, after the cows delivered their calves, all three newly married couples, plus Seth and Hester Stroud, flew to

Dundee, Scotland for their official honeymoons. Wynda and Archie MacKenzie served as their guides for a two-week tour of the United Kingdom countries of England, Scotland, Wales, and Ireland.

After a number of legal hoops, Jace and Reba eventually got full custody of Jip and DeLisa and adopted them in 1994, the same year their Maidie Pearl was born.

Pearl Cahill served two terms as mayor of Road's End. She continued to ride the fences of the enlarged Cahill-Runcie Ranch and drove truck during harvest. She also managed the many programs of the church, Vincent at her side, often asking prayer for stamina. She certainly didn't rust out. She simply wore out June 2011, still doing all the work she loved.

Hanna Jo Cahill's first residents of her Mercy Home for wounded women included Quigley's mother, Eleanor Dalton, and Blair Runcie, Champ's widow. She gained a reputation all over the Pacific Northwest as a women's abuse advocate and horse healer.

Tim and Sue Anne Runcie spent years as Bible teachers and church planters in Montana, Wyoming, and the Dakotas with their three children, Kaitlyn, William, and David Daniel. Then they settled once more in Road's End to become the church's full-time pastor after Pearl Cahill passed away. Tim officiated at her funeral.

Sergeant Elliot Laws became a policeman for the Nez Perce tribe and his nephew, Malik, passed the bar as a lawyer to specialize in tribal reservation legal issues. Reine Laws still plays her flute at pow-wows, rides an old, beat-up crew cab dually pickup, and makes the best fry bread and beans in town. She farms thirty cows and thirty hogs, renting land from the Cahills.

Johnny Poe II's offspring included a buckskin mare and a black stallion, Johnny Poe III, who sired Johnny Poe IV.

Abel McKane lived until age eighteen with his father, Hugh, and stepmother, Jodeen, but spent every summer in Road's End. He and Malik Laws kept tracking Bigfoot. They plotted to make big money by capturing and exhibiting this monster and showed a photo and video of the creature, including their proposed proof of huge paw prints, to anyone who hinted an interest.

Abel wrote about their adventures for travel, science, and animal magazines. He caught the attention of a travel TV channel that filmed a documentary of the two. In their hunt for Bigfoot, they uncovered lairs of cougars and several other herds of wild horses in the canyons surrounding Road's End. Hanna Jo and crew promptly corralled them. The horses have all been tamed and trained at the Cahill-Runcie Ranch by Michael Cahill, Reba Mae Cahill McKane, or Hanna Jo Cahill-Cahill.

The young men also discovered two of the biggest black bears ever sighted in Idaho, but absolutely persisted in their claim that neither was their hairy, upright walking, ape-like Bigfoot creature.

So far, Bigfoot alleged sightings number nearly a dozen in the Pacific Northwest's region beyond Road's End.

MAJOR CHARACTERS & PLACES
DOWN SQUASH BLOSSOM ROAD

CICELY **BOWERS** – OWNS & RUNS ROAD'S END B&B. ORIGINALLY FROM SEATTLE

ANTJUAN **BUNT** – QUIGLEY'S CELLMATE; CONVICTED OF ARMED ROBBERY; INFAMOUS JEWEL THIEF

COLE **CAHILL** – LATE HUSBAND OF PEARL CAHILL; REBA CAHILL'S ADOPTED GRANDFATHER

GRIFFIN **CAHILL** – FORMER HUSBAND OF HANNA JO CAHILL HANNA JO CAHILL – MOTHER OF REBA MAE CAHILL

HANNA JO **CAHILL** – MOTHER OF REBA MAE CAHILL

MICHAEL **CAHILL** – HALF-BROTHER OF REBA; SON OF HANNA JO CAHILL

PEARL STROUD **CAHILL** – MOTHER BY ADOPTION OF HANNA JO CAHILL; GRANDMOTHER OF REBA CAHILL; WIDOW OF COLE CAHILL.

REBA MAE **CAHILL** – DAUGHTER OF HANNA JO CAHILL; GRANDDAUGHTER OF PEARL CAHILL

CASA **TIERRA** – FICTIONAL CALIFORNIA COAST TOWN NEAR SANTA DOMINGA WHERE JACE MCKANE'S FATHER AND FAMILY LIVE

DAX **DALTON** – INSURANCE CLAIMS BUSINESS; AMBULANCE CHASER; MARRIED TO QUIGLEY'S MOTHER

ELEANOR **DALTON** – QUIGLEY'S MOTHER

QUIGLEY **DALTON** – HITCHHIKER; STALKER; MURDERER; ESCAPED PRISONER

POLLY **ENG** – CHINESE CITIZEN OF ROAD'S END; MOTHER OF KAM ENG; EMT; MANAGER OF APARTMENTS; CATERER

MAIDIE **FORTRESS** – BIRTH MOTHER OF HANNA JO CAHILL; NIECE OF SETH STROUD

GINNY **GEORGE** (NICOLI) – WIFE OF PARIS NICOLI;

daughter of Roco and Olympia; sister of Marina and Teddy; friend of Reba Cahill; publicist for George Industries

Alfred T. James – Road's End barber who took over Seth Stroud's shop

Enoch James – Reba's former boyfriend

Richard James – Reba Cahill's hairdresser who created the Curly Cue treatment

Brock Lomax – Road's End deputy

Archie MacKenzie – university student and trick bike rider from Scotland; twin brother of Wynda

Wynda MacKenzie – university student and trick bike rider from Scotland; twin sister of Archie

Adrienne Mathwig – adept at general house repairs and carpentry; co-owner with triplet sisters of Road's End Hotel; former dentist

Beatrice Mathwig – co-owner with triplet sisters and main manager of Road's End Hotel

Charlotta Mathwig – caterer; co-owner with triplet sisters of Road's End Hotel; home and garden tips newspaper columnist

Abel McKane – 10-year-old half-brother of Jace and Norden; son of Hugh & Yvonne

Agatha Finley McKane Hempthorn – first wife of Hugh McKane; mother of Jace McKane

Hugh McKane – businessman who lives in Casa Tierra, California; estranged husband of Yvonne and ex-husband of Agatha; father of Jace, Norden, and Abel

Jace McKane – son of Hugh McKane and Agatha; half-brother of Norden & Abel; owner of Outfitter's Shop in Road's End, managed by Norden

NORDEN **McKANE** – YOUNGER HALF-BROTHER OF JACE; MANAGES OUTFITTER'S SHOP IN ROAD'S END

YVONNE **McKANE** – ESTRANGED WIFE OF HUGH McKANE; MOTHER OF ABEL AND KAYLOR

LISL **MONTE** - POSTMISTRESS OF ROAD'S END

ATCH **MURDOCK** – LIBRARIAN TOURIST ON VACATION AND STAYING AT THE ROAD'S END HOTEL

TUCKER **PADDY** – HUSBAND OF IDA; FATHER OF AMOS & PICO; OWNER OF PADDY'S TRAILER PARK IN ROAD'S END

SOREN **PATRICK** – HORSE BREEDER IN NEW MEADOWS, IDAHO

VINCENT **QUAID** – WIDOWER FRIEND OF PEARL CAHILL FROM BOISE; FILLING IN AS FOREMAN OF CAHILL RANCH

QUIGLEY – HITCHHIKER IN BOOK 1; REBA CAHILL'S STALKER IN BOOK 2

ROAD'S END – HIGH PRAIRIE NORTH-CENTRAL IDAHO TOWN AT 4,200 FT. ELEVATION WHERE THE CAHILLS AND RUNCIES RANCH

RODRIGO **RODRIGUES** – FATHER OF JIP AND DeLISA

BLAIR **RUNCIE** – WIFE OF CHAMP; MOTHER OF DON; GRANDMOTHER OF TIM

CHAMP **RUNCIE** – RANCHER AND MAYOR OF ROAD'S END; HUSBAND OF BLAIR; FATHER OF DON; GRANDFATHER OF TIM; ALLEGED FATHER OF HANNA JO CAHILL

DON **RUNCIE** – WIDOWER SON OF CHAMP WHO HELPS HIM ON THE RANCH; ALLEGED HALF-BROTHER OF HANNA JO CAHILL; ALLEGED FATHER OF REBA CAHILL

SUE ANNE WHITLOW **RUNCIE** – WIFE OF TIM; MOTHER OF WILLIAM (3) AND KAITLYN (6)

TIM **RUNCIE** – HUSBAND OF SUE ANNE; FATHER OF WILLIAM AND KAITLYN; SON OF DON; GRANDSON OF CHAMP; WORKS ON RUNCIE RANCH.

SANTA DOMINGA – FICTIONAL COASTAL CALIFORNIA TOWN WHERE THE GEORGE FAMILY LIVES AND SITE OF GEORGE INDUSTRIES HEADQUARTERS, PROMINENT IN BOOK 2, *DOWN SQUASH BLOSSOM ROAD*

HESTER OWENS VAUGHN **STROUD** – NEWLYWED BRIDE OF SETH STROUD WHO OWNS RANCH IN NEW MEADOWS, IDAHO, THAT SOREN PATRICK MANAGES

SETH **STROUD** – B. 1900; UNCLE OF MAIDIE FORTRESS WHO HE RAISED FROM INFANCY; NEWLYWED HUSBAND OF HESTER OWENS VAUGHN

JESSE **WHITLOW** - SUE ANNE RUNCIE'S YOUNGER BROTHER; FRIEND OF LADONNA YOUNGER

MONROE 'BUCKHEAD' **WHITLOW** - SUE ANNE RUNCIE'S FATHER; OWNER OF WHITLOW GROCERY

LADONNA **YOUNGER** – CLERK AT OUTFITTERS SHOP IN ROAD'S END; TEEN DAUGHTER OF LLOYD AND URSULA

LLOYD & URSULA **YOUNGER** – ROAD'S END TARGHEE SHEEP RANCHERS; PARENTS OF SEVEN CHILDREN

PATSY ELLEN **ZINK** – 17-YEAR-OLD FAN OF QUIGLEY'S WHO RAN AWAY WITH HIM AFTER HE ESCAPED FROM A CALIFORNIA JAIL

ABOUT THE AUTHOR

BORN IN VISALIA, CALIFORNIA, JANET CHESTER BLY RECEIVED HER BACHELOR OF SCIENCE DEGREE FROM LEWIS-CLARK STATE COLLEGE IN LITERATURE & LANGUAGES AND FINE & PERFORMING ARTS. SHE IS A CITY GIRL WITH A COUNTRY HEART WHO DOESN'T CORRAL HORSES, WRANGLE COWS, OR EVEN MOW HER OWN LAWN.

"I'M NOT A WOMBA WOMAN," SHE SAYS. "BUT I LOVE TO WRITE ABOUT GALS WHO ARE."

SHE FOLLOWED HER LATE HUSBAND, AWARD-WINNING WESTERN AUTHOR STEPHEN BLY, TO COUNTRY LIVING IN NORTH-CENTRAL WINCHESTER, IDAHO TO WRITE BOOKS AND MINISTER TO A SMALL TOWN CHURCH. WHEN SHE LOST HIM, SHE STAYED TO MANAGE BLY BOOKS ONLINE AND THROUGH THE MAIL. SHE ALSO RAKES LOTS OF PONDEROSA PINE NEEDLES AND CONES AND SURVIVES THE LONG WINTERS, ONE SNOWSTORM AT A TIME.

SHE AUTHORED AND CO-AUTHORED WITH STEPHEN 40 FICTION AND NONFICTION BOOKS FOR ADULTS AND KIDS 8-12 YEARS OLD.

CHECK OUT HER WEBSITE FOR MORE INFO ABOUT THE BLYS AND THEIR BOOKS AND THE BLOG STORIES BEHIND THE STORIES: WWW.BLYBOOKS.COM

HER EMAIL: JANET@BLYBOOKS.COM

Reading Group Discussion Questions
Beneath A Camperdown Elm

1. Do you think you'd like living in a town like Road's End? Why or why not?

2. For Road's End, fire is the most dreaded natural disaster. What natural disasters do you deal with where you live? How does that affect lifestyles or resources?

3. Have you ever lived in a small town? What do you think are the advantages and disadvantages?

4. Have you ever been part of a committee building process? What were the obstacles and blessings?

5. When has weather ever coincided with a life event for you?

6. When was the last time you experienced pure joy like Reba at the beginning of the novel? How long did it last? Why do you think joy is difficult to maintain?

7. In what can you relate to the loss Reba Cahill felt about losing the ranch?

8. Why was it such a challenge to Reba to trust Jace when he left to go to California?

9. WHAT TRAILS DID REBA MAE CAHILL RIDE IN THIS STORY?

10. WHICH CHARACTERS JOURNEY OF THE HEART DID YOU RELATE TO MOST? AND WHY?

11. HAVE YOU EVER HAD TO DEAL WITH A RELATIONSHIP WITH SO MUCH BAGGAGE IT SEEMED IMPOSSIBLE TO MAKE A HEALTHY BOND, SUCH AS REBA AND HANNA JO WITH THE RUNCIE FAMILY?

12. HAVE YOU EVER TRIED TO TAME A DIFFICULT ANIMAL, SUCH AS THE CAHILL WOMEN DID WITH BANNER AND JOHNNY POE? WHAT DID YOU LEARN FROM THE EXPERIENCE?

13. HAVE YOU EVER OWNED A HORSE OR OTHER ANIMAL FOR WHICH YOU FELT A SPECIAL ATTACHMENT? EXPLAIN.

14. HAVE YOU EVER BEEN TO SCOTLAND OR BEEN AROUND SCOTTISH PEOPLE? WHAT IMPRESSED YOU MOST?

15. HAVE YOU EVER HEARD OF OR SEEN A CAMPERDOWN ELM? ARE YOU ACQUAINTED WITH A MUTANT TREE OR PLANT OF ANOTHER KIND?

16. HAVE YOU OR SOMEONE CLOSE TO YOU EVER DEALT WITH SEVERE DEPRESSION? OR PERHAPS COMMITTED TO A MENTAL FACILITY? HOW WOULD YOU DESCRIBE THEIR SITUATION?

17. HAVE YOU EVER KNOWN A PERSON ROUGH AROUND THE

edges like Tucker Paddy who 'got religion'? What was the result, positive and negative?

18. What did you think about Pearl's students' adventures in evangelism? Which do you believe would be most effective?

19. Share some phrases from the book that grabbed your attention.

20. What was the most touching moment in the story for you?

21. What was your favorite scene? Favorite line?

22. Reba admits to a number of fears. How many different ones can you recall? Which one can you most relate to?

23. Abel and Reba face their fears about Quigley and later Antjuan. What has been the scariest moment in your life so far? How did you handle it?

24. Which character would you like to know more about?

25. Which was the most romantic scene for you?

26. How would you have related to Champ Runcie, if you'd been Hanna Jo Cahill?

27. DID YOU EMPATHIZE WITH CHAMP RUNCIE AT ALL WITH THE CHALLENGES, HARDSHIPS, AND DISAPPOINTMENTS HE FACED? WHY OR WHY NOT?

28. WHY DO YOU THINK CHAMP CALLED SETH STROUD TO HIS HOUSE WHEN HE OVERDOSED ON MEDS?

29. WHAT IS YOUR RESPONSE TO THE STATEMENT— RELATIONSHIPS ARE THE HARDEST THING WE DO?

30. DO YOU DETECT A LONG LIFE OF HAPPINESS OR A TENDENCY TOWARD IMPENDING CHALLENGES FOR ANY OF THE NEWLYWED COUPLES? EXPLAIN.

31. DID ANY PART OF THIS STORY GIVE INSIGHT INTO ONE OF YOUR OWN OR A LOVED ONE'S STRUGGLES?

32. WOULD YOU HAVE CHANGED ANY PART OF THE STORY? IF SO, HOW AND WHY?

33. WHAT WAS THE MESSAGE TAKE-AWAY FOR YOU IN THIS NOVEL? WHAT DO YOU CONSIDER THE MAIN THEME?

34. WHAT SURPRISED YOU MOST ABOUT THIS STORY?

35. IS THERE ANYTHING YOU'D LIKE TO EXPRESS TO THE AUTHOR OF THIS SERIES?

Beneath a Camperdown Elm

Notes

If You Enjoyed This Story...

Tweet about it.
Share on Facebook.
Share on Goodreads or any other social media.
Leave review on your favorite online bookstore sites.

If you liked this story, you will also appreciate The Horse Dreams Series:

Memories of a Dirt Road Town
The Mustang Breaker
Wish I'd Known You Tears Ago

Find them on the Bly Books website bookstore page under "Contemporary Fiction"
www.blybooks.com/product_category/contemporary-fiction/

Almost Monthly Bly Books News ...

Sign up for the Almost Monthly Bly Books email report on other books, including free chapters, giveaways, and family news.
Subscribe here:
https://www.blybooks.com/contact/stephen-bly-books-newsletter/

Contact info for Janet Chester Bly:

Bly Books
P.O. Box 157
Winchester, ID 83555
email: janet@blybooks.com
website: www.BlyBooks.com

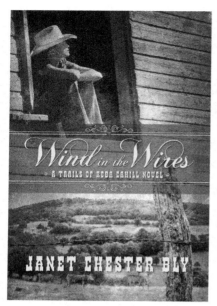

Wind in the Wires, Book 1, Trails of Reba Cahill

In 1991, cowgirl Reba Mae Cahill searches for love and her mother, Hanna Jo, who abandoned her at the age of three with her grandparents at the Cahill Ranch in Road's End, Idaho.

Elderly Seth Stroud goes on a road trip in his purple Model T to seek justice for two cold case murders.

Reba and Seth, with a caravan of others from Road's End, travel together to the Nevada desert. And Reba and Seth uncover lies and betrayal with consequences for them both.

Excerpt:

Seth reached into his pocket and handed her a slip of paper.

Keep it, Reba was tempted to scream. She wanted nothing to do with her mother. No matter what, she wouldn't change her mind. She refused to take a slow boat to anywhere. Or a snail's pace Model T trip to the Nevada desert. She gaped at the folded note, not much larger than a man's thumb, as though torn from a scratch pad. Whatever the words, they could not begin to make up for years of silence. Or abandonment.

Why bother? Why deepen the wound?

Reba Cahill loves ranching with Grandma Pearl in north-central Idaho. But there's a lot of work and only two of them, most of the time. Can she find a man worthy of her attentions and capable enough to help her run the ranch? She finds few prospects in the small town of Road's End.

But Reba is also missing her mother. Deserted by her and never knowing her dad, she feels a sense of longing, loss, and bitterness.

When elderly, quirky Road's End citizen Maidie Fortress dies, Maidie's Uncle Seth presents Reba with an expensive gold and turquoise squash blossom necklace that turns Reba's world upside down. She is thrust into a journey with Seth that exposes dark family secrets.

Down Squash Blossom Road, Book 2, Trails of Reba Cahill

Cowgirl Reba Cahill's schedule is full.

Save the family ranch.

Free her mom, Hanna Jo, from a mental institute.

Take another road trip.

Solve a kidnapping and murder.

Plus, evade a stalker named Quigley.

Can she also squeeze in romance?

Reba Cahill thought she could focus on the duties of the Cahill Ranch, to help out her widowed grandmother, Pearl Cahill. But a crippled Champ Runcie in a wheelchair seeks revenge for the accident that put him there, by a lawsuit against Reba and their ranch.

Meanwhile, a letter from her estranged mother in a Reno mental institute forces Reba and Grandma Pearl back on the road: *I can leave now. Come get me. Love, Mom.*

When they arrive at Reno, her mother balks and refuses to return to Idaho. She and Reba head west instead to California, while Pearl returns to Road's End to fight the lawsuit. In California, Reba and Hanna Jo connect with Reba's childhood friend, Ginny George, whose marriage is on the rocks. And Ginny's family's deli chain business is threatened, as family squabbles turn deadly.

Reba digs deep to find courage to forge a relationship with her mom and also faces an uncertain future as one potential romance ends before it begins and another blossoms after a surprise confession.

Finally, her mother consents to go home to Road's End.